D1506990

BOOKS IN THE RENEGADE STAR UNIVERSE

The Orion Colony Series with Jonathan Yanez:

Orion Colony

Orion Uncharted

Orion Awakened

Orion Protected

The Last Reaper Series with Scott Moon:

The Last Reaper

Fear the Reaper

Blade of the Reaper

Wings of the Reaper

Flight of the Reaper

Wrath of the Reaper

 Will of the Reaper (Nov. 2019)

The Fifth Column Series with Molly Lerma:

The Fifth Column

The Solaras Initiative

Resonant Son Series with Christopher Hopper:

Resonant Son

Resonant Abyss

STAY UP TO DATE

Chaney posts updates, official art, previews, and other awesome stuff on his website. You can also follow him on Instagram, Facebook, and Twitter.

Search for **JN Chaney's Renegade Readers** on Facebook to join the group where readers can come together and share their lives and interests, especially regarding Chaney's books.

For updates about new releases, as well as exclusive promotions, sign up for the VIP mailing list. Head there now to receive a free copy of *The Other Side of Nowhere*.

https://www.subscribepage.com/organic

Enjoying the series? Help others discover *The Last Reaper* series by leaving a review on Amazon.

WRATH OF THE REAPER

BOOK 6 IN THE LAST REAPER SERIES

J.N. CHANEY

SCOTT MOON

CONTENTS

LIST OF ACRONYMS

- **AI**—Artificial intelligence
- **AWOL**—Absent without leave
- **BMSP**—Bluesphere Maximum Security Prison —Ultramax IX
- **CD**—Climbdown Day
- **CIM**—Computerized Inmate Monitor
- **CV**—Curriculum Vitae
- **DM**—Dreadmax Marines (inmates on Dreadmax, often falsely imprisoned, who have prior military experience and protect people from gangs and cannibals)
- **Feg**—Fredrick Eugene Grady
- **HDK**—Highly Destructive Kinetic (weapon / rifle)
- **HDK 4**—Shortened (11 inch barrel--from the

trigger assembly) HDK commonly used by spec ops and law enforcement

- **HDK 4 Dominator**—Full length (16 inch barrel--from the trigger assembly) HDK with double high capacity magazines and a grenade launcher under the barrel)
- **HUD**—Heads up display
- **LAI**—Limited artificial intelligence
- **LED**—Light Emitting Diode
- **LZ**—Landing zone
- **MRE**—Meals Ready to Eat
- **NG**—Nightfall Gangsters
- **QRF**—Quick reaction force
- **RC**—Reaper Corps
- **RSG**—Red Skull Gangsters
- **SD Regulator**—Slip drive regulator
- **UFS**—Union Fleet Ship
- **UPG**—Union Prison Guard
- **X-37**—Halek Cain's Reaper AI (limited)
- **YT**—Galdiz 49 rifle, sniper model. (YT is a randomly generated model number)

SHIP AND CHARACTER NAMES

SHIPS

RWS = Republic of Wallach Ship

Bright Lance of Xad

- Flagship of the Xad fleet
- Captured from the Union in Flight of the Reaper, TLR 5
- **Captain:** Cynthia Thomas Younger
- **Executive Officer:** Commander Bernard Gile

RWS BATTLE AXE

- With *Jellybird* scouting new system after Macabre
- **Captain:** Don Hunger

RWS JUMPING FOX

- **Captain:** Jaime Peterson

RWS SPIRIT of Wallach

- Flagship of the Republic of Wallach fleet
- **Captain:** Quincy Drysdale
- Ship the President of Wallach, Amanda Coronas, travels on. (She does not command the ship.)
- Ship that carries General Karn's main army

HUNTER OF XAD

- With *Jellybird* scouting new system after Macabre

- **Captain:** Omon

CHARACTER NAMES

Asis - soldier First Class of Xad

Bug - A KID from Dreadmax

Beaufort - REPAIRMAN on the Bright Lance of Xad and member of EVA work crews

Ben, Amon - Soldier, First Class. Xad citizen. Currently serving on the *Bright Lance of Xad*.

Cain, Olivia Anna – Halek Cain's mother

Cain, Halek - The Last Reaper

. . .

CAIN, Hannah – Halek Cain's sister

DAY, Orson - Formerly a Corporal in the Union, now serving on the *Bright Lance of Xad*.

DRYSDALE, Quincy - Captain of the RWS *Spirit of Wallach*

FEIST, Theodore - Lieutenant, maintenance and supply officer, fourth watch, section 2.

GILE, Bernard - Commander / XO of the *Bright Lance of Xad*. Executive Officer for Captain Younger. Citizen of Xad.

HUNGER, Dan - Captain of the RWS Battle Axe

HUTTON - ADMIRAL of the Wallach Fleet

JUNKBOSS, Michael - Ensign on the *Bright Lance of Xad*. Controller for Elise during the repair mission of the RWS *Jumping Fox*.

. . .

MOORE, Major Hubert Moore - ship doctor of the *Bright Lance of Xad* (formerly the *UFS Dark Lance*.)

LARGO - soldier First Class of Xad

OBERON, Charles - Lieutenant

OMON, Keeper - Captain of the Hunter of Xad

PETERSON, Jamie - Captain of the RWS *Jumping Fox*

SUN, Suzan - Warrant Officer on the Bright Lance of Xad. Flight deck control supervisor. Formerly of the Union. Has applied for Xad citizenship and been vetted as trustworthy.

ULURU, Sergeant - security chief of the *Bright Lance of Xad* brig.

WALKER, Kyle - Ensign on the Bridge of the *Bright Lance of Xad.*

. . .

YOUNGER, Cynthia Thomas - Captain of the Bright Lance of Xad. Citizen of Xad.

XERES, Samantha - Doctor: Chief Medical Officer on the *Bright Lance of Xad.* Formerly a Union citizen, now applying for citizenship with Xad.

PREVIOUSLY IN FLIGHT OF THE REAPER

HALEK CAIN and his friends arrived in a strange system full of ship debris to rescue the *Bold Freedom*, a modified freighter that they'd last seen leaving Dreadmax with a desperate crew of survivors. After a last-ditch gamble to outsmart their pursuers and deliver needed fuel, they learned their ultimate enemy had them dead to rights and would show no mercy.

Cain proved himself to the scavengers of Xad, united them with the exodus fleet from Wallach, and defeated Vice Admiral Nebs and his elite team of Archangels. When it was all said and done, Cain, Elise, and Path acquired state of the art battle armor and the people of Xad and Wallach took over a Union stealth carrier.

But it wasn't over. They discovered a dark secret. Nebs's scientists were conducting dangerous research and holding

Cain's family in cryo-sleep pods that can't be opened. With the fate of two exodus fleets on the line, Cain must now find a new home for thousands of people and find the codes to awaken his mother and sister.

1

X-37 SOUNDED an alert only I heard, and by heard I meant the vibrations to my cochlear implant brought me to my knees. Everyone should have a limited artificial intelligence to ruin their day. It's fantastic.

I climbed to my feet and placed my untasted whiskey on the little bar at the edge of the *Bright Lance* observation deck. "This better be good, X."

"Doctor Jaxon Ayers is in a state of cardiac arrest," X-37 explained. "I believe Vice Admiral Nebs implanted nerve-ware kill switches in all of his critical staff. Most of the high-ranking officers, special technicians, and spies in the lower ranks have died of heart attacks within the last fifteen minutes."

I gave the bartender a friendly wave as I pushed back

from my usual spot, then strode from the room. "Why now, X? Why not right after we took control of the ships?"

"The most likely scenario is that we have located a secret Nebs did not want us to find even if he was dead," X-37 said. "Eliminating key people, like Ayers, has a high probability of hiding the dead vice admiral's darkest secrets. It is also possible that the reset of the ship's AI has mitigated the worst of Nebs's sabotage efforts."

"The doctor can't die until I figure out what his dead boss had him on this ship for," I said.

"He was a medical officer, Reaper Cain. The cryo-pods are one of his many responsibilities," X-37 said.

"There's more to it than that," I said. "And he better not die before my mother and sister are revived or I'll find him in the afterlife and kill him again."

"I will place that on your post death agenda."

"Sometimes I can't tell if you're joking," I said.

"It is a mystery."

"Yeah, like I need that. Tell me more about these kill switches and why you think they're going off now," I said.

X-37 chattered in my ear about the sketchy and illegal experimentation Ayers had performed before facing a court-martial on about a hundred criminal charges. My LAI trying to be helpful without understanding my anger and frustration.

I was running by the time I reached the hallway to the medical bay. That dangerous sense of foreboding I'd felt since first seeing the man on surveillance cameras was growing faster than I could sprint.

"Reaper Cain, please compose yourself," X-37 demanded.

Stopping at the door, I took a breath, then I let it out and went inside.

Henshaw, Tom, and Elise were standing in the emergency room over Ayers. Their faces were pale. Most alarming of all was my speechless protege. I hadn't thought she'd ever run out of opinions, swear words, and tactless comments.

"What's going on, Elise?" I asked, standing beside her to look at all the IVs and machines connected to Ayers. A team of Union trained nurses came and went, forcing us to step back whenever they needed to check something or adjust his meds.

"He was ranting and raving, saying we couldn't let him die because he'd brought them back," Elise said. A shiver passed through her. She crossed her arms and took a step back.

Henshaw looked hungry for knowledge but also terrified —not the bedside manner I expected, even though I tried not to underestimate the man's curiosity in all things scientific. He had sacrificed his own eyes for his research.

What a nutjob.

Tom's expression was as grim as I'd ever seen it. Of all my crew, Tom was the most caring and—normal. Yet he was every bit the seeker of knowledge that Henshaw was without all of the pathological sneakery.

"Did we ever figure out what Ayers was researching before they banned it?" I asked.

"Alien xenobiology and advanced cloning," X-37 said.

"I really don't like the sound of that, but tell me all of it, X. What do we think he was doing for Nebs?" I asked. "And why didn't you tell me he's a xenobiologist *and* a cloning expert?"

"Based on the small amount of data I have at this time, I believe he was in fact attempting to bring back an alien race through cloning," X-37 said, "despite hundreds of years of failed clone projects and laws against the practice."

"He needs to have an alien to clone one," I said. "Did we check all of the pods?"

"That would freak me out," Elise said, looking way more intrigued than freaked out. "Please tell me we don't have a box of monsters someplace on this ship."

"There are only humans in the cryo-pods. That doesn't prevent Doctor Ayers from having a DNA sample—from an archeological site or something," X-37 answered. "I must remind you we have not found Nebs's secret vault, despite evidence from your initial interviews with Ayers that such a place exists."

"Let's get him stabilized and find that vault," I said.

Elise crossed her arms as she stared into me with angry suspicion. "When were you going to tell the rest of us about this?"

I spread my arms, the model of innocence. "I didn't tell you?"

"No. You didn't," Elise said, moving forward like a master interrogator. Combined with steady eye contact, it was a good tactic. I wondered where she had learned it.

"X, didn't I ask you to remind me to share the existence of a secret vault with Elise...and these other characters," I said, waving at Henshaw and Tom, hoping to divert Elise's attention.

X-37 responded on our team channel. "You did not, Reaper Cain."

"Well anyway, I was just about to ask all of you for your input," I said.

Elise rolled her eyes in disbelief.

I pressed onward. "X-37 believes that Nebs recruited Ayers—kidnapped might be a better word for what transpired —to conduct some very dangerous research on this ship."

"That doesn't surprise me," Elise admitted, letting go of her annoyance. The longer we knew each other, the quicker we were to get over these types of personal slights.

"I've had a really bad feeling since we captured the *Dark Lance*," I said.

"*Bright Lance*," X-37 said. "AI Mavis does not like the old name and neither does Captain Younger."

"Whatever." I didn't want to argue. "Let's divide into teams and search the ship—room by room and data file by data file. We need answers and we need them now."

BRION REJON, the leader of Xad, stood with us. He wasn't as tall as many of his people, but he had that slender, slightly out of proportion appearance of someone who spent most of his life in space. The man wasn't the ultimate authority on the *Bright Lance*, but near enough. Captain Cynthia Thomas Younger of Xad allowed him free reign of the ship, and her crew respected him—which made our search of what had been the *Dark Lance* easier.

Before us was a blast door very similar to what protected the Archangel armories. We waited until Tom and Henshaw arrived.

"X, can you fill everybody in?" I asked.

"Certainly, Reaper Cain," X-37 said. "I have worked with ship AI Mavis to access all parts of the *Bright Lance*. This door, however, has been unbreachable. Reaper Cain would like your combined assistance to gain access."

"You brought us all here to help you steal more Reaper toys?" Henshaw asked. "Or have you discovered this vague and mysterious threat that has you shaking in your Reaper boots? The one you weren't going to share with the rest of us?"

"You're free to get on your ship and leave anytime," I said, not in the mood to argue with a butthurt scientist.

Henshaw ran one hand through his neatly trimmed hair, diverting attention from the way his cybernetic eyes scanned the door. The man had a simple LAI that X-37 said barely deserved the name. When we'd met, he'd been using the technology to win at gambling on Roxo III—which had gotten him into a lot of trouble and prompted our relationship.

"I think this is where Nebs and Doctor Ayers concealed their experiments," I explained.

"Well, that is interesting if true," Henshaw said. "This vault door is on its own power grid. If I were concealing a top-secret laboratory, I would put similar security measures in place."

"I thought that might grab your attention." I knew the man couldn't resist such an intellectual challenge, and that he would also seek new tools to use against the Union. The ocular engineer and unorthodox scientist understood how to work through dangerous situations. He was an intellectual opportunist who came at problems from creative angles.

Tom lacked formal schooling or a limited artificial intelligence but was one of the most innovative engineers I knew. He studied new things and had a very broad base of knowledge. Together, I was sure we could get through this seemingly impenetrable barrier.

Henshaw rubbed his chin. "Too bad we can't have Doctor Ayers here."

"Prior to his myocardial infraction, Doctor Jaxon Ayers stated he did not have the code," X-37 said.

"Maybe your Reaper interrogation was too much for him. I'm not convinced Nebs put kill switches in his people," Henshaw said, visible lights rotating counterclockwise in his dual cybernetic eyes. "If Nebs could do that to his people, how am I alive? I betrayed him long before we met."

"No idea. Maybe you should have a full medical check-up. Wouldn't want you to keel over right when I need you for something." I moved closer to the vault door, studying each detail, looking for something I'd missed on previous attempts to breach it.

"Perhaps a check-up would be a good idea," Henshaw said, his tone subdued, his eyes dimmed.

Elise joined me, squatting down as we tested the bottom seal. "Want to try the lock picks again? You probably wouldn't get shocked this time. And if you did, you survived the last time, right?"

"You're trying to get me to zap myself," I said.

She shrugged and made innocent eyes. "It might work."

I faced her, keeping my expression neutral and unreadable.

"We should get more information from Ayers," she said. "That might be safer for you, and it also might help avoid any self-destruct mechanisms he might have in place to keep his research out of the wrong hands."

"That would be an outstanding idea if Doctor Ayers were available for an interview," X-37 said. "AI Mavis informs me he remains in serious condition."

"Can we wake him up?" I asked.

"Possibly, Reaper Cain, though it is not recommended."

"Can we... drag him down here and force him to open the vault?"

X-37 made a series of meaningless clicks. "Are you trying to kill him?"

"No, X. I need him." Crossing my arms, I asked a serious question of my LAI. "What are those clicks, X? Are you all right?"

"Did the noises in question not convey chastisement?" X-37 asked. "My analysis suggests this would mimic a nonverbal mannerism. I have tried such things before with mixed results."

"You're doing that crap on purpose?"

"I am, Reaper Cain. We commonly refer it to as communication."

I laughed. "All that time I thought you were breaking down."

"To be accurate, there were instances of malfunction and less than optimal performance, but the combined efforts of Henshaw, Tom, and the various ship AIs we've befriended since Dreadmax have much improved my ability to assist you. AI Mavis has been helpful as of late."

"Problems?" Elise asked, raising one eyebrow. Henshaw also watched me with interest. Not all of my conversation with X had been shared with them.

"No. I'm good. X, check with Mavis and see if we can talk with Ayers."

"Standing around isn't solving this little conundrum." Elise backed away from the vault door. "Let's head for the hospital now."

"I'll stay here and take measurements; maybe compare what is in the ship schematics to what is actually here," Tom said.

"Send Path or one of Rejon's people down to stand guard once we relieve him from guarding Ayers." My impatience to get inside needed tempering, which made me glad my friends were here. They held me back when I tried to rush things like this, and they brought a fresh perspective to everything.

"Path," Elise said on the comm channel. "We're coming to you now. How's the doctor?"

"Safe," Grigori "Path" Paavo answered. "And awake. He's threatening to leave the medical bay."

"Don't let that happen," I ordered.

"We will both be here when you arrive," Path promised.

CREW MEMBERS of the *Bright Lance* greeted us and stepped aside as we moved through the narrow hallways. None of them saluted, and they were back to work seconds after each encounter.

"I haven't figured these people out," Henshaw said. "And I consider myself an accomplished student of human behavior."

"What is there to figure out?." Elise asked.

"My first impression of Xad citizens was of homeless vagabonds capable of surviving in an extraterrestrial junk-yard. My second impression was of a hard-working colonists. What I'm seeing here is a group of very formal soldiers and crewmen wearing the same tattered rags their grandparents must have worn," Henshaw said.

"Some have new uniforms," I said. "The *Bright Lance* has recycling facilities near the hydroponics deck. Before you know it, their rags will be good as new."

"Sure," Henshaw argued, "but they can't decide on the design or even color scheme. They are half professionals—serious about tradition and formalities—and half feral survivalists."

"Does any of that matter?" I asked, wondering what the ocular engineer was getting at.

"I'm a scientist. I observe and hypothesize explanations," he said.

"They're a work in progress." My training in how to observe and analyze people was for a different reason but I'd noticed most of the same things as Henshaw.

We arrived at the medical bay, bypassing the high security hallway that led to the cryo-pod area where my family and others were held in a kind of stasis that was hard to look at.

"The doctor is awake." Path stepped away from Ayers as we entered the doctor's room.

The appearances of Path and Ayers were as different as they could be. The sword saint had crazy hair, wild clothing, and eyes as serene as still water. Doctor Jaxon Ayers wore a perfectly maintained jumpsuit and had neatly trimmed gray hair, but his eyes were as crazy as a Tagron beast of Xad in an arena fight. A cumbersome medical bracelet on his wrist allowed the medical staff to keep tabs on his health.

"Are you going somewhere, doc?" I asked.

"Am I a prisoner?"

"As a matter of fact, you are. Can you believe this guy, X?" I asked.

X-37 didn't answer. Elise and Henshaw flanked Doctor

Ayers but held back from the conversation—watching and listening for the right moment to join in.

"What do you want, Reaper?" Ayers asked.

"We found the vault. I want in."

"I told your LAI I have no more codes, for cryo-pods or anything else." Sitting on the edge of the bed now, he looked pale but determined.

"What's inside that door?" I placed one hand on his shoulder.

He shivered at my touch. I sensed Elise and Henshaw shifting foot to foot, probably wanting to interrupt with their own questions before I scared the man into not talking. What they didn't understand was that it was more difficult to lie during physical contact.

"Nebs ordered me to end my research," Ayers said. "I did everything he wanted, fixed all of his problems, did my job perfectly. All I wanted was to test my theories."

"What theories?" I demanded. My friends relaxed slightly, evaluating every word, movement, and hesitation of Ayers.

"It would be easier to show you," he said.

"Agreed, but you don't have the codes to open the cryo-pods or secret vaults or anything else." I crossed my arms, making sure my cybernetic arm was on top.

He looked at his feet, hugging himself as he rocked back and forth on the edge of his hospital bed. A bead of sweat broke on his forehead.

"I'm not an idiot, Reaper. I knew better than to trust Nebs, so I hid the codes to the research vault on a planet called Macabre. If you can take me there, I can introduce you to the first round of test subjects, recover the secrets within the vault, and change our understanding of the galaxy forever," he said. "I also stashed back-up codes for the cryo-pods."

"Why Macabre?" I asked. "What is there that makes it a good place to hide things?"

"Your heart rate is entering fight mode," X-37 said. "Proceed with caution, Reaper Cain."

"There are sections of the galaxy non-human aliens of incredible knowledge and power once ruled. Maybe they had their own exodus—just like your precious Xad and Wallach coalition—but some of them died first. I found viable examples of their DNA in an archeological site on Macabre and brought them back," Ayers said, a sly grin forming as he spoke. "After a fashion."

2

No one spoke. No one moved. No one wanted to drag Doctor Jaxon Ayers into an interrogation room right now and squeeze him for information more than I did. Ventilation and other sounds I normally ignored roared in my ears as adrenaline flooded my system. Even X-37 was at a loss for words.

"You built your own aliens?" I asked.

Ayers must have sensed my mood, because his grin vanished. "What are you afraid of, Reaper? That they might be better than us? Are you worried humans aren't meant to rule the galaxy? Maybe they even have a replacement for someone with your unique skills."

"We need to put him someplace secure, or increase the guards of this section," Elise said.

"Agreed," I said. "X, call the on duty medical supervisor and get us cleared to move him."

"Right away, Reaper Cain."

Moments later, Doctor Samantha Xeres marched into the room. She froze me with her gaze. Behind her came an army of nurses, orderlies, and two guards.

"Good evening, Doctor," I said.

"What is the meaning of this?" she demanded.

I held up both hands. "It's not what it looks like. I'll respect your decision, but I also need to put him in the brig for security reasons."

Rejon and a squad of his soldiers arrived in the hallway. "AI Mavis alerted us there may be a problem. Can we be of assistance?"

Xeres looked at Rejon and his men, then crossed her arms as she stepped toward me. "What security reason?"

"We may have located some illegal research Ayers was trying to hide," I said. "The entire ship could be in danger."

"Everything is a danger to the ship for you security types. I'd hoped this would be better than working for that tyrant Nebs," Xeres said, motioning for her assistant to check Ayers and the man's medical wrist monitor. "But I will admit that Ayers has basically recovered from his incident. If you will please wait in the hallway, we will prepare him for a transfer to the brig. The medical monitor must stay here, so we need to be sure he's eligible to be released."

"Thanks, Doc," I said.

She stepped close. "I know what the man was into, but he is still a patient. I don't have to like him to care for him."

"What do you know about *what he was into?*" I asked, voice low enough that it was just me, her, and X-37 in the conversation.

Xeres didn't hide her annoyance. "I don't know the details. Several of his volunteers had to be admitted to the emergency room after his experiments."

"Where are they now?" I wanted to hear her answer, even though I had a good idea what it would be.

Her expression hardened. She held my gaze like I wasn't a Reaper but someone she was ready to battle. "They died of heart attacks, which I assumed was something he did." She nodded at Ayers. "Now I know whatever is happening is even worse."

"Would you be willing to share medical histories of the patients?" I knew what her answer would be.

"Why did you even ask that question, Reaper Cain?" X-37 asked.

I ignored my LAI and Xeres couldn't hear the question.

"You know I can't do that," Xeres said. "But I can discharge this patient. He will need checkups. Also, Reaper, you and your people should be ready to submit to a complete medical examination. You can't avoid my staff forever."

"No problem," I said. "X, mark that on my agenda."

"Already done, Reaper Cain."

"It must be nice to have an LAI," Doctor Xeres said.

"You're not convinced the recent deaths are because of Nebs," I said.

"An astute observation, Reaper," she said. "I'll need to watch what I say around you. Please remember that every life on this ship, and in this fleet, matters to our long-term survival."

X-37 LOCATED Bug and explained I wanted him to start spying on Ayers as soon as he could hack into the security cameras. Two guards, one Union turncoat who knew his way around the ship, and one Xad soldier led the way to the brig.

"Do you gentlemen have names?" I asked.

"I am Corporal Orson Day, formerly of the Union."

"Soldier, First Class Amon Ben of Xad."

"Path and Elise, you're with them. The rest of Rejon's soldiers can be our rear guard in case Ayers has confederates waiting to liberate him when we move."

"None of that is necessary," Ayers insisted. "Where would I find confederates among these dredges?"

"Be quiet, Ayers," Henshaw said. "Security isn't my specialty but I'm with the Reaper on this."

I leaned close enough to Henshaw to lift a cigar and a lighter from his jumpsuit pocket. "Keep your eyes open. Watch the doctor. Tell me if you think he's up to something."

Henshaw stood a little straighter. "Certainly, Reaper."

"You are being ridiculous," Ayers said. "Not even Nebs treated me like this. I'm not a prisoner."

"You *are* a prisoner, Doc. Get used to it," I said. "Give me a second, then we're moving."

Rejon took me by the arm. "You have my soldiers for as long as you need them, but I want to visit some of my people while I'm here. Some will never recover from the battle to take this ship."

"Thanks, Rejon. I wish it had been easier," I said.

"It is what it must be," he said. "Please keep me informed. I do not trust Doctor Ayers."

We moved out, creating more of a spectacle than I had planned. Prisoner transfers weren't something I had prepared my team to handle. This was on-the-job training but at least we had Xad soldiers for support.

Crew men and women—polite and serious, as most Xad workers were—gave us room as we moved from one hallway to the next.

I'd come a long way since Dreadmax. Now *I* had a prisoner.

"This is for your safety as much as ours," I said.

Ayers didn't agree. "I see what is happening. You're angry about the cryo-pods. That wasn't my decision. I didn't even put them there. Technicians did that, and all I did…"

"What's the matter, Doc, Reaper got your tongue?" I asked. "What did you do that the technicians couldn't—set the codes that keep them as frozen prisoners?"

Ayers looked at his feet as he walked. "Nebs forced me to do it."

"Don't lie. I bet there wasn't that much coercion. He promised to fund your research, and you did whatever he asked. What do you think the penalty should be for a man who froze a Reaper's family? Rule one, don't mess with a man's mother. Rule two, don't go near his little sister."

"She is a very capable adult," he said.

"Still my little sister," I said, genuine anger heating my words.

"That is just like an ignorant trigger man to oversimplify a complex set of circumstances." His expression was resentful, but it also concealed something. "You're just a killer with no thoughts for building a better future."

"Is that what you're doing?" I asked, doubting altruism was a primary motivator for Ayers.

"Humans must embrace other sentient forces in the universe," he argued.

"What if we're alone?" I asked, knowing my question would goad him into talking. Hopefully, it wouldn't give him another heart attack.

"I have nothing to prove to you," Ayers countered. "You will accept the truth or you won't. Either way, people like you are irrelevant to the future of humanity."

"We'll see," I said, watching him.

He quit talking. Every instinct warned me this conversation wasn't over.

No one accustomed to playing high level Union politics and intrigue gave up this easily. He was planning something— an escape, sabotage, or a direct attack.

"You're a smart man, Ayers," I said, unleashing a cigar from my pocket and firing it up with a minimum of extra movements. Sleight of hand could be practiced a hundred different ways, and this was one of my favorites—invisible movements ending in a flourish of smoky goodness.

"The smartest you'll ever meet," Doctor Ayers responded.

"Can you believe this guy, X?" I asked.

"His arrogance is unmatched. He does not seem to fear pain or death," X-37 said. "My analysis suggests this will cause a problem with your future interrogation efforts."

"It's so quaint when the over muscled killer has to ask his LAI for help," Ayers said. "It's a definite limitation of humans."

Instead of responding to his jab, I took a long pull from my cigar, breathing in the smoke and relaxing as the nicotine hit my system.

The man was fearless, despite his propensity for fidgeting and backing away when I got angry. It was hard to blame him for that; it was about the smartest thing he'd done since we met.

Some of his behaviors made him look unsure, frightened, or ruled by nervous energy. I saw through his act. X-37 had explained that some of the man's eccentricities might be the result of neurological trauma he'd experienced over the years. I just thought he was a sneaky, double-dealing bastard.

We reached the brig and passed through security, double checking Ayers for concealed weapons or other hidden devices before locking him in a cell. I instructed the detention supervisor to monitor Ayers and be aware he had just come from the medical bay.

Bug whispered in my ear. "I've got eyes on this weird old man. How long do I have to watch him?"

"Indefinitely," X-37 answered for me. "You do not need to whisper. No one can hear you but Reaper Cain."

"And you, right? Don't sell yourself short, X. You're pretty awesome," Bug said, too loudly this time.

"Thank you, Bug. That is a nice thing to say, if totally unnecessary," X-37 responded.

I gave my LAI a hand signal to shut down the conversation for now.

The rest of our escort returned to their regular duties. I noticed that each Union turncoat had a Xad partner—Corporal Orson Day and Soldier, First Class, Amon Ben being an example. It was a simple first step to integration that might work—or go horribly wrong, depending on the various levels of culture shock they were experiencing.

"What now?" Elise asked.

"We let him sit for a while while we compare notes," I said. "Let's hit the gym and grab some food."

X-37 and I had a private conversation while Elise and Henshaw were reviewing security footage in the next room. I could see them through the monitor and guessed they would be a few moments.

"The man is a hot mess," I said. "Ideally, I would have a lot more background information to go on before we began. I think he's a typical scientist, a one trick con artist only concerned about his research. Those types are easy to intimidate but I'm never sure if he's scared of me or just playing a role."

"I believe many of his behavioral inconsistencies are products of his experimentation. The man, much like James Henshaw, has served as his own test subject more than once," X-37 said.

"You think he's like Henshaw?" The thought had occurred to me more than once. Both men had worked for Vice Admiral Nebs and both had conducted plenty of illegal research.

"Not precisely, Reaper Cain," X-37 said. "My recommendation is to base your evaluation of Doctor Ayers on direct evidence only."

"Noted." It had taken me a long time to trust Henshaw. "I doubt I will ever trust Ayers."

X-37 continued the analysis. "There is plenty of direct evidence that he helped imprison your mother and sister, and that he believes he can bring back an alien race we know nothing about. There is *no* evidence that he understands human psychology, sociology, or politics as much as he thinks he does. For Doctor Ayers, the only worthwhile goal is resurrecting a lost, intergalactic civilization."

"Maybe we should force him to watch some alien invasion holos or read some of that pulp fiction Tom devours between technical manuals," I said. "Then maybe he would stop and think about how wrong his experiments could go."

I took a moment to clear my head before entering the cell. "I want you to watch and listen, maybe take notes. If you have a question or observation that is important, have X-37 relay it to me."

Elise and Henshaw nodded, then went to the observation room. When I stepped inside the cell, Doctor Ayers was ready for me.

He maintained a perfect jumpsuit, the remnants of a uniform from when he had been in Nebs's good graces. His hair was neat, his fingernails trimmed, and his posture schoolboy perfect.

But his eyes looked too many places, and he often seemed to stare at something far in the distance. Even when he was talking to somebody as dangerous as me.

He was skilled at this game, resisting interrogation. I removed a stogie from my jacket and took my time nursing it to life. The room was dimly lit except for a circle of harsh light around the two of us. Nebs had kept all the cells prepped for interrogation. The environment almost made me uneasy, and I was definitely a person most rational people feared.

Exhaling smoke, I leaned back. I wasn't trying to breathe it in his face. That was cliché, an amateur tactic better left in holo vids. I wasn't trying to intimidate him, or gag him, or whatever.

There were a lot more tools in my toolbox than that.

"It's been a long time since I was with the Reaper Corps," I said.

He nodded, focused on me now and listening intently. I wasn't sure if it was something I said, or just the distracted thought process for a man thinking such big, crazy thoughts.

Either way, we were almost talking like normal people. "You are going to awaken my mother and sister, ensure their safety, and help me protect the people of this fleet," I said.

"That is acceptable and necessary," he answered. "I appreciate the fact that you have not threatened me this time. As long as I can pursue my research, I will do anything you ask."

"I need you to be a little more specific on what that research is about," I said. Every time we broached the subject, my gut tightened, and I felt a sense of dread.

"The universe is large," he said. "Humans are not the only sentient life that exists. In this galaxy—or the next—there are wonders you can't imagine."

"Show me some evidence," I said.

The smile he gave me was unnerving. "We've been through this before. And I'm sure your limited artificial intelligence has briefed you on all the applicable theories regarding sentient, nonhuman life-forms that must exist."

"Yeah, I've been reading all the conspiracy theories from crazy people like you," I said.

This didn't offend him. He smiled and nodded as though he expected my reaction.

"I will never trust you, Ayers," I said.

"That is not a commodity I require. If I need you to believe in something, I will prove its existence," he said.

"When?"

He held my gaze. "Soon."

3

I'D SEEN a fleet assemble before, but not like this. This wasn't a Union armada on its way to destroy enemies and conquer new worlds, this was a ragtag collection of transports and out-of-date warships moving people toward hope.

The exceptions were the *Nightmare* and the *Bright Lance*. It was these state-of-the-art Union stealth ships, carrier-class vessels designed for long-range missions, that would give us a fighting chance if we were attacked.

I spent most of my time on the *Bright Lance of Xad*. That's where my mother and sister were still in cryo-pods. The *Jelly-bird* and some of my best friends—people I didn't deserve to know—stayed close and ready to take me where I needed to go within the fleet.

As a Reaper, I felt like I was semi-retired, not having a mission that involved violence, interrogation, or secrecy. That was best for everyone, but I was bored as hell. My intellectual dueling with Doctor Ayers only relieved part of my restlessness.

"You can't smoke on the bridge," said Cynthia Thomas Younger of Xad, the captain of the *Bright Lance*. "I shouldn't have to tell you that, Reaper."

I held the cigar ready but didn't light it, while towering over her, shrugging. "Sorry. You're right. Rules are rules."

She was a small woman, and I was a big man. X-37 advised me many times not to think this meant anything in terms of absolute power.

She possessed a lot of it. Brion Rejon, the leader of Xad, appointed her with the approval of the Xad Council. She'd taken command of the *Bright Lance* and made sweeping changes. Everyone seemed to like her firm but fair style. Even some Union turncoats took oaths to follow her orders—and were paired with capable soldiers loyal to Younger until they were vetted.

The woman was the polar opposite of Vice Admiral Nebs, the man who led this fleet out here where we defeated him.

Captain Younger stepped away from me then faced the main holo display. "XO, are the fleets aligned?"

Commander Bernard Gile shifted uncomfortably in his uniform that lacked patches or rank insignia. The people of Xad, including their military, had been scavengers for hundreds of years. Repurposed items were commonplace. This uniform, by contrast, was fresh out of the ship's fabric recycler and was stiff with newness.

Commander Gile was fit and very young for his rank. I was skeptical of him and many other Xad fleet officers. Rejon explained they were a special class—individuals dedicated to learning ship operations from simulators and the few functioning large vessels they hobbled together over the years. Basically, they grew up on holo games, rigorous schooling, and military discipline.

Xad Star was a dangerous system, a forgotten nexus of slip tunnels where hostile forces converged to gain resources and subjugate anyone who opposed them. It hadn't just been the Union. There were other dangers in the galaxy, including the Alon—enemies to both the people of the Xad and Wallach systems.

Gile was a very serious, very professional young man. "Yes, Captain, the fleets are aligned perfectly. It took a great deal of negotiation with the Wallach ship drivers, but we managed."

Captain Younger nodded with her arms crossed, aware of all that had transpired but wishing for her young protégé to articulate his report. "They do things differently, don't they?"

"Yes, Captain," Gile said. "In time, we can teach them all the secrets of surviving in space."

I watched them and the other bridge crew officer discuss ship order, slip tunnel approach, and standard operating procedures.

"Are you bored, Reaper Cain?" X-37 asked.

"Yeah. You can tell that?" I asked.

"You know that I can," my LAI said. "It would be an

insult to my very existence if I lacked the ability to monitor your moods, and if I could take offense I would. Would you like me to reactivate my hurt feelings simulator protocol?"

"No, unless it's necessary for your overall functioning and interaction with humans," I said, cringing at the memory of that LAI experiment.

The limited artificial intelligence was woven into my nerve-ware at a molecular level. He could communicate with me privately, or use various methods to speak to my friends on a public channel. I upgraded his software whenever possible, which these days meant the LAI constantly worked with Jelly or Henshaw to improve his efficiency. The AI of the *Bright Lance*, Mavis, was also proving to be more helpful than her counterpart on the *Nightmare*, Necron. The system resets that came after Nebs died affected each of the ships differently.

"Why are you standing here, Reaper Cain?" X-37 asked.

I exhaled roughly, aware that this was something Elise and others often took as a warning sign I was in a mood. I hadn't realized I was anything but bored. "For starters, I'm frustrated that we haven't figured out the cryo-prisons yet. You're the one that keeps telling me I can't sleep on the floor of the medical bay where they are keeping my family."

"Sleeping on the floor is bad for your back and the foldout cot is too short," X-37 said. "I suggest you spend more time training with Elise and take better care of yourself."

"All she does is attempt to integrate her Archangel armor with her micro-fighter," I said.

"Or perhaps you might arrange a meeting with Tom on

the observation deck for whiskey and cigar time," X-37 suggested, ignoring my arguments.

"He hasn't stopped working since we launched the Xad fleet," I pointed out.

"Then spar with Path and improve your blade skills," X-37 offered, as patient as a machine.

I looked at the ceiling with just my eyes, an expression I needed to stop doing around Elise, because she always called me out on it—usually with a sharp suggestion to act my age and stop stealing her teenage thunder. "I'm tired of getting hit on the head, X. Are you trying to get me knocked unconscious?""

"You have an 11.3% chance of rendering yourself unconscious despite the fact that we are not on a mission," X-37 said. "I ran this figure several times to be sure. I suspect there may be an error in my calculation, as I did not account for inebriation, only blunt force trauma from training or fighting."

The activity on the bridge of the *Bright Lance* focused to a single moment. Brion Rejon, Leader of Xad, entered and took his place near Captain Younger.

"We are ready to begin the slip tunnel transit," she said. "This is a momentous day. What will be our destination?"

"Hail the *Spirit of Wallach*," Rejon ordered.

"We have a connection, sir," Commander Gile said.

President Amanda Coronas of Wallach came into view, looking as presidential as ever. It had been a while since I'd seen her in person. The memory made me smile. I had smoked a cigar in her palace, which tradition required her to reciprocate. This was a big deal on Wallach—exploding through their social networks like the scandal of the decade.

All the leaders made appropriate greetings, observing formalities necessary between the two leaders.

"It seems like it's been a long time, Halek Cain," Coronas said. "My advisors have informed me that you wish to go to a location identified as Macabre."

All of this had already been discussed ad nauseum. Everyone knew where we were going. I was getting tired of the dog and pony show but liked Coronas too much to give her a hard time. "Going there will be the best thing for the fleet."

Coronas consulted her officers and advisors before turning back to me. "Very well, Reaper. We'll plot a course based on the minimal information we have in this region of the galaxy."

"Thanks, Mrs. President," I said, then gave them some space.

"I would feel much better about this if you were scouting the slip tunnel with the *Jellybird*," X-37 said.

"They need to do it themselves," I said. "That's not my job."

"Of course not," X-37 said.

"Don't start with me, X."

"I wouldn't dream of it, Reaper Cain. However, I must point out that many lives are at stake," X-37 said.

I knew what my digital friend was getting at. The leaders

of both peoples had offered me jobs, a combination of scout, guardian, and mentor role with full honor, pay, and benefits—something I hadn't thought about for a very long time.

The situation was surreal. Not once did they imply that they might need me to fix a problem my actual training had prepared me for. They were treating me like a normal soldier, not a cybernetically enhanced freak that was only good at one thing.

Six corvette class cruisers of Wallach approached the slip tunnel opening. Over the last week, Xad ship soldiers had joined their crews as part of a joint operating agreement. After generations of living, fighting, and salvaging in space, the Xad fighters were uniquely qualified to serve in this capacity. They were tough and creative, and they valued teamwork during a crisis.

Their skill and bravery were what turned the tide against Nebs, who should have destroyed us with his superior technology and veteran warfighters.

I watched the half dozen ships disappear and wished I was with them. X-37 and I both knew the real reason I wasn't going. My family might not wake up from whatever Nebs had ordered Doctor Ayers to do to them, and I needed to be here.

"Captain, if I'm not needed on the bridge, I would like to attend to other matters of importance," I said, mimicking their formal way of speaking in the Xad fleet. For a civilization of scavengers, they maintained a lot of formalities.

"Of course," Captain Younger said, dismissing me politely.

In the hallway, I let some of my frustration show—striding forward, clenching and unclenching my fists. "Let's review the situation with Ayers. He needs to understand that if we don't find the codes to awaken my mother and sister, he better magic up a better solution or get Reaped."

"Would you like me to send a holo of some of your more creative kills?" X-37 said. "Perhaps that has been missing during our previous attempts to communicate with Ayers. He needs to fear the Reaper."

"I like where your head is at, X, but that's psychotic even for me," I said. "Let's try another round of directed conversation. I don't want to scare the man too badly and risk losing the chance to get my family back."

I CALLED Henshaw on my way to the cell where we were holding Doctor Ayers. "Are you still on board *Bright Lance?*"

"I am, Reaper," Henshaw said. "It's the most interesting ship in the fleet right now, and Captain Younger has been kind enough to allow me to park the *Lady Faith* on her flight deck while we are in the slip tunnel."

"Are you with the Lady now? I'm heading to talk to Doctor Ayers in his cell," I said.

"I'm on my way," Henshaw said. "To be honest, I can't stop thinking about the man's theories. Tom and I spent most of last night comparing notes from our research. As your LAI would say, proving the existence of aliens has been attempted over a dozen times since the Union was formed. I never realized humans were so obsessed with the existence of life in the galaxy."

"Really?" I said. "If we've tried this DNA trick before, why hasn't it worked?"

"None of the alien DNA samples were actually from alien races, which is a very interesting discovery in its own right," Henshaw said, sounding a lot like Tom—his voice full of naive wonder.

The ocular engineer couldn't resist a new challenge like this. He'd done things in his career to gain access to technology available nowhere else. I didn't think he regretted working for people like Nebs, even if he eventually did the right thing.

I understood Henshaw. His world was an ordered place, so well ordered that his subconscious rebelled to keep a healthy balance—prompting him to gamble just to introduce a little chaos into his reasoned mind. X-37 had explained I did the same thing, but I vented my frustrations by nearly getting myself killed and taking on lost causes.

"Get Bug on the line," I said.

A moment later, X-37 explained the kid was sleeping in front of his computer, cheese crackers spilled in his lap. "He seems to be taking his job to watch Ayers very seriously."

"We can't have him falling asleep," I thought out loud. "Is there anyone he can split shifts with?"

"I have suggested this to him, but he is resistant to the idea," X-37 said.

"Figure something out, X. This is going to bite us in the ass. For now, wake him up and put him to work," I said.

"Right away, Reaper Cain."

I arrived at the brig first, greeted the guard by name, and was admitted to the high-security area for this type of prisoner. When I had the place to myself, I dimmed the lights. There was a reason I waited hours or even days between my attempts to interrogate Doctor Ayers.

The man was as thoroughly insane as anyone I'd ever encountered, and in a completely unique way. There was no questioning his conviction in what he believed. It was almost like he saw humans, including himself, as a historical footnote to something far greater. As in empires of strange alien conquerors different.

He didn't allude to that belief often, but when he did it filled my nightmares with dire possibilities. He provided detailed reports on DNA that X-37 didn't locate in any database. No amount of questioning could get him to disclose where the Union had obtained the petrified samples.

Henshaw arrived, stepping into the darkened room and looking around. Both of his eyes were artificial. In the dimness, the lights that rotated around his pupils were more pronounced. One circled clockwise and the other counterclockwise. He'd never admitted to doing this on purpose, but I wondered if it wasn't more for aesthetics than because it was actually necessary for proper functioning of his optical enhancements.

What did I know? I was just a Reaper with a heart of gold.

"What are you laughing at, Reaper Cain?" X-37 asked. "This seems to be an inappropriate time for humor. And if I may point out, you are keeping very unique company."

"Don't worry about it, X. Sometimes I crack myself up." Explaining my funny bone to my LAI wasn't worth the effort.

"Are you going to talk to your LAI the whole time we're here?" Henshaw asked, annoyed.

"You have an LAI," I countered.

Henshaw, who I had originally contacted to fix my left eye, was supported by his own limited artificial intelligence. It was a rudimentary unit that might or might not be some sort of high-level do-it-yourself job. Of course with Henshaw, that meant something entirely different from most people.

"I don't talk to mine like you do, and I never uploaded a personality profile," Henshaw said. "It is just a tool for me."

"Well good for you," I said. "Do you think that Doctor Ayers has an LAI?"

Henshaw considered this for a moment, crossing his arms so that he could hold his chin in the fingers of one hand. "I don't think so. But now that you bring the subject up, that's based on a hunch or even worse, an assumption."

"Before you ask, Reaper Cain, I am not able to directly scan the prisoner," X-37 said. "I am running an analysis of our past interactions with the doctor, looking for clues in his speech pattern or behaviors. Thus far, I have found nothing of interest on the subject."

"Why not ask him?" Henshaw asked.

I went to the door without responding. Henshaw didn't seem to take offense, possibly because I hadn't meant any and we had been working together for a while now. Did either of us trust each other? More than we used to, but he was a skeptic and I was a Reaper.

The two of us traversed the short hallway to Doctor Ayers's cell. Neither of us spoke when we moved into the man's living space—which was gloomier than the hospital room he'd been in prior to this.

He stood at the very back of the small cell practically bouncing with nervous energy. I'd seen this before. His moods and his energy levels were often erratic. I thought he looked like there were too many big ideas bouncing around inside his head.

"When can I resume my research?" he asked.

"Which research are you talking about this time?" I asked, somewhat annoyed he jumped ahead on the expected dialogue.

"I've explained to you many times that this galaxy wasn't meant for humans," he said. "The cryo-pod prisons are not research, just a tactic Nebs used."

"That you helped him use," I didn't raise my voice or attempt to be menacing. We'd been through this dance dozens of times by now.

"I had no choice," he said. "They will be fine once we get what we need from Macabre."

"They better be more than fine," I said.

"You are a very tedious man, Reaper," Ayers said, ignoring Henshaw completely.

I stepped back, faced away from Ayers, and conferred with X-37.

"Doctor Ayers has made one hundred and ninety-two references to the existence of nonhuman aliens during your past interaction with him," X-37 said. "Statistically, that is significantly higher than should be noted in any rational conversation. He has never seemed concerned for the welfare of your family or other individuals stuck in the cryo-pods. We need to see what is in the vault."

Stepping past Henshaw, I leaned into my prisoner's personal space. "Actually, Ayers, we're just here to call your bluff."

Doctor Ayers stopped jittering and locked his gaze on mine. "And what bluff would that be, Reaper?"

The distinct feeling the man was several steps ahead of me in this conversation was disturbing. "We're on our way to the Macabre system. I'm just saying, it better not be empty when we get there."

"That's the only place to find the codes to open the cryo-pods," he said, sounding relieved. "I want to do that as much as you do."

"Warning, Reaper Cain. I have detected a variance of his voice modulation in this last statement," X-37 warned.

"Way ahead of you, X," I said, practically touching Ayers now I was so close to him. "I almost believe you, but that doesn't make any sense. What do you care about my mother and sister?"

"They are both fine individuals. I will not pretend to have any special care or concern for them," Ayers said as though this type of honesty was intended to convince me of something. "It's hard to explain."

"You're a scientist," Henshaw said. "You should be good at explaining things."

Doctor Ayers started fidgeting again, his nervous energy having no place to escape.

"You don't have to be a prisoner," I said. "But I can't have you running about the ship if I don't trust you."

This brought Doctor Ayers back. He stared at me with naked hope in his eyes. "Could I continue my research?"

"Once you've told me what it is, no bullshit, nothing left out this time—maybe. If you remain closely supervised. Like under an armed guard and restricted from contact with the ship AI," I said.

"My research is DNA matrixes and xenobiology—a harmless pursuit," he said.

"Unless you're trying to resurrect a potentially dangerous alien race through DNA splicing," Henshaw said. "I have read all of your research."

"I seriously doubt that," Doctor Ayers said.

"I'm a fast reader," Henshaw stated.

I moved back a step and let the two scientists go at it. Neither X nor I heard anything useful, but it was part of the process. We needed more observational data of the man to understand, as a gambler would put it, his *tells*.

"Did you get that, Bug?" I asked under my breath.

"Sure did, Mister Reaper," Bug said in my ear. "That dude is strange. Watching him on the ship cameras has been entertaining."

"Just don't fall asleep, Bug," I said. "You need an assistant."

"Elise could help me," Bug said.

"She's busy," I answered.

"Okay, that's cool. I'll handle it myself for now," Bug said.

"Finding an appropriate assistant for Bug has been problematic. We can't just ask Captain Younger for a communications tech. This type of spying on a prisoner is highly unethical," X-37 said.

"So is building a super-secret alien out of thousands of years old DNA snippets," I said, still trying to keep my voice low. "You know that is what Nebs had him working on."

The argument between the scientists ceased. Ayers stared at me almost angrily. "You're half wrong. The DNA we archived isn't old, and that is exactly what Nebs wanted. He always demanded I make a weapon for him."

"What do you mean it wasn't old," Henshaw asked. "Our entire conversation has been predicated on the fact that you are working on ancient civilizations that were located during archaeological missions."

"I did pull a lot of evidence from archaeological digs on dozens of planets during my career," Ayers said. "But Nebs ranged outside of Union control more than once and found things that are now lost to us since you killed him and destroyed one of his ships."

"I don't like where this is going, X," I said.

Ayers, who apparently had very good hearing, directed his attention toward me. "I may have unintentionally been misleading you, or you may have jumped to the wrong conclusions. The aliens I'm interested in haven't been in this part of the galaxy for eons, but that doesn't mean they're extinct."

"So what's the point of growing one from a DNA sample?" Henshaw asked.

"The crazy old dude wants an alien pet," Bug whispered in my ear. I could hear him eating cheese crackers as he listened in on our conversation.

Ayers took his time answering. He seemed genuinely confused that we didn't get it, that we didn't want what he wanted. "I want them here with us, not in some distant corner of the galaxy. How can we learn from them if they are that far away?"

"There's a serious flaw in your logic," Henshaw said. "They won't have any of the cultural knowledge, even if you can recreate them perfectly, which you can't, because you don't have a viable stem cell from their species."

"I disagree. We can learn many things from them in the way they solve problems. Once we get a full examination of their biology, and how it actually works in a controlled setting, we can make valuable conclusions," Ayers said.

"I'm sure the real aliens won't mind us screwing around with their genetic offspring," I said.

"They will never know, Reaper," Ayers assured me. "We have never acquired a living specimen."

"Somehow, that doesn't reassure me," I said.

4

Elise struck the top of my helmet with her practice sword, sending stars through my vision. Pain glanced down my neck, my spine, and into my limbs.

"Pay attention, Reaper," she said.

"What the hell was that? Are we sparring, or trying to kill each other?" I asked.

"You're going to get us killed if you don't train to your full potential. Isn't that what you always tell me?" She moved with her practice weapon, ready to emphasize her point. "Honestly, you're starting to freak me out and piss me off. And annoy the crap out of me. And a bunch of other stuff."

"All that it once?" I asked.

"Yeah, Reaper. You haven't been right since we found your mom and sister," she said. "I get it, but in this room, we *train*."

"She's not wrong, Reaper Cain," X-37 said, sounding at least as distracted as I had been a moment ago. This meant my LAI was processing a lot of data.

I circled the training mat, practice sword held with both hands, not looking at my feet but remaining aware of everything Elise was doing and anything that entered my peripheral vision. We had the place to ourselves. I wasn't the only one who disliked getting smashed on the head with the practice sword.

Unless ordered, no one trained with Elise, me, or Path. Some Wallach and Xad soldiers would watch but it was rare for anyone to take a beating. Only when we made it clear that it was a technique session did we draw a big class.

"Ready?" Elise asked as she attacked.

It was a lame trick, but I had to hustle to stay ahead of it. I was off my game. What would my mother or sister think if they could watch me doing everything half-assed?

Elise smashed my training helmet again then spun and swept my legs out from under me with her right heel.

"Third time is a charm!" she shouted, dancing back as I came to my feet, pissed off and ready for some payback.

"That was lucky," I grunted.

"You said that the first two times." She circled me, her practice weapon ready for action. "You also said that if I could do it a third time, that meant it was skill and not luck."

"You're such an opportunist," I said. "Attacking a man when he's preoccupied."

"That seems like the best time," she argued, then came at me again.

This time, I parried and moved out of the way with my usual energy and skill. The sound of our swords clacking grew louder and faster. We kept at it for a long time, so long that I realized we had drawn an audience without realizing it. Men and women trickled in to watch the spectacle until there were twenty or thirty soldiers and crew members lining the walls.

Eventually, we broke apart and saluted each other.

"That was good work, Elise," I said, aware that she needed praise but that too much would be taken as sarcasm or belittlement. Dealing with the young woman could be like balancing a feather on a razor blade.

"Ah, thanks, Reaper. It's so sweet that you realize I'm kicking your butt," she said.

"Don't get carried away, kid," I said. "Leg sweeps are good. You might even use the technique in a real fight some-day. When you can shoulder-throw me, then I'll be impressed."

"Three times?" she asked.

"Yeah, three times," I said. "Don't get cocky. Even if you catch me with my head someplace else, I'm twice your size. If you use sloppy technique, you'll not only fail to throw me, you will hurt yourself."

"You're right," she said. "We should have a technique session." She faced the growing crowd. "Who's up for some technique? Nothing too rough."

Awkward laughter spread through the crowd, but we had a few takers. The rest of our session was spent practicing shoulder throws and other takedowns.

THE OBSERVATION DECK of the *Bright Lance of Xad* was crowded. As a gathering space for a much larger ship, there were many people relaxing and talking in low voices. I found a small table with chairs around it and took a seat. Tom joined me. Henshaw, Elise, and Bug straggled in one at a time.

"Aren't you supposed to be doing something important, Bug?" I asked.

"Yeah, sure. But I'm trying something new. An automation sequence I worked up with Tom's help. Tells me if a certain person is awake or asleep. Did you know that dude sleeps standing up sometimes?"

"Tell me about it later, Bug." I wasn't sure why he was here. Going out in public wasn't his thing. He liked places that reminded him of where he'd grown up secure in a fortified tower.

The Dreadmax kid looked uncomfortable. I expected him to antagonize me about whiskey and cigars, demanding his own taste of them, despite his age. Instead, he sat in a chair that looked too big for him and kept his hands in his lap. His posture was terrible. He slouched as though if to make himself small and inconspicuous.

I pulled out a cigar, considered it, then clipped off the tip with a small knife from my pocket. I could do it with my Reaper blade, but it would draw a lot of attention in our current environment. Lately, I had been using the cigar ritual to smooth out my sleight of hand, drawing attention one way, and getting it lit so it almost seemed like a magic trick.

Practice made perfect. Chronic pickpocketing, for example, kept me sharp for missions in urban areas. I wondered if I would ever see a city again. Moving through crowds with my stealth cloak activated and my Reaper mask boosting my LAI seemed like it would be a vacation compared to the stress of moving a fleet across the galaxy.

"I have to say, I enjoy this observation deck," Tom said. "The background music is about perfect."

I found the low melodies and rhythms soothing but hadn't thought about it until he mentioned it. This place was like a cocktail lounge in space. One enormous wall showed a view of the slip tunnel outside the ship. The twisting green fields of energy—or whatever they were made out of—could put a person in a trance for hours. I'd spent hours staring at them.

"Did you find out anything new from Doctor Ayers?" Elise asked.

I waved her comment away. "Rules."

She made a face, drawing back in annoyance at my tone. "Rules? What the… are you talking about?" she asked with an embarrassed look at Bug. He had heard strong language before and used it, but in person, he looked even younger than he was. Everyone treated him like a child most days.

Tom answered for me. "Cigar and whiskey time is for relaxing, maybe talking about an interesting book. Not that I've been able to get Hal to read one."

"I read, just not that trash you like so much," I said.

Tom laughed and took this harassment well.

I sipped my whiskey. We all watched the slip tunnel for a while and listened to the conversations around us. No one was close to our little table, but the volume in the room increased as more people filed in.

"I miss the *Jellybird*," I said.

"Too many people?" Elise said. "Why don't you just jump up and wave your blade around. That will clear the place out."

"They're not bothering me, I was just talking," I said. The Gronic Fat I had managed to buy off one of the Union turn-coats—a quartermaster—tasted good. I was nearly out of them, so I enjoyed it, thinking of other times on planets I hadn't appreciated while I'd been there. I realized then that we had left the Union and the Deadlands and everything we'd ever known far behind.

"So what do you losers do here? So far, whiskey and cigar time seems boring," Elise commented.

"Especially if you're not drinking whiskey or smoking cigars," Henshaw said, leaning forward from his chair to refresh his glass. "Perhaps we should play a game of chance."

"That would make it whiskey and cigar and cards time," I said.

"I've never played," Elise said. "Bug, have you played?"

The Dreadmax kid looked at me nervously, then back to Elise. "I don't even know what you're talking about."

"Warning, Reaper Cain," X-37 said in my ear. "My analysis suggests they are trying to hustle you. There is no evidence that Henshaw is behind this, but I believe he will be coming into this ruse soon."

I gave X-37 one of my hand signals that no one else could detect, although now that I thought about it, Henshaw was a gambler and might detect my minute hand gestures better than most people. The man was always looking for somebody's tell. That was one reason I had included him in my last interrogation session of Ayers.

"If we only had some cards," Henshaw said.

"Maybe they have some at the bar," Bug said, sounding like he was executing a canned line from a situational comedy —*this from a kid who didn't know what playing cards was.*

His confederates glared at him, then tried to cover the faux pas.

"Why don't you run and check," Henshaw said. He waited a few seconds until the kid was away from our little gathering. "I hate teaching kids to play cards. Very tedious."

"I bet," I said. "X-37 is telling me I'm needed elsewhere."

"I am?" X-37 asked privately. "Oh, yes, Reaper Cain. I understand your intent now."

Elise stood from her chair, casting a glance at Bug's quest for cards. "What kind of example are you setting? He's going to think you're avoiding him, or that you don't care. The little guy has been through a lot."

"Little guy? Yesterday you were complaining about what an annoying little preteen he was, and I told you that thirteen makes him a teenager," I said.

"Yeah, I know. But whatever," she said.

"Why don't you show him the basics and we can play next time if anyone is still interested," I said.

"Fine," Elise said. "You're no fun."

Henshaw and the others acted like nothing had happened and went about their rest and relaxation. I left the room and slipped into my stealth cloak, then I circled around to the other side and entered while keeping to the shadows. Just as I suspected, their little group disbanded not long after I left—completely uninterested in *learning* how to play cards.

"They're after me," I said.

"I agree, Reaper Cain," X-37 said. "You should use the utmost caution if you don't want to lose your shirt."

THE EQUIPMENT ROOM was empty when I arrived, which suited my mood. Elise and the others were constantly working with their equipment, making improvements, and maximizing their chance of success in battle.

It'd been a while since I was that enthusiastic.

But that wasn't why was here. I was wandering the hallways and decks, trying to unwind and go with the flow. A long tour of the ship had brought me here.

"Would you like to contact the armorer? The man is formally of the Union, but has passed all of the vetting and loyalty checks required by the Wallach and Xad coalition."

"No need to wake the man," I said, opening one of the larger lockers with the access code X-37 had acquired from Mavis during our last visit to this room.

When the doors opened, I felt some of the same youthful excitement that I felt when I first went into spec ops. The weapon inside was massive, something that required a very strong man or mechanized armor to support.

After lifting it with some difficulty, I put it on the work-bench and examined it with a smile.

"Your biometrics indicate that you like this gun," X-37 said. "It's the Z1A Destroyer, a belt fed, crew-served weapon for squad tactics or bunker emplacements."

"Two questions," I said. "Can we mount it on the back of my Archangel armor, and can we try it out on the virtual range?"

"Yes and yes," X-37 said. "You will need to consult with Tom and Elise to know how to use it with the Archangel armor and a micro-fighter."

"I'm not worried about that right now," I said. "To be honest, X, this is just for fun. I might even smoke a cigar while I try it out."

"Past experience with this type of testosterone charged

activity suggests I cannot stop you from doing either," X-37 said.

"Warm up the VR range," I said, picking it up from the workbench and making sure there was no live ammunition anywhere near it.

I stepped onto the VR lane, aimed it, then shifted its weight side to side on the harness. "This is going to be fun, but I think outside of the range I'll need armor to support it."

"I agree completely," X-37 said.

Holding the weapon with the assistance of the support straps, I fished out a cigar with my right hand and managed to light it on the first try. Puffing smoke, I put away the lighter, smiled dangerously, and aimed at the virtual targets.

"Let's rock out," I said, and started blasting.

"If it's all the same to you, I will be researching our language lexicon for the meaning of this particular colloquialism while you *blow shit up*," X-37 said.

I laughed at the feel of the weapon doing its work. "It's been a while! I need to get down here more often and relax."

"The activities you find relaxing are contrary to logic," X-37 said.

"You know you like it," I said, reloading a virtual ammo box.

"I like nothing," X-37 said. "I am a limited artificial intelligence. As part of my programming, I will make a note that this is an enjoyable activity to us."

"Good enough," I said, puffing another cloud of smoke with the cigar held between my teeth. "Get some!"

This time I emptied the entire magazine box in one trigger pull. The smoking barrel was a virtual special effect, but a good one. Someone had put a lot of loving attention into these simulations.

5

"CAPTAIN ON THE BRIDGE," Ensign Kyle Walker announced, prompting everyone to stand. I was already on my feet, off to one side of the well-staffed bridge.

Captain Cynthia Thomas Younger strode into the room. Her crew responded with the unique professionalism that I still thought contrasted with their not-very-uniform uniforms —standing and facing Younger for the moment it took her to wave them back to their posts. Not for the first time, I thought the ship crews of Xad overcompensated for the shabby, repurposed clothing most of them wore.

"Reaper," she said to me by way of acknowledgment.

"Captain," I said.

Her attention turned back to the task at hand. One of the Wallach ships was struggling. "Commander Gile, what is the situation?"

"The Republic of Wallach Ship *Jumping Fox* is reporting engine troubles. We are the closest ship to that is ready to render aid," Gile said. "The RWS *Spirit of Wallach* is prepping a repair team but also requests our help."

"Open a channel to the *Spirit*," Younger ordered.

"Hailing the *Spirit of Wallach* now, Captain," said an ensign.

A man I now recognize as Captain Quincy Drysdale appeared on the holo. Middle-aged, his uniform was well-tailored, and he had the look of someone who still played contact sports during his leisure time.

"Thank you," Captain Drysdale said. "We are preparing a team but welcome your assistance. All reports indicate your people are skilled at this type of operation."

"We are glad to help," Captain Younger said. She glanced down at a screen, then back to the holo. "We are deploying a shuttle now. You should receive our ship telemetry and an itinerary of how the operation will proceed."

I watched until I saw the shuttle arrive at the malfunctioning Wallach ship. To my surprise, the heavy-duty EVA suit that Path was so fond of these days emerged first. Three other people followed him, also in the beefed-up, ready-for-anything equipment.

Captain Younger saw my expression. "Your weapons master always volunteers for spacewalks. He's extremely good for someone not raised in the Xad system."

"He's a strange one," I said. X-37 berated me privately at the implication of my statement. I made a quick course correction. "My people aren't as comfortable in the void as yours. For Path, floating in space is the ultimate form of meditation."

Captain Younger smiled knowingly. "I've had several very interesting conversations with the man. His appreciation for the beauty outside of the ship is sublime."

"Beauty, terror, it's hard to draw the line sometimes," I said.

She laughed, but I noticed more than a few members of her crew seem to resent my casual conversation with their captain. This made talking to X-37 difficult, unless I wanted to make a scene. Which was always an option.

Younger turned back to her work, seeming like she was in a good mood. The crisis on the *Jumping Fox* didn't bother her much. "Has anyone figured out what a fox is?"

"Some type of animal, I believe," Commander Gile said.

Younger glanced back at me.

"It's like a small dog with a pointy face. Very clever," I said.

"You've seen one?" she asked.

"Only in books. I took a sabbatical for a while, did as much reading as was allowed," I said, not wanting to get into the whole convicted murderer and two years on death row thing right now.

"Allowed? I can't imagine a situation where someone told you what to do," Captain Younger said. "I'm not saying you're a bad soldier, but there is something about you."

"Reaper Cain, Elise has volunteered with the backup

crew," X-37 said. "I thought you should know, given her record for getting into trouble when outside of a ship."

"Thanks, X. That's good news. She been spending far too much time tinkering with that micro-fighter," I said.

This time, the crew of the *Bright Lance of Xad* ignored me, preferring to focus on their assigned jobs.

"I believe Elise is concealing her involvement in this rescue mission," X-37 added.

"I couldn't stop her from volunteering if I wanted to," I said. "And it's not like she's doing anything. Standby is what it is, mostly just waiting around."

"You may have just jinxed her," X-37 said.

"Look who just got superstitious," I said. "I didn't think that was in your programming."

"I believe you understand what I mean," X-37 said. "What you explain away as superstitious presumptions, I treat as an evidence-based prediction. Many times when you have relaxed, and thus spoke casually about our chances, things have gone horribly wrong."

"That's not enough to show causation," I said, watching several of the holo screens, looking for Elise even though I knew she was just standing by, not getting involved. She knew what she was doing. We'd been through EVA missions more dangerous than even the people of Xad were accustomed to taking on. That didn't mean I wanted her getting involved in this. Mixing her freewheeling style with the long-established methods of the Xad salvagers could be a real headache.

"We have a problem, Captain," Commander Gile said.

I edged as close to his workstation as I could without being in the crew's way. Captain Younger also shifted her attention. I felt the energy in the room go up. Something was wrong and everyone saw it before I did.

This was their world, not mine. I'd been doing so many ship-based missions that I had become overconfident. I forgot that people like Captain Younger devoted their lives to ships and what they could do.

"What am I looking for, X?" I asked, trying to stay out of everyone's way.

"Power output is fluctuating on the RWS *Jumping Fox*," X-37 said. "It won't be long before one or all of the engines fail. They are also having trouble with maintaining course, which should not be even the slightest issue without there being a serious internal problem."

One of the small ship's engines cut out, causing it to turn.

"In any other circumstance, this would not be a problem," X-37 said.

"I get it, X," I said. "Why can't they compensate for the change?"

"Unknown," X-37 said. "I am listening in and it seems to be a hardware issue, something that must be repaired on the exterior of the ship, preferably while docked at a space station."

"Of course," I said. "Nothing can be easy."

Slip tunnels were easy to use. Once a vessel was inside, the pilot only needed to keep going until the end. One thing everyone knew, however, was that touching the wall of the slip tunnel was deadly. The deviation and course that the *Jumping Fox* was making would have been invisible if they were in normal space. As it was, a collision with the green wall of energy appeared to be imminent.

"This is Captain Peterson of the *Jumping Fox*," a man said, voice only on the communications link. "We're cutting all engines to avoid further course deviation. The more course corrections we make, the greater the error in our navigation. Please direct your crews to the steering jets on the port side. We can handle the main engines. My engineers believe it is the small thrusters that started the problem and continue to aggravate it."

"Understood, Captain," Younger responded. "We are directing our teams now."

Peterson replied distractedly, then ended the conversation to work on more pressing issues on his end. The bridge of the *Jumping Fox* sounded like there were a dozen crew persons jumping from one crisis to the next.

"Captain, I suggest sending all available EVA teams to deal with the problem. There will most likely be more than one navigational thruster that needs attention," Commander Gile said.

"Agreed," Captain Younger said.

I watched as the alert went out inside.

"So much for Elise staying out of trouble," X-37 said.

"We should have just sent her first thing," I said.

A half dozen shuttles with as many EVA teams surrounded the *Jumping Fox*. I couldn't see what they were doing without looking over the shoulder of one of the mission controllers who was watching through individual EVA video feeds.

"At least they're not being shot at," I said.

"Agreed," X-37 said. "But thanks for bringing up that possibility. If I had the capacity to worry, this would have caused me distress."

"Maybe I should have you upgraded," I said, immediately deciding that would be the worst possible personality upgrade I could force upon my X unit.

Captain Younger supervised without interfering with her subordinates. She walked the deck with the practiced bearing of a professional officer. Eventually, she stopped near me.

"Now we have two of your people working with mine," she said. "None of you lack for bravery."

"That's one way to look at it," I said. "It's easy for Path. Elise has faced her death more than once in that type of environment. She's the one I'm worried about."

"I would like to learn your weapon master's secret," Younger said. "How does he stay so level headed?"

"His actual name is Grigori Paavo. He's a sword saint, all meditation and calmness in the face of death. Very annoying sometimes," I said. "If you don't watch him, you'll find him floating in his spacesuit with star fields all around him happy as a pig in—"

"What's a pig?" Younger asked, then waved back my explanation with a wink. "We also have this phrase. I'm toying with you."

"We have another problem," Commander Gile announced.

"PARTIAL HULL DECOMPRESSION on the *Jumping Fox!*" Gile said, raising his voice for the first time. "Their crew is fixing it from the inside, but we have several of our people floating free."

Alerts sounded, and I saw them spring into action on what they called a floating free immediate action response or FFIA. Several members of the spacewalking repair team were recovered in seconds, which was important because while the relative speed of the *Jumping Fox* and items near it was nearly constant, it wasn't exactly the same.

Several dots drifted from the repair site.

"Check on Elise," I growled at X-37.

"I'm doing my best, Reaper Cain," X-37 said.

I heard one of the small clicks that my limited artificial intelligence hadn't made for quite a while now. This indicated he was working at his maximum capacity.

"There is too much data flow," X-37 informed me. "Each unit has an emergency tracker and there is a large amount of information about the repair still flowing between ships. It's a mundane issue, but very critical to life-support systems on the *Jumping Fox*. They are also scrambling all relief efforts toward the people floating toward the wall of the slip tunnel."

"Is one of those people Elise?" I asked.

"Unknown." X-37 clicked and popped, working more

energetically than I've ever heard him, even when he'd been trying to save my life and in some very impossible situations.

At least I hoped that was what was happening. It had taken me a long time to get my LAI and all of my hardware working smoothly. Thoughts of the malfunctions I'd endured since Dreadmax weren't reassuring.

"I have a vector," Elise's voice said over the main channel. Everyone on the bridge was listening to her now. "But my safety line isn't long enough. I'm going to jump and knock Specialist Beaufort off his current course."

"What the hell are you doing, Elise," I muttered. "And who is Beaufort?"

"She is attempting a rescue without the proper resources," X-37 said. "Beaufort is a member of the repair team."

"Good luck, Elise," a member of the bridge crew said.

I wanted to punch him.

"Are you thinking of punching the comms officer of the *Bright Lance*?" X-37 said. "Your biometrics correlate with past incidents of senseless violence."

Ignoring a reaper LAI wasn't impossible, especially when all of my attention was on my reckless protégé.

The scene unfolded in slow motion like everyone was moving underwater. Additional personnel arrived on the bridge. Every sensor and communication channel was manned. Several conversations began at once.

Elise wasn't the only one taking action to save her fellow team members. I focused on what I needed to hear, hoping I would catch anything else relevant or that X-37 would monitor the other conversations.

"I just need to run at it," Elise said. "Once I catch him, I'll expend all of my steering jets to change his course. Can you give me an update, *Bright Lance*?"

"I'm streaming the bare minimum of telemetry to your HUD. Please don't deviate from that information, as we have a very busy bandwidth right now. I won't be able to make alterations on the fly," her controller said.

My knuckles popped as I clenched both fists. A second later, the blade in my left arm snapped out.

"Control yourself, Reaper Cain," X-37 said.

"I'll get right on that." Standing, retracting the blade, I tried not to interfere with the crew. I needed to get out there. This was the last time I'd let the kid go solo.

I moved as unobtrusively as possible to stare over the shoulder of the young man talking to Elise. He didn't have video for me to spy through. I could, however, hear her breathing increase as she sprinted across the deck of the *Jumping Fox*.

"You're doing great," her controller said. "You're quick. Where did you learn to run like that in space gear?"

"She's been on missions," I answered, startling the young ensign. "Xad doesn't have a total monopoly on extra vehicle activity skill."

Elise's controller nodded, shaken by my looming presence, and went back to work with his calculations. The screen he used was simple, dots with predicted paths of each unit, including Elise. Her icon was brighter than all the others on his small holo screen. Her target, Beaufort, was also emphasized as he drifted toward the edge of slip space.

"I hope this Beaufort character is worth it," I grumbled.

The man at the control terminal glanced back over his shoulder, again more nervously than I liked. "The girls all find him stunning."

"What?" I shouted, drawing the attention of several other mission controllers.

The bridge of the *Bright Lance* was far larger than the *Jelly-bird* or other small ships, but still very compact compared to a full-sized Union worship. Right now, it was full of people working to save lives.

"I'm sorry," the controller said. "I... need to get back to work helping Elise."

"Are you telling me the kid is risking her life to save some boy she has a crush on?"

The controller ignored me, face reddening second by second. He bent over his work screen and typed furiously, double and triple-checking his calculations.

"Leave it be, Reaper Cain. It would be natural for Elise to have interest in the opposite sex," X-37 explained. "And now is not the time to address the issue."

"We are definitely going to talk when she gets back," I stated, then crossed my arms. Shifting my weight from foot to foot, I felt like a nervous wreck. The sensation was alien to me. I couldn't even punch the wall or stalk the deck or smoke a cigar in this environment.

6

GREEN-DOT-ELISE MOVED THROUGH THE VOID, out of range for an argument. She approached red-dot-Beaufort at a maddeningly slow rate. Sure, the interior of the slip tunnel was a big place and they were falling behind the *Jumping Fox* slowly, but it was aggravating to wait for news.

On another, larger holo view, a fleet coordination officer was scanning the rest of the area for similar problems and found nothing. I wasn't interested in that scene, but the image of hundreds of ships trailing back into the slip tunnel stuck in my mind. I only hoped Elise didn't slam into one of the ships that was now moving faster in relative terms.

"Sir?" Elise's controller said nervously.

"What?" I snapped, moving close to him as I searched for whatever was on his screen that had alarmed him.

"Elise will contact Beaufort in fewer than two minutes,"

the young ensign said. "Once her course intersects with his, we should know if my calculations were correct. And they will be, don't get upset. Once she bumps him off his current course, they will both remain within the slip tunnel for eventual pickup."

"Your calculations?" I asked, staring into his eyes.

"Yes, sir," he said.

"Are you good at your job… what's your name?" I asked.

"Yes, sir. Very good, sir," he answered. "My name's Michael Junkboss, Ensign Michael Junkboss."

"I'm not even going there," I said, but couldn't resist. "Your family name is Junkboss?"

"It's a common name among my people," he said. "I'm the first in my family to become an officer."

"As long as your telemetry calculations for Elise are perfect, you'll be fine," I said.

"My analysis suggests that intimidating the boy will not improve his performance," X-37 said.

"You're doing a great job, Michael," I said, patting him on the shoulder with my cybernetic left hand. "This Beaufort character, however, is going to have some explaining to do when I get a hold of him."

"I've done a quick scan of Xad social media and cannot find any evidence that Elise and Beaufort are an item," X-37 said.

"I don't need evidence," I said, stepping back from Ensign Michael Junkboss to let him concentrate.

"My relationship algorithms recommend choosing your

80

words wisely, or better yet, dropping the issue entirely," X-37 said. "Whether she finds Beaufort or anyone else attractive should have little or no effect on future missions."

"I disagree," I said. "Stuff like that can get into an operator's head and ruin his or her concentration."

"There is an idiom in my conversational database that suggests you should not borrow trouble," X-37 said. "My advice is to not worry about things that have not happened yet."

"You're right," I muttered, watching the dots collide.

The green dot and the red dot touched, then parted ways. Michael Junkboss banged his fist once on his terminal and exclaimed his excitement.

"Yes! That was perfect," he said, and I realized he wasn't talking to me. "Good job, Elise."

"Are you talking to her?" I asked, not realizing that was possible.

He looked embarrassed and unsure of what to say to me.

"Tell her I'm gonna talk with her when we're done."

"I advise against starting this argument now," X-37 said.

"Um, I don't think I should do that," Michael Junkboss said.

"Tell her," I repeated.

He muttered something into his mic that I couldn't hear even with my enhancements.

"X, did you get that?" I asked.

"Of course, Reaper Cain. I can hear him perfectly," X-37 said.

"Then what did he say?" I asked.

"I'd rather not tell you, because you are being an asshole," X-37 said.

"You can't refuse to answer me," I said.

"On the contrary, I am often required to filter information in a way that protects you and keeps you on task to complete any given mission," X-37 said. "That is what I am doing now."

"Bullshit!" I shouted loud enough to draw attention from other rescue mission controllers.

"Calm yourself, Reaper Cain," X-37 said. "If I were a person, I would be quite embarrassed by your behavior."

"Patch me through to Elise, X!"

"You know that is much more difficult now that the *Bright Lance* belongs to Xad," X-37 said. "And it would not be helpful to the situation."

"I don't want excuses, X. I want to talk to Elise right now." I needed to pace the deck but there wasn't room. Bumping into people would probably get me banned from the bridge.

"There is literally nothing you can do. Leave it to the professionals," X-37 said. "For someone who's terrified of the void, Elise certainly does spend a lot of time out there. My analysis suggests she will be fine."

"She's facing her fears. I get it. You can't let something like the freezing atmosphereless expanse of space get the best you," I said. "Do we need to go through Younger to put me through their system?"

"That will not be necessary, Reaper Cain," X-37 said. "Since you are going to cry and whine about it, I managed to find access to a suitable communications channel. I am contacting Elise and her EVA unit now. You might be interested to know that it is an Archangel unit."

"Check yourself, X. I'm about one more argument from having your personality reset. And what did you say about Archangel armor? We're still figuring out what that stuff can even do," I said.

"Do you want to talk to her or not?" X-37 asked.

I groaned, then dove into the conversation. "Elise, this is Cain."

"I'm a little busy," she snapped.

"Doing what, floating?" I asked.

"That's funny, Reaper. Very reassuring. Michael told me I have at least an hour before I drift into one of the other ships in the exodus fleet," Elise said.

"We need to get to a planet where I can keep better track of you," I said. "This is stressing me out."

"*Hello*, I'm the one drifting through a slip tunnel. It's not all about you, Reaper," she said.

"Who is Beaufort?" I demanded.

"Random," she shot back.

"You know who I'm talking about. The guy you risked your life to save," I said.

"I didn't ask what his name was before I made my decision," she said, sounding more serious. "You would've done the same thing in my place."

I didn't answer. Suddenly, I felt out of my depth. What had gotten into me? I wasn't her parent or even her guardian. Operationally, I might be her mentor or unit commander but that would assume she actually listened to me half the time.

"X, I didn't sign up for this," I said.

"If you are referring to the semi-parenting role that you assumed, that is correct. Your original mission was only to save Doctor Hastings and had nothing to do with Elise," X-37 said.

I gave X-37 a hand signal, requesting confirmation that we were speaking privately.

"Yes, Reaper Cain, I did not think that Elise would appreciate this particular aspect of our discussion," X-37 said.

"Was there a point to your interrupting my mission?" Elise asked.

"I just..." The right words wouldn't come. "I was checking on you. Next time could you warn me?"

"I can do that, Reaper," she said, sounding calmer than I thought she had the right to sound.

"Reaper Cain, we have a serious problem," X-37 said.

"What was your first clue?" I asked as I watched the rescue procedures. They were scrambling a second wave of shuttles. A tone of fresh urgency spread through the room.

"What's going on, X?" I asked, moderating my tone, trying to be less of a jerk because I was now more worried than I had been when this entire disaster started.

"New calculations are coming in," X-37 said. "The safe zone, as previously conceptualized, was calculated improperly.

No one, not even the people of Xad, possess much experience operating like this within a slip tunnel."

"For fuck's sake," I said, moving for the door.

"After a careful analysis, my recommendation is to pull Elise from the void as quickly as possible," X-37 said in his extra neutral tone that conveyed the cold logic of an LAI.

I ran for the flight deck as X-37 explained it to me.

"Elise is far outside their operational envelope. Commander Gile has sent rescue ships but there are more people needing rescue than there are rescuers," X-37 said.

"We've got to get to her before she drifts into the wall of the slip tunnel," I said.

"Colliding with other ships in the exodus fleet is the greater danger now," X-37 said. "Ensign Michael Junkboss did an outstanding job plotting her intercept course of Repairman Beaufort."

"Is that a rank in the Xad military?" I asked, panting slightly as I ran.

"It is, Reaper Cain," X-37 provided. "My analysis suggests you could run a bit faster without crashing into any of the crew."

I sprinted onward.

IT TOOK me three tries to close the micro-fighter canopy when I finally reached it. The flight deck of the Bright Lance was a flurry of activity. Shuttles were coming and going, either to rescue people or bring them in after they were recovered. The stealth carrier wasn't made for this type of traffic. Most of the ships attached to the outside with the landing and launch bays being used only for specific purposes or in emergencies.

The flight deck supervisor, Warrant Officer Suzan Sun, quickly checked my ship, then waved me toward the launch area.

Not waiting to be told twice, I was soon in the void rushing toward Elise. There was one shuttle closer than I was, but I was going to get there first. The micro-fighters were extremely fast over short distances and could maneuver around larger ships with ease.

"X, can you patch me into Elise?" I asked.

"With difficulty," X-37 said. "The rescue operations are running smoothly now, but there is still a lot of comm traffic and ship to ship data transfers to coordinate everyone."

"Do what you can, X," I said, as I fled around other rescue operations and lumbering transport vessels.

Elise was well into the main fleet now, barely missing a freighter. I noticed, as I passed, that they had tried to collect her but missed. The people of Xad were good at this sort of thing but overwhelmed by the volume of search and rescue to be done.

"How did one ship malfunction turn the entire armada into a beehive of screw ups?" I asked.

"It's a good reminder that anything can happen," X-37 said.

"That's not helpful," I said as I banked the micro-fighter

around a medical vessel while heading the final distance toward Elise.

"When we get closer, you may use a direct link to communicate with Elise," X-37 said.

"Great. Let me know when we have a connection."

The exodus fleet looked strange with the green walls of the slip tunnel all around it. Some of the ships were large, not leaving a lot of extra room for maneuvering. When I finally had a visual of Elise, she looked like a mere spec with danger all around her.

"How you doing, kid?" I asked.

"Not a kid, Reaper." She twisted her Archangel armor to face me.

"How is the EVA functionality on that hunk of junk?" I asked.

"Only you would consider state-of-the-art battle armor junk," she said. "To answer your question, I don't have a lot of air left. Did they get Beaufort picked up?"

"No idea," I said. "X, can you check on that?"

"He was picked up by rescue shuttle. He wishes to convey his thanks to whoever saved him," X-37 said.

"Let's tow you to the *Jellybird*, unless there's another ship close enough to help," I said.

"I am on final approach to your location," Jelly said. "I will prep the cargo bay to accept Elise."

We were extremely close to the slip tunnel wall now, so near it that all I saw was a shimmering green energy field with

Elise so close it seemed impossible she wasn't touching it. "You're in a really bad spot."

Her answer was more subdued than normal. "Yeah, I know. That's why none of the other rescue attempts were able to pull me in. They're a little squeamish about getting this close to death. The crew has hundreds of stories about what happens if you run into the wall."

"Most of them are completely wrong," I said.

"Because you have lots of experience running into slip tunnel walls," Elise said, but she sounded out of breath.

"I'll tell you what, just stop talking. I'll tow you back from the wall so you can get on the *Jellybird*," I said, steering toward her with the micro-fighter."

"Thanks," she said.

X-37 assisted by plotting approach vectors and suggested throttle settings as I piloted. When I finally reached Elise, it was anticlimactic. I dropped a line, she fastened it to her armor, and I carefully pulled her to safety.

Jelly approached none too soon. Elise had quit talking completely to conserve air. The sense of relief I felt when she was safely on board the *Jellybird* was enormous.

THAT EVENING, I stayed up way too late talking to Warrant Officer Suzan Sun, the flight deck controller I promised a drink after rescuing Elise. How many years had it been since my last conversation with a member of the opposite sex who wasn't the focus of a mission or part of my team?

After the first couple of drinks, we told stories and watched the slip tunnel. There hadn't been as many people on the observation deck as previous evenings. The semi-disastrous rescue mission had taken a lot of manpower, and people were tired or still doing work.

"You shouldn't have stayed out so late," Elise said the next morning, holding back a sly chuckle.

"I wasn't on a date," I said.

"You were drinking with a woman and trying to be funny, right?" Elise said, pointing at me. "People talk, Reaper."

"Wasn't a date."

"Whatever." She smiled, shrugging as she turned away to climb into a flight simulator. "I'm going to own you in this dogfight."

I went through the start-up procedures, paying careful attention to each step. The value in a simulator lay in its user. Or that's what I thought until I observed the souped-up ship Elise was using.

"What is that?" I asked, scrolling through the readings my imaginary micro-fighter provided.

"I uploaded the actual schematics of my micro-fighter," Elise said.

"You can't incorporate Archangel armor into a micro-fighter chassis," I said. "Or can you? X, why didn't we try that?"

"Elise asked me not to tell you until after this contest," X-37 said.

"Traitor." The closer I came to my enemy in the simulation, the more readings flowed into my HUD. Elise had in fact incorporated the Archangel armor into the micro-fighter system.

"Did you wish me to improve your micro-fighter's design," X-37 asked.

"Always, X. Always get me the best equipment you can. I shouldn't have to tell you this."

"Noted," X-37 said.

The ships were small and now I saw how they had been developed from accessories to combat armor. The possibilities were intriguing. I didn't know where she found the time to get such complicated work done.

"Let me ask you this before we start, Elise," I said. "Did Tom help you?"

She laughed. "Everyone helped me, especially Tom. Prepare to get owned."

"My analysis suggests it is a good thing this is not a real contest," X-37 said.

"It's okay, Mister Reaper," Bug said. "I didn't help her. I wanted to, but I didn't think you would like it. And I was kind of embarrassed at how bad you were going to lose."

"X, why is Bug on this channel?" I asked. "He's supposed to be watching Ayres."

"I can do both," Bug said. "Trust me, he's not going anywhere without me knowing."

"X?" I wasn't sure which annoyed me more—that Bug was multitasking when I wanted him to focus on Ayers, or that my duel with Elise had become common knowledge.

My limited artificial intelligence gave me the bad news. "Someone mentioned there would be a contest in the flight simulator arena. One person told another, and now there are a lot of people watching your dogfight with Elise."

"Is there betting involved?" I asked.

"That activity has been concealed through various means, but I suspect your hypothesis is correct," X-37 said.

"Can everyone talk to me?" I was already in trouble. From what I could see, Elise could make that micro-fighter move even faster with her Archangel armor integrated into its frame. "Because that will be distracting."

"I'm the only one who can talk to you without authorization from Captain Younger," Bug said. "You know that's what I do."

"All right then," I said. "See if you can help me win."

"Hey, that makes us a team!" Bug's excitement was over the top. "You better watch out, Elise. I'm on Mr. Reaper's team."

"Good luck, Bug." Elise maneuvered her fighter in a long powerful arc, then aimed at me. "Come at me Reaper!"

7

"I'm looking after this kid, Mom. I hope I wasn't ever this much of a pain in the ass," I muttered, my words slurred.

My mother didn't answer, which was a good thing, because I was sure she would argue the point. I'd been no end of trouble. From stealing cookies out of the oven before they finished cooking to getting in fights and running from the police.

The room rotated, or seemed too. Whiskey warmed me. The melancholy mood that came from long nights sitting with my family was strange and addictive. I was too familiar with the medical research room that kept my family alive.

I had always been a connoisseur of whiskey, never a hard drinker. Slow sips on the observation deck with a cigar in one hand and good company and conversation to pass the time was more my style.

"How do you feel, Reaper Cain?" X-37 asked.

"When you're right, you're right. This isn't helping," I said, looking at my mother's cryo-pod in the dim light. It was *ship night*, not that it mattered to anyone in the room.

On my left was my sister's cryo-pod. I held the cigar but didn't smoke—this was a medical research bay after all, and I wasn't a total animal.

"Can you ask Mavis to play some music? Something that might give them good dreams," I asked.

"Of course, Reaper Cain," X-37 said. A few moments later, the AI of the *Bright Lance* caused classical music to come through the public address speakers in this section of the ship.

I couldn't remember the composer of the slow concerto, but it was something with strings and it seemed right.

"Strings are a strange way to make music," I commented without thinking.

"It is a primitive method of causing sound vibrations," X-37 said. "Would you like me to research the origin of this music?"

"Maybe later," I said.

Sitting here had become my ritual. I tried not to think, but when I did, the whiskey took me back to Boyer 5. It always started with a happy scene in the kitchen: me teasing my sister while my mother caught up on work at the table—lots of reading, taking notes, and muttering profanities she hadn't realized I could hear.

The image of her typing and scribbling notes on an old tablet remained vivid. In these memories, it was always my night to cook—a tradition among our family. My sister, who was a good deal younger than me, harassed me as I brought food to the table.

"X, I have a question," I said.

"I have an answer, Reaper Cain," my limited artificial intelligence said.

"Why isn't my father in these memories? I sit here every night thinking about home, but he never shows up," I said. Again, this was an impulsive question—something that just came out.

"Contrary to what you've suggested in our previous discussions, I cannot read your mind; therefore, I have no direct observational data of your imagination," X-37 said. "Are you angry at your father? Did you have a poor childhood?"

"No, X, I had it pretty good, all things considered. All of my misery was self-induced—running with gangs, not running with gangs, not listening to anyone," I said.

"You have made contradictory statements unless you are talking about more than one unit of time in your past," X-37 said. "How can you run with gangs and not run with gangs?"

"They had just as many bullshit rules as school and society and the military and all of it," I said. "They claimed once you were in, you couldn't get out without a beating or being killed. And yet, I was kicked out of at least three that I can remember. Always some rule violation."

"That correlates well with your adult behavior," X-37

said. "My humor algorithm is alerting me that this is funny or ironic."

I took a deep breath, held it, then let it out. "Run the analysis of the cryo-pods again," I said. "The more I sit here, the more I think this is ridiculous. Why can't we just wake them up?"

"Patience, Reaper Cain. We are en route to Macabre where we will obtain the proper codes," X-37 said. "They have been like this for a long time. A few more days or weeks will have little effect on their health."

"It's wrecking my health," I said.

"I agree that it has increased your consumption of alcohol and the frequency of your moodiness has become somewhat alarming," X-37 said. "I recommend that you cut alcohol intake by point 09 percent."

"So specific," I said.

"Apologies, Reaper Cain. The actual number is point 0908123457," X-37 said. "I wasn't prepared for your sarcastic response."

"Don't ever change, X," I said.

"I won't," my limited AI answered.

"You know what, I'm feeling pretty good now," I said.

"Is this one of your metaphors for inebriation?" X-37 asked.

"No, but maybe that's part of it." I considered everything about the moment. "You're right. My family could be in a lot worse shape. We'll get to Macabre and get the codes. Doctor

Ayers won't freak out or prove to be a lying psychopath. All good."

"I can make no promises," X-37 said.

I DIDN'T DRINK beer in the shower this time. The recycled water relaxed every muscle in my body, especially since X-37 disabled the timer. That wasn't fair to the rest of the *Bright Lance* crew, but I was guessing the amenities on the ship were far better than they were accustomed to.

"What's on the agenda, X? Have we had any more ship repair emergencies or annoying kids floating around inside the slip tunnels?" I asked.

"None, Reaper Cain," X-37 said. "Captain Younger has requested that you assist her with the Union crew members who have applied for Xad citizenship. Also on your calendar is a training session with Elise and maintenance of your cybernetics."

"Sounds exciting," I said. A short time later I was dressed and geared up for the day. Getting ready quickly was a habit I didn't see any reason to abandon. I kept the stealth cloak and Reaper mask in a slim pack that I wore under my jacket. The chances of using it today were slim, but I'd long since learned that carrying these items concealed was a skill that needed to be practiced as much as possible.

"Captain Younger is waiting for you in the security room of the brig," X-37 advised.

"Great," I said, walking briskly toward my destination.

"Your biometrics are exceptionally good today," X-37 said.

"Thanks, X, you're not so bad yourself," I said.

"I was not giving you a compliment," X-37 said. "I was merely relaying information as is my mandate."

"Don't go losing your personality now, X," I said.

"Understood, Reaper Cain. Adjusting my humor and personality algorithms. Please standby," X-37 said.

The guards to the brig saluted, which I wasn't accustomed to even now. I imitated their salutation, raising my hand level with my eyes—palm facing them because I didn't want to use the Union salute that I've been taught in basic training.

In the control room to the section, Captain Younger and one of her aides waited. Her uniform was red today, or mostly red. The striping on her arms was the same as always. The crew was still going through a transformation with the fabrication capabilities of the *Bright Lance*. Some people were having more fun with the fabric manipulation devices than others—part of a competition they were having to decide on the final design of their uniforms.

"Thanks for coming, Reaper," she said.

"No problem," I said, nodding to her outfit. "You and your crew are looking more squared away every day."

"Thank you, Reaper," she said, as dignified and officer-like as ever. "The *Bright Lance* has an extraordinarily efficient laundry service and uniform repair function. I'm not sure it was meant to redesign and tailor jumpsuits for the entire crew, but so far it seems to be working. We put old clothes in the recycler, adjust some settings, and next thing you know, we are all facing decisions we've never had to make—like what to wear."

I knew all of this but didn't interrupt.

"Can I ask you something?" I ignored X-37 warning me away from this line of conversation. He chattered in my ear, but I was pretty good at blocking him out.

"Of course," Captain Younger said.

"Why red? Yesterday it was blue and the day before that black with the same stripes down the arms," I asked.

"I wasn't aware that Reapers were so fashion-conscious," she said.

"Attention to detail. Target description is important in my line of work," I said.

"Am I your target? That will alarm my security detail," she said.

"You understand what I'm talking about," I said, feeling relaxed and non-confrontational. The woman had a certain charisma that was undeniable. This wasn't like flirting or small talk. Speaking with the captain of the *Bright Lance* was a unique experience every time.

"My crew jokes that we are setting a bad precedent by having a uniform of the day, completely opposite to our more frugal lifestyle before you and your enemies came to our system," she said. "In reality, it's a test and evaluation sched-ule. At the end of each week, we vote on which uniform works best."

"Very democratic," I said.

"My assistant today, Lieutenant Paul Oberon, will keep track of your interview style and some questions you direct at the Union applicants. Our goal is to develop a reliable screen process that can be replicated on a larger scale," she said.

"Sounds like a plan," I said. X-37 agreed. "X-37 told me you have a new batch of Union turncoats. Intuition told me they would come around."

Younger's expression cooled. "They don't like that term."

"They've been called worse, just like I've been called worse. And, more importantly, they know the drill. If you didn't take their switching sides seriously, they would lose respect for you and your people."

"Where would you like to start?" Captain Younger asked.

I looked at Oberon, raising one eyebrow while opening my palm to signal him it was his turn to make a decision. The nonverbal communication took a second, but he got it.

"I think starting with an officer would be best. Most of the enlisted crew members switched sides early on with very convincing declarations of intent," he said.

"Rule one, don't trust any of their very convincing declarations," I said. "Action not words."

"Are you suggesting we keep a careful eye on them for an extended period?" Lieutenant Oberon asked.

"That is exactly what I'm suggesting. It's time-consuming and resource draining, but necessary," I said.

"Any member of my crew who was formally associated with the Union is assigned a mentor and guard. This protects them from accusations of disloyalty, and also acquaints them with our rules and customs," Captain Younger explained. "It is time to begin."

"Let's start with somebody who wasn't excessively dangerous—a supply officer or something. Maybe that will help with your uniform transition."

The man Captain Younger and Lieutenant Oberon selected was named Ted or Theodore or something I really didn't care about. Guards brought him into a small, comfortable room with a table and comfortable chairs. Once everyone was seated, a crew member from the galley brought a tray of snacks and cool drinks.

"Seriously?" I asked.

The Union officer looked as alarmed and wary as I was, eyeing the gifts with clear suspicion.

"It is a tradition among our people to be good hosts whenever possible," Lieutenant Oberon said, serving each of us. "Can you please restate your name and rank, sir?"

"Lieutenant Theodore Feist, maintenance and supply officer, fourth watch, section 2," he said, then recited his rather long unique identification number.

"Is that a number that is important? Your personal identification, perhaps?" Lieutenant Oberon asked as he took his seat and crossed one leg over the other, holding his drink very properly in his right hand. Captain Younger also sat with excellent posture, though she left her beverage on the table near her.

I leaned forward, planting my elbows on my knees. "Listen, Ted, we have a lot of people to talk to. You have about five minutes to convince us why you suddenly want Xad asylum."

"I know who you are," he said, watching me like I was a dangerous killer or something. "Why am I talking to the Xad captain? What is all of this food?"

Oberon interrupted me, which I found annoying since he was supposed to be observing my technique. "The ship AI indicated this was a common snack, not an actual meal, and that it would be appropriate for an intimate conversation."

"Ask the ship AI about campaign rations," Theodore Feist said. "Check the discipline log for violators and Nebs's personal penalty enhancements that were instituted the moment we left Union space."

Captain Younger made a note on her work pad but said nothing.

Lieutenant Oberon nodded thoughtfully.

I had assumed I would take the lead, but that wasn't how the interview was turning out. Before long, I settled back into an intimidation role—basically just staring at the man like I would as soon space him as look at him.

Oberon did all the talking, sounding like he was reciting a personnel management questionnaire pulled straight from a book. Captain Younger paid careful attention and took notes.

I signaled X-37, asking what he thought. Prompting my LAI with nonverbals was second nature now. The more I was around people, the less I wanted them to believe I was a crazy person who talked to himself all the time.

"I am detecting a pattern to their interview style," X-37 said. "Should the methods fail, you can step in and be your usual self. Until then, I would continue to glare at the man. It is giving me a very clear visual reading of his physical indicators."

I prompted X-37 for more, still leaning back in my chair. My casual, almost careless posture contrasted sharply with that of the Xad officers.

"From what I can read of the man's biometrics, and analyze from his speech patterns, he did genuinely resent Vice Admiral Nebs. I have insufficient information on this individual to determine whether he can be trusted," X-37 said. "And yes, Reaper Cain, I can stream this information to the tablet that Captain Younger is using."

A few moments later, she looked up at me, held my gaze, and then smiled subtly. She went back to work making notes and listening to the turncoat.

We conducted three more interviews this way and sent each of the individuals back to their cells until the results could be analyzed.

8

THERE WERE times I just wanted X-37 to do what I asked and skip the analysis of my every burp and fart. "Please, X, check on them."

"Right away, Reaper Cain." X-37 paused for several seconds. "I have confirmation that Elise is waiting for you in the gym. I can also assure you that James Henshaw is in the middle of a card game at the back of a storage area. Shall I check on your other friends?"

"You're quick, X. That's exactly what I want. Find anyone who might try to talk to me and make sure they're busy," I said.

"Without specific instructions, I can only report on their status," X-37 said. "Normally, I am on the same screen as you, but I'm at a loss. What is with your sudden need to micromanage your friends?"

"I'm going to talk to Ayers and I want to do it alone. Is that so difficult?"

"Stand by." X-37 took a few seconds to accomplish each task I had assigned him. "My analysis suggests there is a low probability that anyone will come looking for you during the next ninety-four minutes."

"Perfect." When I arrived at the maximum-security wing of the brig, I spoke with the guard and was admitted. We were on a first-name basis at this point and he didn't flinch that I came alone.

The hallway was dark, narrow, and had a low ceiling, something I suspected Union shipbuilders had done on purpose. If I'd been imprisoned here, the ambiance of the place would have been intimidating.

Each cell had an observation window. Further down this direction was a cluster of interrogation rooms and two offices that could be used for research between sessions. The lights were off, but I instructed X-37 to make sure no one was working in them. When I was sure we were alone, I stood before the cell of Doctor Ayers.

"What are you waiting for, Reaper Cain?"

"I'm just waiting for it to feel right. I don't want to rush this." We had covered a lot of ground with Ayers. Henshaw and the others had often offered questions I might not have thought of myself.

But I wasn't here because I had a specific question. Something was bothering me, and my gut told me I needed to press this guy.

When I was ready, I entered without knocking or announcing my presence. Doctor Ayers stood in the middle of the room facing me, calmer and less fidgety than I'd ever seen him.

"He may be sleeping," X-37 advised. "It is not impossible to sleep standing up with your eyes open, but it is rare. Would you like to know the exact statistical probability of this behavior?"

I didn't answer, choosing instead to watch my target for clues.

"Filing statistical probabilities for a later discussion," X-37 said. "The doctor has awakened."

"Yeah, he's awake," I said. "Aren't you, Ayers?"

"I wasn't asleep when you entered, but working through a complex hypothesis," he said.

"Screw it, I'm just gonna ask you. Do you have a limited artificial intelligence in your nerve-ware?"

I had argued with Henshaw on this point. The ocular engineer was convinced no one could be this smart without assistance. He conducted long solo interviews with the man, which was alarming for about ten different reasons, and come away breathless after some of their debates. All I needed was a secret coalition between the two scientists.

Doctor Ayers held my gaze when he answered. "I have no augmentation. It is possible to train the human mind to a very high level of functioning. This will be necessary for all people to obtain if we are to stand on equal ground with the many alien races that must exist in this galaxy and in the next."

"You think these imaginary friends of yours are smarter than our entire race, is that it?" I asked.

"It is a possibility," he said. "I admit, however, that nothing is a certainty. Even their physical appearance has been somewhat surprising."

The doctor's haunted look stabbed through me like a knife. "Did you just say what I think you said? Where are your test subjects?"

Doctor Ayers said nothing, seeming to stare straight through me.

"Answer me, Ayers." It took all of my self-control not to grab him by the throat.

"You are smarter than you look. That is for the best. If you don't mind, I must sleep now."

"I do mind. And let me promise you this, sleeping will not be restful if you try to nod off while I'm talking," I said, restraining myself from a more dire threat, not because I believed it would be ineffective, but because the thought of it turned my stomach.

I was getting soft. Threatening the man with sleep deprivation, and following through with that threat, would be effective. There were few coercion methods more miserable than long-term sleep deprivation.

Having been subjected to it three different times, I knew what it did to a person.

The interrogation wasn't going well. I was losing my edge. Leaving without explanation, I waited for X-37's inevitable question.

"Is something wrong, Reaper Cain?" X-37 asked.

Watching Ayers sleep standing up, I considered what he said, what it meant, and what I needed to do about it. "We're done for today."

I moved into the hallway, then leaned against the wall to review the interview. The gloomy atmosphere fit my mood. "You understand why I'm worried, don't you, X?"

"It seems obvious that he used alien DNA on human test subjects and something went wrong," X-37 said.

9

THE UNIFIED XAD and Wallach fleet departed from the slip tunnel in a disorganized fashion. It started out well, but it was clear not everyone understood the chain of command or the post slip tunnel formations the leaders of both fleets had agreed upon.

Two-thirds of the ships lined up in order of the operational plan. Another group started to patrol and set up defensive contingencies, while a third headed for an asteroid belt to search for resources.

Captain Younger was the highest-ranking officer in the Xad fleet and had operational command. Gen. Karn and Admiral Hutton of the Wallach forces would also get a turn every ninety standard days.

Captain Younger had requested my presence on the bridge for the exiting of the slip tunnel. We had discussed best practices and then watched as the best-laid plans unfolded in unexpected ways. I admired the way she worked, taking control when needed but not interfering with her subordinates. As captain of the Xad flagship, and leader of the unified fleet, she was in control of the entire operation.

She approached when she had a free moment. "My apologies for the disorder. It seems the mission to Macabre will be delayed unless you can take a smaller team on your ship to investigate the claims Doctor Ayers has been making."

"I can do that Captain, but I will need to take Ayers," I said. "I doubt he has told us everything, and if there are surprises, I'll need to ask him some questions."

"As long as you can provide enough security to keep him from escaping custody, then you may take him where you like," Captain Younger said. "I will advise my security chief to assist you in any way needed."

She went back to managing the larger situation.

I left the bridge and headed for the brig. On the way, I made sure X-37 contacted my team and sent them to the *Jellybird*. We had expected something like this, and everyone knew what to do. My job was to work with the Xad guards to move the prisoner to the *Jellybird*.

Doctor Ayers wasn't happy to see me, but he complied with the guards and did what he was told. Soon we were on our way to the flight deck.

"You surprise me, Ayers," I said.

"In what way, Reaper?"

"To be honest, I thought you were maneuvering toward

Macabre. It makes sense that you left something there and want us to do your dirty work to retrieve it, but I expected you would demand to go there yourself," I explained.

"It's a horrible planet," he said. "I suggest you take people who are expendable."

"What?"

"That came out wrong," he said, "but you know what I mean. It is very dangerous. People will die."

"Maybe fewer people would die if your life was also at stake."

"Nebs would've sent his Archangels." He seemed very distracted and had a tremor in his left eyebrow. "They are better suited for the environment."

"X, how many suits of the Archangel armor do we have unlocked?" I asked.

"As many as you need, Reaper Cain. I make this assessment based on the maximum number of people you can transport on the *Jellybird* and the *Lady Faith*," X-37 said.

Ayers waited until I concluded my internal conversation. After that, he spoke more like a normal person. "I am thankful to be out of my cell, but it does me little good without access to a ship AI to assist me."

"Assist you with what?" The last thing I was going to allow was a mad scientist messing with our ship.

"Processing my theories and assisting the away team in a remote capacity. I'm better suited to be in the control room providing my expert analysis than stomping around on the planet surface," Ayers said. "I would only slow you down and

I have no fighting experience or training in harsh environments."

"Well I guess it will be on-the-job training for you because you're coming with us," I said. "I'm not going down into whatever mess you created without having you close at hand to give me answers when I need them."

THE *JELLYBIRD* SLOWED as she approached Macabre, establishing a high orbit. Both Elise and Tom were on the bridge. Path guarded Doctor Ayers in our makeshift brig.

Two Xad soldiers, Largo and Asis, both Soldiers First Class, and two Wallach soldiers, Horvath and Carrie Decker, we're on standby on the *Jellybird* to provide security on the ship or in case we needed more guns in a fight on the planet. Carrie was a good pilot and would be an extra resource for an away mission. We also had a shuttle and two micro-fighters attached to the *Jellybird* now.

Not far from us, Henshaw piloted his yacht, the *Lady Faith*, in case we needed a second ship. It also made it easier to control Henshaw's access to Ayers, which I thought was necessary. They seemed far too interested in each other's work.

Two Xad soldiers had volunteered to assist on the *Lady Faith*. The opulent amenities of the yacht probably stunned them. I also assigned Bug to Henshaw's ship, mostly to annoy him. He had been too lax in his duties monitoring Doctor

Ayers. I hoped pulling him off the job for a time motivated him to do better in the future.

"I have completed an initial scan, Captain," Jelly said. "From a geological perspective, this is a very interesting planet, though I must advise against going down to the surface if it can be avoided. There is a great deal of seismic and volcanic activity."

"I see what you mean," I said, looking at the images of molten lava and collapsing ridgelines. "There must be some-place the Union could have squirreled away the research."

"Maybe Ayers was lying," Elise said.

"That's a possibility we need to think about," Tom said. "I can't see any place they can have a base or even a storage facility. Hopefully, we will learn more as we complete subsequent passes around Macabre and continue to run scans of the surface."

I stood and prepared to leave the bridge. "This is exactly the reason I brought Ayers with us."

"Do you need my help?" Elise asked.

"Path and I can handle Ayers. Get ready for the away mission," I said.

Her eyes went wide. "Down there?"

"Start working out an operational plan, then hope we don't have to use it," I said. "Worst environment imaginable. A perfect place for the Union to hide something. I will get the rest of the story from Ayers now…or die trying."

"This planet is so far outside of Union territory it's ridiculous," Elise said. "If what Jelly is telling me is correct, we're even farther than we were in the Wallach or Xad systems."

"Nebs left Union space for over two years and never accounted for what he did during that time. We should be ready for anything," I said.

"You're right, Reaper," Elise admitted.

My mind was spinning by the time I joined Path outside of the makeshift brig. Images of the glowing red planet reinforced my belief that Ayers had tricked us somehow. Despite what I had told Elise, I doubted there was any way the Union could use this planet. It didn't even have moons. I'd been to several worlds where the moon was more hospitable to humans than the planet.

"Good morning, Reaper," Path said. "Did you know the doctor sleeps standing up sometimes?"

"Sometimes he's just thinking deep thoughts," I said. "It's hard to tell the difference."

"I can tell," Path said, keeping his attention on the scientist who had lured us here.

"Are you awake, Ayers, or shamming?" I asked.

The man eyed me. "I am a doctor, you know. Not one of your rough friends. I would appreciate a little more respect."

"I will address you by your honorific as soon as my family is safely awakened from the cryo-pods," I said. "We have arrived at Macabre. It's an interesting planet. I'm wondering how the Union could have any type of facility here."

"I understand your skepticism. Too bad the engineer in charge of building the facility on Macabre died when you destroyed the UFS *Black Wing*," Ayers said. " It's submersible. What better way to hide something than sink it in an ocean of lava."

"I bet Nebs loved that," I muttered, struggling to imagine how we would reach this facility.

"Jelly, contact the *Nightmare* and any other ship that might have an expert in this field," I said.

"Right away, Captain," Jelly said.

"Have you located the satellite?" Ayers asked.

"Our prisoner says there's a satellite we need to find," I said.

Jelly responded immediately. "I will endeavor to locate it. With your permission, I would like to ask Doctor Ayers direct questions."

"That's dangerous, Jelly. I don't trust him, and he seems far too interested in gaining access to an AI."

Ayers waited patiently, only hearing half of the conversation. His version of calm meant an almost spiritual serenity that would rival Path on a good day, interrupted at random intervals by twitching and nervous sweats.

"I can look after myself, Captain," Jelly promised. "I will report any attempts he makes to act inappropriately to X-37."

"Jelly, I trust your judgment." I made eye contact with Path. "What happens if Ayers attempts to pull a fast one?"

Path tapped his sword hilt.

"I'm no good to you dead," Ayers said.

"My sword saint is very accurate. He'll take a finger at a

time. But don't worry, you won't even feel it until after it happens," I said.

Ayers paled. A tremor swept through his body from head to toe. I made a mental note to get him another medical check as soon as we were back on the *Bright Lance*.

"I have located one functioning satellite of the planet Macabre," Jelly announced. "There is, however, no way to access it remotely. This is strange and defeats the purpose of having a satellite. What can it do with no way of communicating from a distance?"

"Is that a question for me?" Ayers asked. The scientist seemed less of a wreck when he was engaged in conversation or working on something.

"Please explain how we can use the satellite," Jelly asked.

"Took the words right out of my mouth," I muttered.

"Jelly is doing an excellent job, Reaper Cain," X-37 said.

"Agreed." With the ship asking the questions, I was able to watch Ayers more and decide whether he was lying or trying to pull a fast one. So far, I wasn't detecting anything nefarious —which made me suspicious.

Ayers cleared his throat. "Can I see what you have found?"

Jelly presented a small holographic representation of the satellite that had been discovered. It looked like a needle about ten meters long that was thicker in the middle. I'd never seen a satellite that was so plain and free of antennae.

"That is the one." Ayers leaned toward the image, eyes

bright with interest and his mannerisms less twitchy and weird.

"There are no others," Jelly said.

"Bring it on to your ship and I will open it," he said. "Inside, there is a pod that will have to be fired from your ship. It will penetrate the surface of the lava sea and seek the floating vault."

"You're telling me that thing contains a drone that can survive in molten rock that has to be well over a thousand degrees?" I asked, crossing my arms.

Ayers tried to back away but there wasn't a lot of space. "For a time. It is a single-use tool. We only planned to come here once, and only in an emergency."

"What type of emergency?" I asked.

"Perhaps you should ask Nebs," Ayers said.

"I don't like your tone, Ayers," I said.

"I hold multiple doctorates. Why must you needlessly disrespect me?"

"What. Type. Of. Emergency," I said, staring straight into his eyes.

He swallowed, revealing he was human after all and feared death just like the rest of us. "We were only to come here in the event that we lost our research."

"Or to wake up my family and the other people locked in cryo-pods," I said.

"That would not have been necessary if you had kept Nebs alive," Ayers argued. "You can blame the condition of your family on your own hotheaded decisions."

"Be calm, Reaper Cain," X-37 ordered.

"You're lucky I still need you, Ayers," I said.

He answered without pause. "I am. An intelligent and rational man like myself would endeavor to remain useful."

"Don't forget it," I said. "Jelly, capture the satellite. Tom, meet me inside the main bay so we can look at this thing."

"Sure thing, Hal," Tom answered.

"I will assist you remotely," Henshaw offered in my earpiece.

"Great. I love it when a plan comes together. Path, keep an eye on Ayers." Nothing about this mission was good but if it had been easy, I would've been seriously suspicious.

Path nodded that he would watch the crazy xenobiologist without fail.

"I'll take Horvath and Carrie to help me modify the Archangel armor we brought," Elise said. "I don't see any other way to operate on the surface. Tom agrees with me it should be able to withstand more heat than maintenance gear or EVA suits."

"Good," I said. "Keep me updated."

10

THE SATELLITE LOOKED MUCH BIGGER LYING across the deck in the *Jellybird*'s main storage area. Tom managed to open it without much difficulty. We were looking at the contents when I received a message from Path.

"Ayers wants to know if we need his help opening the satellite," Path said.

"We already have it open," I answered.

A pause followed.

"He doesn't believe you," Path said.

"He's never seen our mechanic work," I said. "Let me know if he says anything else useful."

"He doesn't understand why he wasn't allowed to be present when the satellite was recovered," Path said. "I told him he hadn't earned our trust and now he seems to be pondering that like it's a scientific theorem."

I watched Tom work. He wasn't in a rush, but he did get things done quickly. The man was confident in his abilities and had such a broad base of technical knowledge. He never ceased to amaze me. His methodical, patient approach was faster than someone who rushed into mistakes and was forced to make several attempts before getting it right.

"We are very lucky to have made such talented and loyal friends," X-37 said to me privately.

I gave my hand signal that I agreed.

Tom stepped back, still looking at his work. He indicated what he had done with one hand, palm facing up. "And there you go, one Union super drone meant to be fired from a ship."

I moved closer and studied the small oblong pod.

"It's a shame to waste a machine like that," Tom said. "The metallurgical uniqueness is fascinating. I wish I could put it in a laboratory and study it with Henshaw's help," Tom said.

"Do you think the Union made it?" I asked.

"I'm sure that's the case, but it is very cutting edge." Tom barely took his eyes off the device as he answered.

"Maybe we'll find another someday," I said. "Can you figure out how to load and fire it at the planet?"

"No problem at all. Once we finish our safety checks, it can be loaded, then shot into the lava sea," he said. "If Ayers is telling the truth and the secret vault does rise to the surface after the drone makes contact, I'm still not comfortable with anyone going down there. We've done a lot of dangerous things, but this is unusually… dynamic."

"Earthquakes and volcanoes are like that," I said. "Good work."

With Tom working on the drone, I checked in with Elise. "How are you doing with your new toys?"

"Not bad," she answered. "But there's a problem—if you want Ayers to go on this mission. I don't think giving him these types of weapons is a good idea. Removing the guns has been difficult."

"If you can't disable the weapons, remove the ammunition and power elements from them," I said.

"We already did that," Elise said quickly. "But these are tightly integrated units. Their limited artificial intelligences are actually just one digital entity networked across all the Archangel gear. It keeps them all functioning at maximum capacity—and makes communication on a squad level freakishly fast. Or that's what our test runs show. As soon as we started taking things off, they began to malfunction—even the units we didn't modify. Horvath, Carrie, and I have worked around the problem, but we will need to practice with them before we jump into a volcano or something."

"We don't have time for that," I said, and immediately felt ridiculous. X-37 and Elise corrected me at almost the same time.

"Actually, Reaper Cain, progressing more slowly would be advantageous," X-37 said.

"Aren't you always the one telling me not to rush to failure? If we take some time to practice, the only thing that's going to happen is that the rest of the exodus fleet will get here and possibly help us," Elise said.

"Okay, okay. We can practice with the Archangels," I said.

We discussed a few more details as I went to the armory and allowed Elise to instruct me on the best way to use the modified gear.

"First of all, I have to give credit to Tom even though he still messing with the drones. He was the one that insisted we bring all the accessories these golden goodies have," Elise said, motioning toward one of the large durable crates near the Archangel armor and workbenches.

I walked around each piece of the armor that was able to stand like Doctor Ayers taking one of his weird naps. The surface of each Archangel had a faint golden sheen, something in the alloy that made it different from other combat armor I'd seen. There were times I thought it was just a reflection of Nebs's vanity, but I wasn't an expert on metallurgy or engineering.

Each piece of gear now had a new layer of frangible armor. "That seems redundant, but I get it."

"The outer layer is a lot like the drone were sending down, single use," Elise said, walking around and pointing at different things she'd done to improve the setup. "The schematics we were able to read thanks to Jelly and X decrypting their security codes advocate a fairly loose connection of these add-ons, allowing for ease of movement. We decided to put more time into it and make every piece fit very precisely, to minimize the amount of molten rock slipping into the cracks and touching the actual armor."

I examined their work and knew it was good. "This should be more than enough protection since we're not actually going to be getting our feet *wet*. So try not to fall in."

Elise gave me one of her special *whatever* grins. "Having said that, and done all of this extra configuring, the Archangel armor itself is extremely resistant to heat and all other forms of physical insult. If we knew exactly what we were getting into, and could keep to a very tight time schedule, we might not need the extra layers."

"This is good work. You're right about not rushing to failure. We will need to practice—some on the ship and some extra vehicle activity drills just to increase the training intensity," I said.

Path brought Ayers to the equipment room we had turned into an armory. There were tools and pieces of armor scattered across magnetic workbenches. Elise, Horvath, and Carrie were already in their modified Archangel armor. I decided to put Ayers in his weaponless outfit next, then assist Path in getting ready.

"Why are you going last, Reaper?" Ayers asked.

"Because I'm the only person who can put this stuff on unassisted," I said. "And I can do the job faster than most."

"I refuse," Ayers said. "Away missions are not what the Union trained me for. My value lies in my intellectual output and willingness to see what others deny as the truth."

"Good for you," I said.

"I'm not going to the surface of Macabre. Send some of your soldiers. That is what Nebs would have done," Ayers insisted.

"I'm not Nebs, and you don't have a choice. Cooperate and help me save my family, and maybe someday you'll get to do your research," I said. "Refuse and I will send you down there by yourself."

"That is unfair, Reaper. You know I must acquiesce. My research is very important," Ayers said.

"Life isn't fair. At least I'm letting you wear protective gear on this mission. I'm told it's theoretically possible to survive where we're going as long as you don't get too close to the edge of the safe zone or get hit by any splashing lava," I said.

"Or fall in a rift when there's an earthquake," Elise added.

"There probably aren't any fire-breathing monsters on the surface," Horvath said.

I nodded like my friends were making exquisitely rational arguments. "I definitely believe you could do this without the armor, Ayers."

"You and your friends are wildly optimistic," Ayers argued.

I shrugged, motioning toward his new ride. "You're going with us, and you're wearing what we tell you to wear."

The Archangel armor opened like a standing clamshell when I issue the command. Ayers gaped in horror. I motioned for him to climb in.

"I'm not a *mechanical* engineer but that doesn't appear structurally sound," Ayers said. The way he said mechanical engineer suggested he thought people like Tom were lesser beings than alien DNA tinkerers like him.

"This makes it easier to get in," I said. "If it's properly closed and latched, it's as strong as it would be if it was all one piece. We're not expecting to fight. This is just an insurance policy for when the Union's clever vault bobs up and down in the lava. Climate control, basically."

11

"I DON'T WANT to go down there," Ayers said. "Nebs never made me go on away missions."

"You're going on this missio—" I repeated, staying calm as I could.

"I can't," he interrupted.

"You can if you want to continue your research," I said.

"I don't believe you."

"You don't have any choice. Don't make this ugly." I motioned for Elise and the others to get ready to run the drill. We needed to practice. The environment we were heading into would not forgive our mistakes.

Ayers climbed into the Archangel armor, stopping when he was halfway in.

Elise gave him crisp, no-nonsense instructions. "Lean into it. See there, the Archangel armor is canted forward. Just lie against it and the back half will come up and close. The less you move, the quicker this will be. Don't squirm around."

A tear leaked from each of Ayer's eyes as he followed her instructions. His body trembled. I thought he looked like a drowned rodent and almost felt sorry for him.

"It's weird the first time," Elise said. "But trust me—once it closes, you'll feel invincible."

"Okay, okay, I'm trying," Ayers said.

I connected to Elise on our private commlink. "So far so good. Remember, you will be his best friend when we do this."

"Next time I get to be the bad guy," she said.

"Keep him alive and make him understand that he owes you his life," I said.

"No problem, Reaper. We've got this," Elise said.

Horvath, already in his armor, stood beside me and leaned over to get my attention. "There's no way this will work with him on the mission. He's worse than a beginner. He's terrified, and that means he's going to make dumb mistakes that will put the rest of the team in danger."

"Agreed," I said. "But if we get down there and there's something he's holding back, we're likely to get trapped in the Union vault or sunk in the lava fields. I can handle him. It might not be pretty, but this is what we have to do."

Horvath seemed to consider that for a moment, then nodded, looking dignified in the Archangel helmet.

"He's in," Elise said. "Your turn, Reaper."

What none of my friends knew was that the basic chassis for the Archangel armor wasn't unfamiliar to me. As soon as they opened it up like this, I understood it was a modification of the killing frenzy armor I had trained on while a Reaper.

Everything was different on the outside, and I hadn't realized the similarities until it opened like an upright clamshell. Being able to integrate with a micro-fighter was one thing, having heat resistant properties capable of withstanding extreme, protracted exposure to heat was another.

The armor had the same step ladder that didn't look like a step ladder. When it was open, a series of small ledges unfolded from the back of each section. There was also a handhold that opened around the neck area. I climbed up, then pulled myself inside, leaning into the gear so it closed around me almost immediately.

"That was about ten times faster than the rest of us did it," Carrie said.

"Sometimes my Union training is useful," I said, regretting the words even as I spoke to him. With Nebs gone, I hoped to avoid talking about the Union for the rest of my life. It would take practice and mental discipline to truly believe I was free.

Once inside, I took two minutes going over the controls and making sure I had full access. "This would've made our fight against Nebs easier."

"Indeed," Jelly said. "I have prepared a simple EVA mission as you requested. Please exit the airlock in an orderly manner, then walk one time to the end of the *Jelly-bird*. When that is complete, I will give you a secondary objective. This exercise is winnable even for first-time users of EVA gear, provided they have had the proper familiarization course."

"I've had no familiarization course at all," Ayers complained.

"One of us will hold your hand," I said.

"Will that work? Are you going to actually hold onto me?" Ayers asked. "Because I would like that."

"Elise, calm the mad scientist, please," I said.

Elise jumped into the conversation, right on cue. "It will be okay, Doctor Ayers. We have some time. Let's take a stroll around the deck and I will give you some pointers."

"Thank you, Elise," Ayers said. "I appreciate your respect and helpfulness. Perhaps we could go on the mission without the Reaper."

"He's my boss, Doctor," Elise said. "It would help me if you would cooperate and let me show you how to run this armor."

"I understand. Life is a struggle and we must overcome the obstacles put in our way. Let me say that I am empathetic of what you're going through with your very unreasonable boss," Ayers said.

They began walking around the room with Horvath and Carrie monitoring their progress, hands up and ready to catch Ayers if he tried to run through a wall or something.

I switched to a private channel with X-37 and Jelly. "Can you monitor his vitals now that he's inside the Archangel?"

"Yes, Captain, I'm able to see what his body is doing quite clearly now," Jelly said.

"My measurements of his heart rate and respiration are also much improved," X-37 added. "Now I can take readings even when we can't directly observe him."

"Good," I said. "We need to get him up to speed on the basics."

"You want to actually train him? My analysis suggests that is a good idea," X-37 said.

"Yeah, I don't want to hold his hand. We can't pass up this opportunity to catch him off guard, however. If he thinks he's going to die, he might let something slip," I said.

"X-37 and I have discussed this training event in great detail. There's no reason we can't achieve both goals," Jelly said.

"Great detail? How long did your conversation take?" I asked as I watched Elise teach Ayers how to move. She was a natural, which surprised me. As a student, she could be stubborn one day and coachable the next.

"A few seconds," X-37 answered. "We wanted to take the time to consider all the variables."

"That sounds right." I crossed my arms and watched Elise take it up a notch.

She incorporated Horvath and Carrie into the drill, asking them to catch Ayers when she pushed him over.

"Is everyone ready?" she asked.

"I am if you think this is necessary," Ayers said.

"It's good practice. If you go off course or fall, you'll know we're here for you," Elise said.

"Ready," Horvath said, hands up in front of him and his

palms facing forward like he was playing defense in an arena game.

Carrie took a similar position on the other side of Ayers and Elise. "Same here."

Elise drew back both fists, paused a second, then slammed them into Ayers, launching him off his feet toward Horvath. The Wallach soldier caught him with moderate difficulty. The armor made him strong enough, but he struggled to find the balance point for the Archangel armor, setting his feet a bit too wide in anticipation of the collision.

Path strolled around the perimeter of the room, then stopped beside me. "She's a very good instructor."

"I was just thinking the same thing. Is that because of you?" I asked.

"Doubtful. Some of it, perhaps. I know little about teenagers and can't remember my childhood or all of the bad choices I made. She seems to be an exceptional person and I am glad that you rescued her from Dreadmax," Path said, the volume of his Archangel gear perfectly adjusted. His voice was loud enough to be heard but not so loud that I couldn't also hear Elise talking to the others.

"How do you like the new armor, Path?"

He faced me. "I find it disturbing."

"I thought you might. Tell me the rest, so I can see if my hunch was on the money." I knew my sword-wielding friend was a purist and a minimalist in most things. What was more difficult to know was why he'd chosen to take this path.

"It bothers me that I might master this ultimate killing

machine and be called to use it often," Path said. "I also worry that I might come to rely on it and lose track of who I am."

"Interesting," I said.

"Were you correct in your assumption?" Path asked, seeming curious.

"Pretty much nailed it," I said. "I'm already wanting out of this thing. I need a cigar."

"Of course," he replied.

Elise strode across the deck, Archangel armor working perfectly with her. The movements were smooth. "We are as ready as we can be. We should start."

"Agreed," I said. "Path, you're first. Horvath, you're last. Elise, I want you to stay close to Ayers."

"That is the most reasonable thing you've said so far. I feel much better that she will be there to keep me from floating into the void," Ayers said.

"Actually, her job is to keep me from throwing you into the void when you annoy me," I said.

"Calm down, Reaper," Elise said, playing her part well. "We need him."

Path approached the airlock, waited for Jelly to open it, then stepped into the darkness beyond. He moved with his usual grace and precision. "I'm standing on the hull beyond your field of vision. There are no obstructions on the exterior of the ship. It is safe to proceed."

Elise, Ayers, and Carrie went next. I paced them, staying a few strides back, not wanting to put Ayers into a cardiac arrest. Horvath followed, doing everything by the numbers. He took EVA missions seriously since his friend had died during one of our first spacewalks together.

"Your heart rate and respiration have increased but are within normal parameters," X-37 said. "Please scan the outside of the *Jellybird* so I can record points of interest for Jelly. She says it has been too long since the ship was given a proper overhaul and has likely accumulated damage over the last several months."

I complied, checking my environment for anything that could go wrong. I wasn't paranoid, I was just always ready to defend myself from an attack. It was one of my more useful habits, especially when it also allowed me to share information with X-37 and Jelly.

Elise and the others moved to the first objective. When they arrived, I let them stand idle for a moment, knowing that it could be stressful for someone like Ayers who was unfamiliar with the unique view from an EVA unit, even if it was state-of-the-art Union battle armor.

Blackness surrounded us. Stars seemed far away while also dominating the view in all directions. There was no light on the outside of the ship to compete with the galactic panorama.

"Okay, Jelly, what's next? How are we going to test our maneuvering capabilities?" I asked.

Ayers stood straighter, alarmed by my implication. "We were already told that it would be a simple circumvention of the *Jellybird*."

"That will be necessary, Jelly said. "However, it is not the next drill we need to accomplish to be certified in these units. Buoy retrieval is next."

"What?" Ayers asked as he retreated, looking back and forth between me and Elise. "This is the Reaper's idea, isn't it?"

"Are you sure buoy retrieval is safe?" Elise interjected. "Doctor Ayers has no formal training and this is his first spacewalk."

"He has to learn some time," I said.

"Warning, Reaper Cain, Ayers's heartbeat has increased by twenty percent in the last few seconds. Blood pressure is also approaching dangerous levels," X-37 advised. "How hard do you want to push him before demanding answers?"

I hesitated, having second thoughts. The plan seemed more humane than the torture Elise and I came up with it. Now I wanted to get it over with.

"Elise, show us how it's done," I said. "I'm not expecting Ayers to do this cold."

"I could watch Elise," Ayers said. "She hasn't led me astray so far. This armor is more comfortable than it looks but I cannot imagine when I will ever be required to retrieve a buoy from the void."

"I almost admire how he's trying to pull it together," I said to X-37 and Jelly.

"Don't be misled by his statement," X-37 said. "His biometrics are still dangerously high. He's merely putting on a brave face."

"Thanks for the update, X." I disagreed but wasn't able to articulate the reason. This felt like we were being hustled. Ayers was either on the verge of panic or was the best actor I'd met for a long time.

I waited until Elise was ready, the buoy was launched, and the drill began. X-37 tracked the speed and trajectory of the training buoy that Elise would recover.

"I'm going to jump forward and use my steering jets as little as possible to correct course," Elise said.

"What if she misses?" Ayers asked.

"She can fly back to the ship with her maneuvering jets. It may not look like it, but this is a controlled environment," I said. "Nothing like that little incident in the slip tunnel."

Elise sailed through the void like a pro, only using a small amount of thrust from her left boot. A moment later, she put both palms toward the buoy and slowed herself with the maneuvering jets in her gauntlets. She contacted the buoy perfectly—like it was a solid object rather than something in the void with spectacular star fields looming above her like the ceiling of a cathedral.

"That was good, right?" Ayers asked.

I could almost see him twitching inside of the Archangel armor. "She's good. We won't need these exact skills on Macabre, but it's a good drill. We're training hard now to avoid failing in the future."

"That is a rational supposition," Ayers said.

"I'm glad you agree." I gripped him by one arm. "Now it's your turn."

He wailed in panic when I threw him.

"You better steer," I said through the commlink.

"Are you trying to kill me!" Ayers screamed as he spiraled out of control, steering jets blasting with far more force than necessary.

"Elise, you're up," I said.

"I'm on my way to bring him in," she said on our private link. "That wasn't nice. I hope this works."

"He's definitely going to see you as his savior, maybe even a confidant," I said.

"Assuming I can catch him. Why did you throw him so hard?"

"I was going to ask the same question," X-37 said.

I didn't bother answering, choosing instead to watch Elise race through the void to grab Ayers and bring him back.

"Elise and Ayers are approaching the safety envelope for this exercise," Jelly advised.

I pointed at Carrie and Horvath. "Standby in case she needs help."

"Should we go now?" Horvath asked.

I could hear the tension in his voice and knew why this bothered him. My honest assessment was that Elise could handle it on her own, but I needed to keep Horvath's situation in mind. "I think she's okay, but I'll let you decide,"

Horvath hesitated, then shifted his stance until he looked ready to jump after Elise and Ayers.

"Let's work this together," Carrie said.

"I'll count us off." Horvath backed up a step, crouching. "On three. One, two, three!"

The Wallach soldiers leapt into the void with much more force than I thought was necessary. "Their adrenaline might have screwed them."

"My analysis of their trajectory and speed suggests they will need to use more thrust than is ideal to slow themselves, but they should rendezvous with Elise and Ayers without excessive difficulty," X-37 said.

"What do you think, Path?" I asked.

"They are learning important lessons," the sword Saint answered.

"I should have guessed you would say that." I checked our timer and reviewed other data, like how much oxygen we had each used and whether we would have a reserve left at the end of this drill.

Elise was right about one thing: the Archangel units were well integrated. I could almost believe I was flying right alongside them. Each of my data queries came back instantaneously.

"Update, Elise has reached Ayers and reversed his course. Horvath and Carrie are approaching in good order and will be able to help them if needed," Jelly said.

"Good," I said. "Elise, are you ready to get some answers?"

"Doing it now, Reaper," she said, then went silent.

I assumed she was now in a private conversation with Ayers.

"All we have to do now is wait," I said.

"What do you hope to gain from this rather unorthodox method of interrogation?" X-37 asked.

"Honestly, I'm not sure. Elise might get him to admit there is a trap or double-cross on Macabre. But it's more of an insurance policy," I explained. "When things go wrong, and they will, I want Ayers to turn to Elise and trust her completely."

"It seems they are off to a good start," X-37 said.

"Let's wait and see what Elise says after this training run is completed," I said, watching Elise, Ayers, Horvath, and Carrie make their way back to the ship for the easy part of this lesson.

We spent the next hour circumventing the ship and practicing very basic skills, some of them in the void and others walking on the exterior of the hull.

Ayers didn't talk to me but seemed to be listening to Elise as though he trusted her.

AT THE END of the day, we were tired but in good spirits. Even Doctor Ayers seemed proud of what he had accomplished. This type of thing was new to him and he was like a proud kid.

I disengaged from the group as soon as I could, drinking a beer in my shower and leaning out to puff on a cigar from time to time as was one of my favorite decompression rituals. X-37 advised me to get some sleep, but I wasn't tired.

Before long I found myself on the observation deck, and I wasn't alone. Tom was there reading a tablet. This time, however, he had a slim pair of reading glasses on his nose.

"Vision problems?" I asked, as I poured myself a glass and sat down to stare at the holo display.

"Getting old isn't fun," he said.

"You're not old."

He smiled. "My eyes are old, and parts of my body. In my head, I'm twenty years younger with all the curiosity of my youth still intact."

"That's a good way to be," I said, meaning every word. Tom had been a loyal and brave friend since the day we met.

"The exodus fleet is getting closer. Every time I look at it, I'm amazed at what we're doing," Tom said. "There are so many ships, and very few of them from the same design."

"None of them are the same except for the stealth carriers," I said.

"Exactly." Tom put aside his book and held his own glass but didn't drink from it.

We watched ships large and small moving in formation toward our location. The view was enhanced, of course, but was as accurate as possible.

The stealth carriers flanked the procession while warships from Wallach took the lead and brought up the rear guard.

There were other vessels that barely looked like they should be moving—like they were a collection of junk we had seen in the Xad system. It was strange to see all these vessels in a star system that didn't have a comet blazing through the center of their numbers.

"Macabre is a clean system," Tom said. "It wouldn't be a bad place if the planet wasn't so hostile."

"Agreed," I said.

"Are you worried about the mission?" Tom asked.

"No more than usual." I paused, gathering my thoughts. "Have you been watching Henshaw?"

"I was going to mention that," Tom said. "He's been reclusive. We normally meet in person or by commlink if we're on different ships to discuss books we've read or theories we would like to investigate about this or that."

"Why do you think that is?" Like Tom, I sensed something was off.

"The problem is Ayers," Tom said. "Henshaw doesn't believe anyone is as smart as he is and now that belief is being challenged. More importantly, the theories that Ayers puts forward are compelling and intriguing on a visceral level."

"That's interesting," I said. "I think I know what you mean, but can you clarify what you're talking about?"

I was still holding my cigar unlit, and my whiskey glass had barely been touched.

"Humans have marveled at the possibility of there being other life out there for as long as we've had the language to ask the question," Tom said. "We've always known there were humans on other planets, and other systems, and maybe beyond that, but what about other forms of sentient life? Ayers passionately believes they exist."

I put down my glass to light my cigar. Before long I was puffing away to get it going.

"The moment we find real proof that Ayers knows what he's talking about, Henshaw will face a crisis of his own scientific paradigms," Tom said.

"That's what I'm afraid of," I said, letting the cigar hang to one side as I retrieved my whiskey glass but didn't drink from it.

"I don't believe it'll be a problem. If Henshaw is as much like me as I assume he is, we will both be rushing forward with questions and testing theories and learning lots of amazing new things," Tom said.

"That's good, I suppose. Not sure I feel great about all of this, but it is what it is," I said. "I want to get the codes to those cryo-vaults and get my family out of them."

"That's all that matters," Tom said. "That, and finding a new home for everyone in the exodus fleet."

12

THE NEXT MORNING, I woke and listened to X-37 updating me on the status of the fleet as I got squared away. Captain Younger, the acting admiral of the fleet, had deployed in the lagrangian point between Macabre and the fourth planet from the local star.

"I've also observed that your morning ritual is significantly less focused on your personal security than it was before your final encounter with Vice Admiral Nebs," X-37 said.

"Are you saying I'm getting soft?" I asked. There had been a reason for me to roll out of bed like I was about to be attacked, but I couldn't remember what it was. I still checked my environment and remained as situationally aware as possible, always understanding that anything could happen.

But I felt safer than I ever had. Why? I thought it was

because I belonged with the people of Xad and Wallach and my friends.

I hoped I didn't let them down.

"Elise and the rest of the team are waiting for you in the launch bay," X-37 said.

"I'm on my way."

We loaded into our archangel gear a short time after I arrived. Elise harassed me for being late, but she seemed to be in a good mood. When I had snapped into my Archangel, I viewed the rest of my team: Elise, Path, Horvath, Carrie, and Ayers. Tom stayed on the ship in a command-and-control function, while the Wallach and Xad soldiers we'd borrowed waited as a reaction force if needed.

They didn't have archangel gear, only the heavy-duty search and rescue equipment provided by Captain Younger. I hope they didn't have to test it on the harsh surface of Macabre.

"I'm launching the probe," Tom advised. "Make yourself comfortable but be ready. There may be a narrow window of opportunity once the process begins."

"Your mechanic is correct," Ayers said. "The vault will rise to the surface of the lava for a short time, then descend to a cavern far below the surface. That's the secret to its long-term survival."

"Good to know. Not that I'm excited about getting trapped miles below the surface of the volcanic planet," I said.

"You have a way with words," Elise said. "And you tell me to think before I speak. Can someone else give our pep talk?"

"Fine. How's this for a pep talk? Everyone get on the shuttle," I said. "Carrie will pilot, Elise is the back-up pilot."

"Why can't I fly the shuttle?" Elise asked.

"You can't pilot the ship and be on the away team. If we get to where you're flying, then something has gone wrong." I reviewed the plan and checked on Tom regarding the status of the drone.

"It struck the surface and disappeared. Jelly can't get any further readings on it," Tom said. "We won't know if it worked until the vault rises to the surface."

"Understood," I said. "We'll maintain a high orbit in the shuttle until you give us the go ahead."

Once we were all loaded up, and we'd completed our safety checks, Carrie flew the shuttle into position. We waited for almost half an hour.

"And... it seems Doctor Ayers was telling the truth," Tom said. "I'm sending you images of the vault. It's emerging from the lava field and seems to be opening. I suggest you move quickly."

I watched the viewscreen, amazed at what I was seeing. The vault was more like a mobile base in the shape of a sphere. There was no instrumentation, and there were no portholes on the lava ship, but once it was on the surface, it began to open.

The first thing that happened was the unfolding of a foundation. My gut instinct was that they were using advanced alloys and shielding technology that rivaled anything found on a starship. How they powered it to maintain a constant defense was a mystery, but there it was.

Once the giant pontoon-boat-like foundation had been put out, the center of it opened up into what looked like a landing strip with retaining walls all around the edges to keep lava from spilling onto the open area.

"That looks big, but I think when we get down there it will feel small," Elise said

"A good portion of the vault is still below the surface, much like the whole of any oceangoing vessel on a normal planet," Ayers said. "Time is of the essence. I recommend that you land, get what you came for, and then have us pick you up in the shuttle."

"Carrie is the only one who's staying on the shuttle. I will need your expertise, and passwords, when we land," I said.

"There are no passwords at this point. No one could access it if they didn't have control of the drone, so further security measures are redundant," Ayers said.

"Right, and the Union never does anything that's redundant," I said.

Elise moved closer to Ayers, the helmet of her archangel armor open since we were still on the shuttle. "There aren't any surprises down there, are there?"

Ayers looked away embarrassed. He covered his mistake, but we all saw what had transpired.

"There's something else, isn't there, Doctor Ayers?" Elise asked. "You wouldn't want us to get hurt, would you?"

Eventually, Ayers looked her in the eyes. "No one would've been hurt. You just wouldn't have been able to get inside. You would've returned to the shuttle and we would've left."

"Without the codes to save my family?" I asked, keeping my voice as dry and sharp as a blade.

"There is a way to retrieve the contents of the vault without going inside. You merely need access to the control panel, and I would've walked you through it remotely," Ayers said. "That's still an option if you're interested."

I shook my head, leaning toward him. "We came all this way, so we might as well have it all."

"I was afraid you'd say that." He closed his archangel helmet. "We might as well do this."

I waited until I was sure the doctor didn't have any other surprises to hit us with, then gave Carrie the signal. "Take us down. The moment we're off the ship, get some altitude. I don't want the shuttle damaged by the environment."

"Can-do, Reaper," Carrie said. Moments later, we were shooting down to the upper atmosphere.

"Doctor, how are you going to open the vault?" Elise asked.

Ayers hesitated, but then spilled it. "The important parts of the vault can only be accessed with my DNA or the DNA of Nebs."

I leaned back, regarding the scene with satisfaction. "When I'm right, I'm right."

"You didn't know it would require my DNA," Ayers countered.

"I knew it would be something."

"We are on final approach," Carrie said. "Be ready to deploy. Touching down in five, four, three, two, one, now."

The ramp at the back of the shuttle opened, and I saw nothing but heat waves and splashing lava for a few seconds. The shuttle rotated until the deck of the Union lava ship was visible.

I went first, jumping down and doing a quick check for traps or other dangers.

"All clear. This place has one door in the center of the deck," I said. "Bring Ayers and let's get this done."

"On the way," Elise said.

Moments later, Elise and Horvath escorted Doctor Ayers down the shuttle ramp. The moment they were clear, Carrie lifted off and climbed for altitude.

I leaned close to the door, examining the nearly invisible seam around the edges, then searched for a locking mechanism. The entrance was barely recognizable as a door despite being in the center of the dome-shaped vault. There was no way I was getting in this one without help.

The deck of the Union facility shifted sideways, sliding across some change in the lava sea around us. Horvath and Ayers stumbled, but Elise was there to balance them, using one hand to steady the Wallach soldier and pick up the scientists where he had fallen to one knee with the other.

Below the ash-gray clouds above us, the shuttle circled at an altitude safe from a shoulder-fired surface-to-air rocket. This gave me more insight into Carrie as a soldier. She was following her training, most likely. Being reliable and brave was important to the men and women of Wallach.

Elise and the others gathered around me. "Made it," she said.

"Ayers, you're up. Get this door open," I said.

He hesitated for a count of three, nodded, and stepped close to the portal. Seconds later he had located a small pinhole off to one side that I wouldn't have found even if I'd known what to look for.

"What are you waiting for?" I asked. "Every second we stand here is dangerous. Open the door."

He looked embarrassed. "I need a small knife or a needle."

"You've got to be kidding me," I said.

"I'm not going to pick the lock, Reaper. I need to cut myself. This will operate on my DNA," he said.

Horvath pulled a long combat knife from the leg of his Archangel armor. Doctor Ayers flinched even though he was safe in his own gear.

"That seems excessive. I was hoping somebody had a small tool I could use to prick my finger," Ayers said, removing his gauntlets.

"When did we teach him to take those off? They are triple-sealed to maintain ballistic integrity, protection from the environment, and to maintain internal temperatures," Elise asked on our private channel. "Huge pain in the backside to deal with."

"Quickly please," Ayers said. "You wouldn't believe how hot the air is."

X-37 answered. "He was not instructed and should not have any skill at using the gear. My analysis suggests that it is a good thing we took the weapons off of his unit. Doctor Ayers has been holding back. He is trying to *hustle* us, Reaper Cain."

I stepped forward, not wanting the man to realize we detected another layer of his dishonesty, then fished a small cigar knife from the storage compartment in my Archangel armor. "Use this, but I'll need it back. Not that I'm excited about trimming a cigar with something you bled on."

"All it took was a mission to Macabre for us to learn what makes a Reaper squeamish," Ayers said. He accepted the knife, drew a small line across one of his fingertips, and milked the wound to produce a bead of blood. Next, he pushed it against the pinhole, and we all watched the blood disappear.

Fewer than twenty meters from the edge of the platform, lava geysered into the air without warning. It shot a hundred meters above us then fell back toward the planet, creating an arc over the Union lava ship. Glowing red and gold mist rained down on us.

Ayers put back on the Archangel gauntlets so quickly it seemed like he had never taken them off. Despite the soft look of the superheated magma, when it struck my helmet it sounded like fist-sized hail.

The door to the wall started to open but stopped when the melted rock splattered across its surface.

"What the hell?" I grunted.

"It's protecting itself," Ayers said. "The vault wouldn't survive long in this environment if we hadn't designed it well. Be patient and it will open. It knows I'm here."

"Creepy." Elise made a sound over the commlink Ayers couldn't hear.

Unaware of our opinions, Ayers composed himself.

"Doctor Ayers seems extraordinarily calm given our prior observations of his behavior," X-37 said.

"Yeah. I think you're right. He's trying to pull a fast one," I said.

"My analyses are usually accurate," X-37 said. "I should add that it is equally likely that he is unstable and could revert back to any number of behavioral templates at any time."

"That doesn't make me feel good," I said, then switched to the main channel. "I'll go first. Elise, bring up the rear. Horvath, stay at the door to make sure it doesn't close."

"How am I going to do that?" Horvath asked.

"You'll figure something out." I moved into the small space and began searching it with the enhanced power of the Archangel optics but also my cybernetic eye. X-37 processed images as fast as possible, giving me concise updates as I moved.

"There are seven steep stairwells circumventing the interior, suggesting the vault can operate upside-down if needed. Lighting is set to emergency power levels. I'm increasing your optical sensitivity. Motion detection is null, but please remain vigilant, Reaper Cain."

I took a stairwell descending along the wall into the bowels of the vault. It was only one room lit by red, low power emergency lighting.

"Freaky," Elise said. "Not on my list of places to visit often."

The floor shifted. It was like being on an ocean-going vessel but more subdued because of the consistency of what we were floating on. I heard the lava ship bump against something large.

"What was that, Ayers?" I demanded.

"Not everything remains molten when exposed to the surface atmosphere. Everything is continually melting and solidifying," he said.

Something rocked the entire ship to one side, forcing us all to fight to stay on our feet.

"We are safe for now," Ayers said. "The ship was made to withstand this environment. That was another geyser."

"Where are the codes?" I asked.

Ayers led me to one side of the vault where there were several small workstations. "I will need to disconnect these properly and transfer data to a single unit, then we can take it with us. Once we are back on your ship, the codes will be easy to retrieve with or without me. However, I recommend you don't leave me here or kill me even though my value will diminish once you have these in your possession."

13

"GET TO WORK, AYERS." I watched him. On one hand, I was paranoid and untrusting of people like Ayers. On the other hand, I was usually right. There was no way I would let him get me or my friends killed while he tried to escape with the codes.

"Reaper," Elise said from another section of the room. There shouldn't be any place to hide, but the multiple staircases and ladders leading down into the center gave it something that passed for corners and the lighting was minimal.

"Are you okay?" I asked.

"I'm fine, I guess," Elise answered. "You need to see this."

"Horvath, watch Ayers. And I mean watch him like you don't trust him," I said.

The Wallach soldier grunted as he replaced me as Ayers's guard. "I *don't* trust him."

Elise stood over a dark shape that had to be a body—a large, motionless body.

"Who did they leave behind? A technician who couldn't take the isolation?" I asked. "A guard? Or just someone who pissed off Nebs and Ayers and got left here to pay the ultimate price."

Elise shook her head as she answered. "I don't think this is any of those things."

I moved around Elise and stared down at a monster. The body had started off as a human, I thought. The more I studied it, the less sure I was. "It looks mummified. There aren't any bugs or animals to speed the decomposition."

"Keep an eye on Horvath and Ayers," I repeated, then knelt next to the corpse. The pre-mortem color of the skin was difficult to determine. Post-mortem, it looked charcoal blue with a striped camouflage pattern. Decomposition had withered the tissue underneath the skin and possibly changed its overall effect, but I didn't know what it had looked like before it died to be sure.

The head was too large, and I had an uneasy suspicion there were a lot of teeth in the mouth. Its lips had drawn back, showing a preview of the horror within.

"What's wrong with its jaw?" Elise sounded nervous and I noticed she was dividing her attention between the dead creature and Doctor Ayers.

"I don't think it's hinged like a human mandible. I read a book during my isolation in Dreadmax; it was a fairytale about Earth, but it mentioned an animal called a snake that could swallow its prey whole. Maybe that is what this is." I said. "X, are you getting all of this? Include Elise in your answer but leave Horvath out of it. I need him to focus on his job."

"The structure of the jawline in the oversized mouth suggests that this humanoid had been able to take very large bites—or possibly swallow three or four kilos of organic material at once. The neck, which seems to have a tougher exterior than a human would, is also enlarged," X-37 explained.

"You're saying this thing has bad table manners," I said.

"Unknown, Reaper Cain. I can conclude it is capable of such an action, but have no way to verify that is its preferred method to consume calories," X-37 said.

"I'm going to bring it back with us," I said. "Assuming it doesn't fall to pieces when I pick it up."

"Doctor Ayers has not concluded his data recovery efforts," X-37 advised. "So you have time to examine the arms of this thing more closely."

I squinted at the arms, leaning closer to see what my limited artificial intelligence had observed. What I found on the left arm were cable-like tentacles lying in a pool of putrid slime.

That this thing's left arm differed from its right set me off balance. It wasn't cybernetic, but for a second, I felt a strange kinship with it. It was a freak that had a mass of spike-tipped tentacles on its left arm. On instinct, I checked the dead creature's left eye that found both of its eyes to be sunken and mostly decomposed.

"This thing is big," I said. "I can lift it with my armor, but it will be awkward."

"Please examine the right arm," X-37 said.

I shifted my attention and saw what my LAI was looking for. The right arm had grooved slots from wrist to elbow where the tips of the organic spike-tentacles protruded. "Wow, X, it looks like the death tentacles could extend themselves—if it was alive."

"I hope this is the only one," Elise said. "It looks mean."

"That's an understatement," I said. "Ayers, are you about done?"

"I have transferred all the codes into one unit that will be easier to carry back to the shuttle," he said.

"Great, let's get out of here," I said, then hefted the corpse onto my shoulder. "Do you know who this freak is?"

"No, not precisely," Ayers said, his voice so quiet I barely understood him even with the Archangel comms gear. "Nebs was looking for test subject 14B before we left Macabre. I would be very curious to know how he was left behind."

"Ayers, there are a lot of things about this place that raise questions," I said. "Elise, take point. Get Carrie down here with that shuttle."

ELISE PAUSED IN THE DOORWAY, contacting Carrie before stepping out onto the deck of the lava ship. "We're ready for pick up. Let's time it so there's as little exposure as possible.

I'm not excited about getting sprayed with molten rock again."

The outside of her armor, and ours, was pockmarked with heat damage. On one section of her back, there was damage all the way down to the gold surface.

"I'm inbound," Carrie advised. "Ninety seconds."

A countdown timer appeared in all of our Archangel HUDs Elise waited for fifteen seconds, then let us out onto the deck. The moment we started to move, the deck came apart under our feet.

The shuttle touched down as Elise sprinted toward it. Just behind her, the deck split as though it had been designed to self-destruct. Horvath grabbed Ayers and pulled him back, saving him from a rather toasty death.

Sections of the lava ship plummeted downward, spraying red waves into the air. Horvath and I shielded Ayers with our armor. The add-on layers sizzled and burned as more and more of the magma splashed across us. All of us were struggling to maintain our feet and not slide off the tilting deck.

"Jump, Ayers," I said, "and don't tell me you don't know how."

His voice caught when he tried to speak. "You're right. I was lying. I'm skilled in the Archangel armor. Nebs made me learn because he thought I might need it someday. But I still can't jump."

"Now is not the time for games!" I growled.

"I'm scared! Jumping over that is impossible!"

"Godsdammit!" I dropped the freakish corpse I was

carrying and grabbed Ayers by one arm. "Horvath, get the other. We'll have to jump with him between us. Ayers, I know you're shitting your pants but try to jump when we do. All this extra protection we covered ourselves with will only make dying longer and more miserable if we fall in."

"I... I... I..." Ayers stammered.

"I'm ready, Reaper," Horvath said.

"On three. One, two, three, jump!" I leaped over the gap, holding Ayers as tightly as I could. The three of us sprang into the air, and for a second, it felt like we would make it.

I cursed, twisting in mid-flight, and shoved Ayers and Horvath as hard as I could. The effect was minimal because I had nothing to push off of, but it was just enough to get them onto the deck where the shuttle had touched down.

They landed in a heap while I hit the edge, smashing the armor so hard it knocked the wind out of me, and fell back.

"Reaper!" Elise screamed, already leaping toward me with a tow cable in one hand while Horvath and Ayers were tumbling across the rocking deck of the lava ship.

I hit the surface of the lava. All of my sensors went blank.

"You have forty-five seconds before the Archangel armor loses integrity," X-37 said. "Please tread water."

"I'm not in water, X!"

Something grabbed me and hauled me upward. Bubbling lava held onto my legs, nearly dragging me back down.

Lights and images on my HUD flickered and popped. The Archangel armor was trying to reboot, fighting for survival as hard as I was. When I heard Elise shouting at me, half of the words were lost, and she sounded like she was far away.

"Can you... can you at least try to climb out of that mess? My servos are overloading. Why are you so big?" she grunted, her words barely understandable. Apparently, I was heavy even with the added strength of her Archangel gear.

"I'm doing my best!" I snapped. "Why don't you try swimming in lava. It's harder than it looks."

Elise started laughing so hard I thought she might be crying inside of her helmet. "You're such a jerk!"

"Less talking and more pulling me out of the fire," I said.

I was halfway out when Horvath came to help. After what seemed like hours but was only a handful of seconds, the three of us tumbled onto the surface between the edge and the shuttle ramp.

"Let's go, let's go, let's go!" Carrie shouted.

I heard Ayers in the background yelling at her to leave us.

"I really don't like that guy," Elise said, panting the words as we all leaned on our knees to catch our breath.

"Me neither," I said. "But you still have to be nice to him. I doubt this is the last secret he's hidden from us."

We staggered up the ramp and onto the shuttle, and Carrie took off. I grabbed Ayers and slammed him into his seat.

"You nearly got us killed."

"I thought Reapers knew what they were doing. You can't blame your incompetence on me," Ayers said.

Elise pulled me back and pointed at a bench along the

wall. "Sit down, Reaper. Buckle in. Let's just get back to the *Jellybird* before you try to kill him."

I complied, glad she had intervened. Turning away, I spoke with X-37 privately. "Can we never do that again, X?"

"I will enter your desire to avoid lava fields in my database," X-37 said as I took my seat and strapped in for the ride back to the *Jellybird*.

14

THE RETURN TRIP to the *Bright Lance* was uneventful. I took a nap right on the bridge of the *Jellybird,* too tired to smoke a cigar first or express how I truly felt about what Ayers tried to do to us.

Elise volunteered to guard the man but mentioned privately she had no intention of talking to him. She wasn't in the mood.

As for Doctor Ayers, we had to coerce him out of his Archangel armor. After that, he sat trembling and refused to look anyone in the eyes. I wasn't sure if he was traumatized by his near-death experience or just worried about what we were going to do to him.

When I awoke, I saw a view of the mad, alien obsessed scientist on the holo view, and I realized he was muttering to himself and counting on his fingers.

"X, is the hotshot genetic scientist actually counting on his fingers?"

"That is correct, Reaper Cain. He has not slept since we put him back in his cell. My analysis suggests it is more of a nervous tick than something he needs to do, but without mind reading abilities, I can't be sure," X-37 said.

"Maybe it's weird, but I feel sorry for him," I said.

"Why would that be weird?" X-37 asked. "I am honestly curious. Clarification would assist me in further communication with you and other biological life-forms."

"You know it creeps me out when you call me a biological life-form," I said.

My limited artificial intelligence, securely interwoven into my nerve-ware, didn't sound repentant. "It is a factual statement. Are you going to answer the question, or should I mark it for the research on my part?"

"Because he nearly got us killed," I said. "That's why it's weird. I should be punching him in the face, but I feel sorry for him instead. The man has made his own choices, but I don't think any of them were easy."

ELISE, Tom, Path, and Horvath gathered around but kept a respectful distance.

"What the hell is going on?" I asked.

"We have the codes to the cryo- pods," Elise said. "You'll be able to see your mother and sister as soon as we get back to the *Bright Lance*."

At a loss for words, I nodded then looked at the floor.

"We want to be with you, or at least in the room," Elise said.

"What do you think I'm going to do? Freak out?" I asked, not really knowing what I was even saying. "I'm sorry. Of course I want you all there."

"We are approaching the *Bright Lance* now," Jelly said. "Shall I advise Carrie to prepare the shuttle?"

"That would be great, Jelly," I said, as I stood and stretched my arms above my head. "We're taking Ayers with us to the *Bright Lance*. I promised Captain Younger he would be returned to their brig."

"That's a good idea. It will be more secure," Tom said.

"Let's do an equipment check, gather up Ayers, and load onto the shuttle," I said.

My team went to work with efficiency that only came when people trusted each other and knew each other's idiosyncrasies. This semi-random collection of people was starting to function as well as a well-trained spec ops unit. Different, but maybe better in all the ways that counted.

THE RIDE to the *Bright Lance* felt like a lifetime. I remembered scenes from my childhood, wondered random things like what my mother and sister would think of my new friends, and worried about what might go wrong.

The *Lady Faith* was docked in the limited space of the

Bright Lance's flight deck. X-37 advised that Henshaw was waiting for us in the cryo-pod wing of the ship hospital and that Bug was ingratiating himself with the ship's internal security teams.

"I almost wish I had time to see that," I said.

"The security personnel of this ship, especially those individuals in the camera rooms, have taken him on as a type of mascot," X-37 said. "They greet him warmly, cheering and calling out his name whenever he appears. It is a uniquely human behavior, I think."

"Keep an eye on the kid. I'm glad he has friends, but it won't be long before he gets himself into trouble," I said. "Will this make his job easier?"

"No," X-37 said. "While he has better access to surveillance cameras, his new friends are always interested in what he is doing, making his surveillance of Ayers harder to keep a secret. My analysis suggests Bug should ask for their help instead of hide his objectives."

"We don't know if Ayers has confederates on the ship, but you're right. Start doing background checks on the security personnel who have befriended Bug," I said.

"Of course, Reaper Cain."

We removed Ayers from the shuttle. He said nothing, even when Elise tried to talk to him. As soon as we were on the *Bright Lance*, ship security helped us escort Ayers to the brig where he was locked down.

I pulled aside the shift supervisor. "Keep an eye on him and notify me if he starts saying or doing anything crazy."

"Yes, sir," the man said. "Are you going to the celebration? We heard the mission to Macabre was successful. A buddy of mine says the holo footage is amazing. It's an honor to have you with us, Reaper Cain."

"Thank you, Sergeant Uluru." I liked the sergeant but signaled X-37 to check him out. Over-friendliness always raised my suspicion. At some point, we had to trust the crew of the *Bright Lance*. Deciding on when that some point was could be tricky.

"Sergeant Uluru is a Xad citizen with an excellent record. None of the Union turncoats have been allowed near the brig," X-37 said for my team only. "The doctor will be unable to cause trouble while locked down."

We moved away from other security teams and entered the main concourse that would eventually lead us to the hospital level.

"What about friends and girlfriends?" I asked. "Uluru might be solid, but what about his private life. Be sure to check his finances."

"Finances are irrelevant in the exodus fleet. Everyone is working together to survive," X-37 said.

"Humans always have something to trade, so finances are always an issue. I learned that in prison. Debt kills. Never forget it, X. That's Reaper school 101." Walking without a hundred pounds of powered armor encasing me was a nice change. "Keep me updated. It seems like we're missing something with Ayers."

"Of course, Reaper Cain."

"What's going on, Reaper," Elise asked, looking back toward the brig. "You're weirding me out."

"I'm checking the boxes, making sure we're not trusting others too much," I said.

"Oh, right. Trust is a bad thing. I forgot." Elise rolled her eyes away from me, which made me chuckle. "They are professionals, Reaper."

"I've completed the preliminary background check of Sergeant Uluru of Xad, Reaper Cain," X-37 said.

"So fast and invasive," Elise said.

"I'm unsure if that is a complement, Elise," X-37 said, then continued without missing a beat. "Sergeant Uluru has a girlfriend formerly loyal to the Union."

"What did I tell you?" I asked.

"Really, Reaper? The guy can't have a life?" Elise asked.

"Sure, but not while he is guarding a high value prisoner," I said. "Send the report to Captain Younger and request Uluru be removed from the guard detail."

"Right away, Reaper Cain," X-37 said.

My friends led me toward the hospital and the cryo-pod wing. None of us spoke. Even X-37 was quiet.

A pair of guards admitted us into the cryo-pod area that consisted of a nexus point in several hallways radiating into the medical laboratories.

Henshaw was waiting. Technicians and doctors who Captain Younger had assured me were the best she had also waited to assist if needed. Younger and a pair of junior officers stood back respectfully.

I approached the Xad officer who was currently in charge of the entire combined fleet but who had made time to be here.

"Excellent work on Macabre," she said. "I've watched the holo several times myself. That jump was amazing." She smiled at Elise. "And that was some quick thinking. It looked like you were already moving when disaster struck."

"Thank you, Captain Younger," Elise said.

"Don't let me or my people get in your way," Younger said. "Everyone here is at your disposal, but I understand you will want some privacy. My XO informed me you have concerns about the security team in the brig. We will look into it."

"Thank you, Captain," I said. "Or should I call you Admiral?"

"We've been discussing terminology, but since it's a rotating position, there have been a few differences of opinion," she said. "Enough about politics and organizational charts. Go to your family."

I nodded, then approached the hallway to the room where my mother and sister waited. Elise was behind me, then Tom and Henshaw and the ship's doctor, Major Hubert Moore, followed.

"How does this work, X?" I asked.

"I took the liberty of contacting Tom and James Henshaw," X-37 said. "They have reviewed all the protocols and understand the codes. I've also worked with AI Mavis and Major Moore. But once we decide to awaken your mother and sister, I will walk you through the progress so you can do it yourself."

"Okay." I entered the room. My friends loitered to the door, watching me.

Everything was in order, the facility perfectly clean and well lit. X-37 recommended dimming the lights slightly for when they awoke, so we made that happen. I pulled a chair close to my mother's cryo- pod and just sat there for a long time. My friends waited patiently.

"Are you certain you're ready to do this, Reaper Cain?" X-37 said. "Your biometrics are remarkably calm given the weight of this moment. I must remind you that there is no rush to awaken them. Their health will not be affected by another day if you need to take some time."

I stood, picked up the tablet with her medical information on it, and hesitated. *Olivia Cain.* The screen also gave her height, weight, and other biometrics. She was a tall woman but according to the tablet, her weight was at a bare minimum after so long in the cryo-pod.

"I thought these things were meant to preserve people," I muttered. "She looks starved."

"That is correct, Reaper Cain. Apparently, Nebs or his staff adjusted the settings for minimal life support in an effort to conserve all possible resources for a long tour in unknown regions of space," X-37 said.

"I really wish I could kill that guy twice." I reviewed each step of the revival process.

When I entered the code, I used more care and deliberation than I had in anything I'd ever done. A message flashed along the cryo-pod's screen. *Revival sequence in progress.*

"Everything seems to be working," X-37 said. "Mavis sends her best wishes and wants to assure you that a significant portion of her processing power has been dedicated to making sure this is a safe and successful procedure."

The first thing that changed was my ability to see through the observation window. Before long, it was like there was no glass between us. My mother's strong face looked more severe than I remembered because her hair was pulled back and her expression was frozen despite the readout claiming she was now in a normal state of sleep.

I couldn't stop looking at her hair. In my memory, it had always been a darker version of auburn with streaks of silver. Now it was like liquid mercury.

"The process is intended to be slow and gentle," X-37 said.

"I know, X. I read the manual several times in case you forgot," I said.

"It is unlikely that I would forget such a momentous occurrence. You really should read more, Reaper Cain," X-37 said.

Gases vented slowly from the side of the long tube. I heard them more than I saw them. My sense of time was probably distorted.

When my mother opened her eyes and saw me, she smiled with obvious effort.

"She won't be able to talk, Reaper Cain. It's important to

ease her back into normality. Rushing the process could damage her vocal cords," X-37 said.

"I know, X." I opened the lid and helped my mother to sit up. She hugged me weakly, her head on my shoulder and her arms feeling far too thin.

"Hal," she whispered.

"Don't say anything, mother," I said softly, holding her like she might vanish if I looked away even for a second. "There will be time for that. Don't strain your voice."

"I knew you would find us," she whispered, her voice sounding harsh from long disuse.

Rocking her gently, I didn't know what to say.

"One last thing, and then I will take your advice," she said. "Your sister will be angry when you wake her up."

"Okay, mother. You need to rest."

We both started laughing, her voice rough and beautiful at the same time. The more we tried to stop, the worse it was. My friends were having similar issues near the doorway, but Elise, I noticed, had tears in her eyes.

WE REPEATED the process after my mother drifted into a normal sleep. Her warning didn't bother me. Of course Hannah would be angry—she was part of the Cain family, after all, and we all had tempers.

"There must be a reason your mother made the considerable effort to warn you," X-37 said. "She understands the danger of straining vocal cords that haven't been used for months. Please be careful, Reaper Cain."

Hannah's hair was much shorter than I remembered, barely reaching the nape of her neck. When she'd been a teenager, it had tumbled down her back in waves, often high-lighted with whatever color suited her mood. As a young woman in her twenties, it had been so rich that it almost seemed magical. Unlike my mother's, whatever Nebs had done to them hadn't changed its color.

"Why is her hair so short?" I asked.

Mavis surprised me by answering. "She was in the habit of shaving her head bald before Nebs resorted to the cryo-pods to control her. The vice admiral comple-mented her hair. She responded by taking a razor to her scalp."

"That sounds like Hannah," I said.

She was nearly as thin as my mother but had been more athletic and robust before getting put to sleep. Like me, both women were tall and athletic. Hannah hadn't always liked being taller and stronger than the boys her age. I wondered if that was still true.

When she awoke, she was instantly alert. Her ice green eyes focused on me like she was sighting a weapon. She touched her throat to indicate she couldn't speak yet.

"It's okay," I said. "I already woke up mom and I know how hard it is for you to talk right now. I think I can hold up the entire conversation."

She laughed silently and it looked like it hurt.

I joined her, fighting back tears. "It's good to see you, sis. I was warned you would be angry."

Her response was hard to interpret because she was still struggling to restrain her mirth. A mixture of emotions played across her face—everything from a type of laughter that only her big brother could evoke to an underlying rage at her situation.

"I killed the fuck out of Nebs." My voice caught, surprising me. Killing wasn't a problem for me but saving my mother and sister made it different, more personal and dangerous, even though I'd already done the deed.

"Good. Help me out of this thing. I hate being in here."

X-37 warned me it was too soon to move her, but I knew there wasn't a choice. In most ways, she was as different from me as was humanly possible, but there were certain personality traits we shared. Being stubborn was right at the top of the list.

I took her hand and pulled her upright. We didn't hug. Now didn't seem like the time even though we had all been a hug friendly family before everything went wrong on Boyer 5.

"Your biometrics are very strange, Reaper Cain."

How did I explain emotion to my LAI? It couldn't be done with hand signals and I didn't want to ruin the moment with my sister.

"Reaper Cain, please respond or I will be forced to call Doctor Moore," X-37 said.

My heart was beating the inside of my chest, tears ran

down my face, and my hands were shaking like I was a scared kid. "I need to talk to my LAI, Hannah."

"Can I get out of this thing first?" Her words were barely a whisper and I thought pain was causing her to sweat. She wasn't looking at me; we saved me the embarrassment of crying like this.

"Let me help you." I held her firmly by one arm and a shoulder, ready to catch her head if she flopped backward. "Don't call the doctor, X. I'll explain later."

"Are you experiencing happiness, Reaper Cain?"

"Yeah, X. That's all this is."

One side of the pod folded away. She swung out her legs and sat with her hands on her knees trying to get her bearings. It looked like she was in pain, every muscle cramping against the sudden movement.

"You should distract her by giving her an update on the situation," X-37 said.

I wanted to tell my limited artificial intelligence that she wasn't a commando, but X was mostly right. I was sure she wanted to know what was going on.

"My friends helped me storm the *Dark Lance* and take it from the vice admiral. They call it the *Bright Lance* now. Some of the Union soldiers and crewmen switched sides."

"Don't... trust the officers." Hannah was still looking at the floor as she wrestled with her discomfort.

"Most of them died. Nebs did something to their cardiovascular systems—some kind of dead man switch that went off when we discovered the secret vault where they hide their research," I said.

Hannah went pale at the mention of the vault. She looked at me with haunted eyes but said nothing.

"We can get to that stuff later," I said. "I want you to meet my friends."

15

It was one of those days that didn't seem to end. Both my mother and my sister had liked my friends, smiling at the exaggerated stories they told about me. Neither of them could keep their voices so they sipped hot tea and tried not to strain themselves laughing.

If I'd been worried about them fitting in, it had been a misplaced concern. The reunion quickly became as festive as was possible in a medical research facility.

The exception was Rejon. He'd arrived after about the first half an hour and loitered on the fringes of our impromptu gathering. I introduced him, of course, and he was exceptionally polite.

But I could tell his mind was elsewhere.

When Doctor Moore finally told us enough was enough

and that his patients needed to rest, we dispersed. I took Rejon aside and confronted him.

"What's on your mind, Rejon?"

"I'm glad that you are reunited with your family. If I have ruined it in any way, I apologize," he said.

"Don't worry about it."

He shifted, clearly choosing his words carefully, and faced me with a haunted expression. "I've been watching the video of your mission to Macabre. What we show the crews of all the ships focuses on the dramatic leap across the lava and flying away on the shuttle with the prize in hand."

"But that's not what's bothering you," I said.

"I'm wondering what type of creature you found inside the lava ship," Rejon said.

My blood ran cold. I'd forced my thoughts away from that particular discovery. "I need to watch the video to see how it appeared to everyone else. X, has Captain Younger edited the video display to the fleet?"

"She has not, Reaper Cain," X-37 said. "Transparency of government is a fundamental principle of both Wallach and Xad. It is one of the things that confirms my theory of them having once been part of the same society."

"Great." One disaster after another grew in my imagination.

"Why would this be a problem, Reaper?" Rejon asked.

"We don't know much about the creature I found in the lava ship vault. There are probably a hundred rumors rippling through the fleet right now." I wondered if I was overreacting, but I could imagine the horror stories that were growing each time someone discussed the creature. The monster had spiked tentacles that looked ready to catch children and eat them in one bite.

Rejon looked at his feet. "I've already received reports of such stories. Fortunately, the people of Wallach and Xad have been hungering for stories of heroism and good news for a long time. So far, most have focused on the successes of the mission."

"I think it's time to check out the vault," I said. "Let's walk. We're going to reveal the *Bright Lance's* secret."

"I suggest you include Captain Younger in this revelation," X-37 said.

My limited artificial intelligence wasn't wrong. I also knew better than to rush to failure. "Let's get the whole team on this. Elise and Path for security, Tom and Henshaw for technical advice, and Younger. Who she brings is up to her, but I suggest it's a small group."

"I would like to see this for myself before exposing my own people," Rejon said. Despite his lanky spacer's frame, he was shorter than me and had to stride quickly to keep up. "I would recommend that President Coronas at least be informed of what we're doing, however."

"Good call." I was feeling awake and energized if not exactly refreshed from the day's events. "X, make sure Path and Elise are geared up in their archangel units. And make sure Path understands that's an order. He may not like the power the AA gives him, but we need him ready to kill the hell out of something."

"Ordering your friends about as though they are Union soldiers is unnecessary and rude," X-37 privately said.

I gave my LAI a nonverbal signal suggesting he understood what I meant and should rephrase my message appropriately.

The messages went out over secure commlinks, and before long we met at the *Bright Lance* vault. Access to the area was guarded by Xad and Wallach soldiers. None of the Union turncoats were allowed on this level, whether inside or outside the restricted area.

Nervous energy rippled through our group. I took Younger and Rejon aside. "I don't know what we're going to find. To be honest, I had hoped to take it slow until rumors started spreading to the ship."

"It's best we find out sooner rather than later," Younger said. "If there are going to be rumors, I want to be informed. I would hate to tell people something isn't true, and then find out I was wrong. That would look as though I was lying to my people, and that is a sin not tolerated among our people."

"It is much the same with the people of Xad," Rejon said.

"If no one has any objections, it's time to see what's inside," I said.

Path and Elise flanked me as I approached the most secret section of the ship with codes that could change everything for us. And probably not for the better.

"I must remind you that leaving that door sealed could be

the best option," X-37 said to me *and* the group. "I understand this is nearly impossible. Curiosity is a nearly unstoppable force for you and your friends."

"You've got that right, X," I said. Nervous chuckles spread
through our group. Except for Path, of course. He was deep
into his pre-fight calm. The man could invoke his meditative
practices at will and be ready to fight in an optimal state at a
moment's notice.

"Does anyone want to back out?" I asked.

No one answered.

Nodding, I approached the vault door and activated the
access panel. There was a place for a palm print and a DNA
reader, which probably meant I could bring Ayers down here
and prick his finger for a little bit of blood to get in if I had to.
"Are you thinking what I'm thinking, X?"

"Unknown, Reaper Cain, but in light of recent events, it
seems we might have to use DNA from Ayers to access this
area if the code Ayers gave us is false," X-37 said. "My review
and analysis of your many interrogations with the man
suggests that only Nebs had complete access to Union ships. It
is probable that Ayers added a way to access the vault on
Macabre without the vice admiral knowing. On the ship,
however, it is much different. The captain is the king and
admirals are their deities."

"That is an interesting way to look at it," Captain
Younger said, not sounding entirely pleased. "We will need to
study Union psychology to avoid being caught unaware of
such mental paradigms."

"You're absolutely right," I said. "There are going to be some growing pains as we learn to live together. I'm going to use the codes now."

Everyone waited, completely focused on the vault door and what I was doing.

I entered the code from memory even though X-37 offered to put them on my projected HUD. Touching each number on the pad deliberately, I regulated my breathing and tried to be as ready as Path was for a fight or whatever happened when the door opened. It was unlikely there were any living guards inside, but there could be traps just waiting to go off in my Reaper face.

I pressed the last button. A light blinked three times, slow enough to almost seem broken, and numbers began down from ten.

"Well now isn't that dramatic," Elise said with attitude.

"Elise and I should stand in front of the opening," Path said. "If there is some sort of countermeasure, our armor will withstand it better than your body, Reaper."

I let my friends step in front of me. The Archangel armor gleamed where it hadn't been marked by molten lava that had breached the external layers we used on the mission to Macabre.

The door slid open revealing a dark chamber that stretched out farther than I had anticipated. "X, adjust my optics. I want to see everything. No surprises."

"My thoughts exactly, Reaper Cain," X-37 said. "I'm

detecting a line of cryo-pods similar to those used to imprison your family over the last several months."

"Elise, Path, and I will clear the room," I said. "Tom you have the codes to open the door if it closes behind us."

We moved quickly but not too fast. I checked between each cryo-pod and looked for doors, finding none. When nothing exploded and no one attacked us, I gave the all clear for the rest of the group to enter.

"There are thirty-six life support units, divided into three distinct groups," X-37 said.

"Yeah, thanks, X." I walked from one end of the room to the other. "Just give me a second to take this in."

The first row contained a dozen men and women who seemed normal except for their size and muscularity. Each was a commander's dream of the perfect soldier: tall, broad shoul-dered, and well developed. Someone had shaved their heads before they were put to sleep, but even in this state there were some biological changes. I made a mental note to ask X-37 and my smart friends about that, because something seemed off.

Or maybe they had been in stasis much longer than my mother and sister. Why were they strong and robust when it seemed these super soldiers were just lying around growing muscle? The answer, when I thought about it, was fairly obvious.

Nebs had restricted calories to my family's pods, and to the other people he had chosen to imprison. These people were weapons, volunteers that would be combat ready soon after being awoken. Or knowing Nebs, maybe they were volun-told to submit to Ayers' lunacy.

I paused at the last subject, looking down into the face of Commander Briggs. It took me a second to recognize him. He was younger somehow. He'd always had buzz cut hair, but it had been thick. Now he was bald, his skin a shade of blue gray that made me think of dead things.

Elise walked up behind me. I casually shifted my stance to divert her attention. This was a complication I needed to face on my own, after I thought about it, and maybe after I threw down a few glasses of whiskey.

The next row changed my hypotheses significantly. These men and women had spiked tentacles growing out of their arms. The monstrous additions were fully extended, frozen in the act of coiling around their limbs from wrists to shoulders, looking like an alien cocoon of strangeness.

Their heads were oversized and their faces grotesque. One had its mouth slightly open revealing rows of teeth. Each of these twelve had different skin tones, apparently changing at a different rate depending on their individual biology.

They were even larger than the first group, nearly filling up the oversized cryo-pods.

The third group were like nothing I'd ever seen, not even the corpse in the lava ship vault on Macabre.

Every one of the dozen monsters filled their pods, faces pressed to the glass and tentacles smashed into all the open spaces. Something was different, so I leaned close to allow X-37 a better view.

"Boo!" Elise shouted, instantly becoming the least popular member of our group as everyone jumped halfway to the ceiling.

"Paybacks are a bitch, kid," I said.

"Sorry, I couldn't resist." She moved toward me. "What's the big deal with this last group?"

Once she saw what I was seeing, her mood changed. Henshaw and Tom began theorizing, chatting so quickly it was hard to follow their conversation. The scientist and the engineer had a theory about every aspect of this horrific techno tomb.

I went back to my careful examination of the creatures Ayers had created from whatever DNA he thought belonged to aliens. "There are a lot more of the tentacled things on these mature subjects. Do they have them in their legs? It looks more like one tentacle interwoven around its lower extremities."

"I believe that is a tail," X-37 said. "For balance while moving or to brace against the floor while striking with hands or feet. In a worst-case scenario, the tail itself could be a weapon."

Tom and Henshaw moved away from the pod they had been studying and stood next to me, looking at the most mature monster in this menagerie.

"I think that is a tail," Tom said excitedly. "This is incredible."

Henshaw rubbed his chin. "The possibilities of its functionality are endless. In nature, a limb like this could be used to prop an organism up, maintain balance will running at high speeds, or lash out as a weapon."

"What did I say, Reaper Cain?" X-37 asked privately. "Henshaw has co-opted my theories."

I didn't comment.

"This is amazing," Tom said, sounding like he might need to throw up despite his curiosity.

"It's the most horrible thing I've ever seen," Elise said.

Captain Younger and Rejon toured the room slowly. Tom and Henshaw began an organized database of notes and observations from everyone in the group.

"One thing is certain," Younger said. "We need to change the locks."

"That was my thought exactly," X-37 said.

"I think you should assign a combined Wallach and Xad guard detail of at least three squads," I said. "They will need to be vetted for security clearances and possibly get some extra training. I'd also include a science officer in that group in case there is a critical decision that needs to be made before they can consult one of us," I said.

"Agreed, Reaper," Younger said. She faced Rejon. "Would you like me to brief President Coronas and our council? They will want to see this. Who among their people need access?"

"Not many," he answered. "Our council will want to know as much as possible. We should continue to work together."

"What about the Union turncoats?" Tom asked, looking up from his work with Henshaw.

"What about them?" I asked, wishing I had a cigar but also feeling weird about the idea of lighting one up in here. It was irrational, but I thought that might invite contamination of some sort.

"We have ten Union officers and scientists who were imprisoned alongside your family. I imagine they ran afoul of Nebs and Ayers at some point. I'm wondering if they can be trusted and if they might have some insight about this experiment," Tom said.

"I'm not even sure we should wake them up," I said without thinking.

Elise shot me a look, which was much more dramatic in the Archangel armor. "We have to wake them up. What the hell are you talking about? How would you like to be imprisoned like that?"

"Yeah, you're right, kid. I wasn't thinking. There has just been a lot to take in today," I said. She didn't snap at me for calling her a kid, which probably meant she wasn't a kid anymore.

"I recommend we seal this area and select an appropriate security team," X-37 said.

"Agreed," I said. Younger and Rejon consented.

"I will guard the exterior until you have selected the proper guards," Path said.

"Good. After that, it's definitely whiskey and cigar time. And sleep. Lots of sleep. And maybe the biggest breakfast that has ever been eaten on the *Bright Lance*."

16

WHEN THE DREAM STARTED, I was running through the metal trenches of Dreadmax. Red Skull gangsters chased me in their noisy vehicles. They fired heavy machine guns into every side alley and doorway. I kept looking back for Elise, but she wasn't there. X-37 told me again and again that she could never fall that far behind because she was a better runner than I was.

So I looked forward, looked ahead, scanned the future for a safe haven. With no warning or transition, the place became Boyer 5. I ran faster because I was smaller, just a kid, but the place was strange because there were no people in it at all. Rows and rows of tenement buildings and graffiti covered transits systems looked as though they hadn't been used for years.

My mother sounded worried. My sense of urgency grew

every time I turned a corner and found a strange street I'd never been on. Vines grew up the sides of buildings, and mysteries lurked in the alleys like shadowy ghosts. Clouds of rust drifted down from a monorail I remembered from the neighborhood I grew up in.

"Reaper Cain," X-37 said. "Are you dreaming or just being difficult."

I stopped and looked around. One building in the distance was filled with light. The really strange thing about the towering structure was that it reached the clouds, stabbing upward toward the sky like a beam of energy. Every level was full of activity. A glowing apartment building that might have been a starship of Xad landed on the surface of a green planet.

Boyer 5 was gone. In my heart, I felt as though Dreadmax had never been. A field of purple and yellow flowers covered the ground from me to the vibrant new buildings that had once traveled through dozens of slip tunnels as part of the exodus fleet.

I looked behind me, unsure why there was a need to look back, and saw two Union stealth carriers moored on the side of a mountain with a team of people stripping it for parts.

What I needed was for X-37 to tell me that my family and friends and allies were all safe in their new home. I felt like everything was better, like I had done right by Elise and the others. But there was no way to know for sure while my limited artificial intelligence was squawking about something entirely irrelevant to this scene.

"Reaper Cain, you have slept one hundred and fifteen percent of your rest phase," X-37 said. "If you do not respond I will be forced to conduct a thorough medical evaluation."

Opening my eyes, I felt the reality of my cabin on the *Bright Lance* and wondered if I shouldn't be back on the *Jelly-bird*. "I'm awake, X. And for the record, I don't even know what kind of thorough medical evaluation you could do that you don't do all the time anyway. Isn't half your job monitoring my biometrics?"

"I was improvising since my other encouragements were not having an effect," X-37 said. "My next option was to use a rather loud and annoying noise to bring you around."

"Is there an emergency?" I asked.

X-37 clicked a few times. "There is not, Reaper Cain. The entire fleet is doing remarkably well and is pulling resources from the volcano planet of Macabre."

"Then why would you wake me up?" I started thinking about the dream, only now realizing how strange it had been. On the surface, it seemed a very obvious pointer to the future. The combined fleet of Xad and Wallach had conquered incredible obstacles. We'd retrieved the codes to awaken my mother and sister, and they seemed healthy and were recovering well.

The future looked pretty good for us. Being a Reaper, I had a hard time with success and safety. I was trained to always look for danger, often seeking it out, and always neutralize it if it threatened me, my mission, or my friends and family.

The monstrosities Ayers had created bothered me and I wasn't sure, but I thought that might've been where the nightmare started. Something kept me from remembering those images.

"There are two reasons," X-37 said. "First, you have slept longer than needed. My protocols are to keep you healthy and avoid unnecessary downtime. Secondly, there have been several messages from your friends inquiring of your welfare. Perhaps these made it into your rest cycle."

I processed all of this information as I fought out of the haze of sleep. At the same time, I did a quick walk-through of my small cabin, checking for anything that looked out of the ordinary. The chances of there being an intruder or any type of danger were virtually nil, but that was what I did.

I jumped in the shower, not waiting for it to warm up. "What do you think about a beer?"

"That is normally part of your end of the day ritual, and I think it would be strange for you to start your morning in this manner," X-37 said.

"Are you judging me, X?"

"I would never dream of it," X-37 said. "And if I did, my analysis suggests it would have zero effect on your behavior."

"You've got that right, X," I said as numbers appeared in the wall above the nozzle. "Ah, come on, X. You didn't turn off the timer?"

"It is against regulations," X-37 said. "And in case you

have forgotten, the combined fleet is far beyond any charted system. It is unknown when we will have a chance to acquire new resources."

"Water is not that hard to find," I said.

"That is a dangerous assumption, Reaper Cain. I believed from your earlier conversations with Captain Younger that you respect her decisions and her rules for the ship. I took the liberty of removing all of the rule breaking hacks you had me install when we first checked into this cabin," X-37 said.

"That's great, X," I muttered. "You do realize that I'm not completely rinsed off?"

"I suggest a towel dry."

"What are we doing, camping? Good thing I didn't try to drink a beer in there. I would've had to chug it."

It didn't take me long to finish up my morning rituals and head out into the *Bright Lance*. What I found was a complete surprise. There were people from Wallach, Xad, and even some of the Union turncoats crowding the hallways and public areas of the ship. They seemed to be having a party.

"What the hell is happening on this ship?" I asked.

"It is what is commonly known as a celebration. The success on Macabre has inspired the people of Xad and Wallach to good cheer, or that is what my database suggests. Every ship in the fleet has declared a holiday."

I moved through one hallway after another, frequently running into happy groups of people drinking some type of nonalcoholic beverage. X-37 explained that there were only a few areas where inebriation was allowed.

"Someone needs to teach these people how to party." I headed for the observation deck.

"My analysis suggests you are the wrong person for this task," X-37 said. "I did a quick search of your conversations with Elise, and she has told you one hundred and thirty-seven times that you are no fun."

"I'm fun." I scowled at a group of people who were in my way and didn't even realize it. There wasn't anything to do but wait for them to unclog the intersection before I could proceed.

"Yes, of course, Reaper Cain. You are a barrel of laughs," X-37 said.

"Sarcasm detected."

"I do aim to please," X-37 said, almost sounding smug if that was even possible for a limited artificial intelligence.

"I need to check your personality algorithm. It seems to be drifting a little bit."

X-37 responded immediately. "I will run a complete and thorough scan."

I understood X's concern and wished I hadn't mentioned he was drifting. Upsetting the emotionless LAI was impossible, but I still didn't want to do it, like that made sense, but whatever. There were strict rules about sentience, or even the strong appearance of sentience, in artificial or limited artificial intelligences. We were far beyond the reach of the Union, but the laws that governed my digital friend were internal. If he crossed the line, the shutdown could happen before either of us realized it was happening.

The observation deck of the *Bright Lance* was packed. I moved through the crowd with skill. It was one of the less glamorous things a Reaper learned during the espionage curriculum. Many covert missions required navigation of social settings and it was best not to alarm everyone by pushing and shoving.

I settled for a small table near the viewing wall, which was a holographic display of extreme clarity. People watched a mock dogfight between Xad, Wallach, and Union fighters.

Two micro-fighters were dominating the contest, zigging and zagging all over the place but always working as a team and always winning. They fired some sort of display ordinance, rounds that glowed with their own light for the sake of the spectators. I'd seen all kinds of rockets, tracer rounds, and energy weapons, but nothing like this.

The event was pure spectacle.

"Where is Elise, X?" I asked, crossing my arms.

"It's funny that you should mention that, Reaper Cain," X-37 said. "She quickly teamed up with Path during the dogfight challenge. As expected, they are winning easily but may not rack up enough points to take the contest before they run out of fuel."

I viewed rows of statistics going down one side of the wall. Shaking my head, I disagreed with my limited artificial intelligence. "At this rate, they can take a break to refuel, get back in the fight, and still win."

"This is a possibility, but it will require them to perform each operation to near perfection, and while Elise and Path practice many things, they have not always focused on refueling and re-equipping their micro-fighters," X-37 said.

"Is there a betting pool?" I asked.

"There is," X-37 said. "Henshaw has placed a variety of bets, not all of them under his own name, but the largest portion is against Elise and Path winning. My analysis suggests that is because the odds and potential payoff are much greater if they lose. Tom has also placed a modest bet on Elise and Path, possibly out of loyalty."

Someone in the crowd recognized me, pointed, and shouted to their friends. Before long, I had a problem.

"It's the Reaper!" the instigator said.

"Get out there and show them how it's done, Reaper!" several other people shouted. Some cheered this idea, others booed it.

I waved them off. "I don't want to mess up the pool. And ship to ship combat isn't my strong point."

"Are you serious?" another person asked.

"Maybe next time." I fended off questions, spending more time arguing with my new friends than watching Elise and Path dogfight. The scene was incredible. In addition to the contest, there were ships flying in all kinds of formations— easily staying away from the more dynamic action. We were only able to see everything due to the powerful magnification and computer recreations of what was far beyond normal visual range.

"If you're interested, Reaper Cain, there are other betting pools. It seems that the people of Xad and Wallach are also having a contest for the most impressive space parade," X-37 said. "It is quite wonderful."

"How about you find me a quiet place where I can relax, maybe with a viewing terminal I can use to keep track of Elise?" I asked.

"There are numerous maintenance bays and other facilities available. Only the bare minimum of crew members are still working, a good portion of them being security and critical staff."

The idea appealed to me, but I was eventually able to draw back from all the attention and just watch without leaving the observation deck. Elise had always been a natural learner and was especially well suited for operating a micro-fighter. Her progress was amazing. With the Archangel armor integrated into the tiny ship, she was a force to be reckoned with. What really struck me was that I could actually see her improving during this contest.

"She'll be better than Path soon," I said.

"That is my analysis as well," X-37 said.

17

THE CELEBRATION SHOWED no signs of slowing when I left the observation deck. X-37 marked several nearly vacant areas of the ship where I could get some peace and quiet, but I walked to the medical recovery section of the *Bright Lance* without thinking.

My sister was asleep, the fingers of her left hand intertwined with her short hair. She looked young and happy in the state, and I hoped she was having dreams of a brilliant future.

My mother, Olivia Anna Cain, sat in a chair next to Hannah's bed, sipping tea. She smiled as I entered, then motioned with a free hand for me to sit.

"We have a lot to catch up on," she said.

I kissed her on the top of her head before dropping into a

chair, and she smiled again. "I'm glad you and Hannah are okay."

She nodded. "I knew you would find us."

"The mask and the clues helped," I said.

This made her laugh gently. "I sent a lot more than the mask your way. There were several weapons caches, a ship, and contacts to a team of commandos I paid a small fortune to assist you. It seems, however, that you managed without all of that."

"What kind of ship?" I asked, a bit stunned.

"A Lightning Star 5000," she said. "But I also had people I trust improve the armor, weapons systems, navigational databases, and they boosted the ship AI by three hundred and twenty-five percent. That's right below the legal limit. I would've gone over, but I thought it would draw too much attention. It's all about trade-offs and that sort of thing."

"I've never heard of anything newer than a Lightning Star 3000," I said.

"I know the developer from before I met your father. He has his flaws, but he was a good friend. Now I'll never know what happened to him or anybody else who risked their lives to help us," she said.

I wanted to talk more about what happened to my father, but there was a pain that came with the thought and I guessed it wouldn't speed my mother's recovery to break open old wounds. We both knew the score now. The Union had taken him out to provoke me and blamed it on the gang members of Boyer 5.

"Tell me about Nebs. Is he really dead?" she asked, and I sensed tension in her voice.

"He's gone. So are most of his officers. They died when I located a secret vault on the ship."

Color drained from my mother's face. "Was it empty?"

I shook my head.

She closed her eyes. Her hand started shaking until I thought she would spill her tea, so I took it from her and placed it on a small table near my sister's bed.

"What did Ayers do?" I asked.

She opened her eyes, clenched her fists on her lap, and looked at me very directly. "He tried to play god. The part that infuriates me is the complete and totally unnecessary nature of it. The man wanted to resurrect aliens from their DNA profiles to prove they existed, when Nebs had already found evidence that they still exist somewhere in the galaxy."

"You're talking about nonhuman, truly alien life-forms?" I asked, fearing the answer.

"I am," she said.

"From what I've seen, they don't look friendly," I said, thinking of the monsters in the secret cryo-pods.

"Our only hope is that his experiments caused them to mutate, which is a distinct possibility. Ayers blended DNA recovered on a lost world with human test subjects. What I tell myself so that I can get to sleep at night, is that this bonding was unnatural and caused them to be freaks."

There wasn't anything to say. X-37 and I had had a similar conversation with Henshaw and Tom, basically trying to convince ourselves that we hadn't just found a deadly new enemy in the galaxy.

"It's more than just a theory," she said. "I know that Nebs was pushing him to make weaponized life-forms he could control."

I interlocked my fingers and stared at my feet for a time, then faced my mother's intelligent gaze. "I told Rejon and Coronas the monsters should be destroyed and the remains jettisoned toward a sun."

My mother looked as though she might be sick. "I gather this idea was rejected. Are they complete idiots?"

"There are the same idiots everywhere, even if we leave the Union fifty slip tunnels behind us. Some of their scientists want to study them. They give different reasons, of course," I said.

"Like being ready for the real aliens when they come? Learning about alien biology? Discovering the secrets of the galaxy for the good of humanity?" my mother asked. "I've heard all of these arguments and I'm not surprised."

"There are three dozen of them."

"What about on the *Black Wing*?" she asked.

"That ship was destroyed," I said.

She seemed relieved. "Good. That was where they stored most of them. There were several hundred on the *Black Wing*. Was it actually destroyed or just lost? Could there be survivors?"

"The *Black Wing* was a total loss. It came apart all around us," I said.

She snorted gently, a sound that was both measured and amazed. "You must tell me the rest of that story sometime. It sounds like it was quite an ordeal."

"Hopefully we'll have lots of time to catch up," I said.

I WALKED the hallways for a long time after the visit with my mother. My sister slept the entire time, her face a mask of peace I could only dream of. X-37 told me I was long overdue for sleep, but I didn't care.

Somewhere between the physical training rooms in the observation deck I encountered Elise at an intersection.

"Why aren't you sleeping?" she asked.

"Are you doing something you don't want me to know about? I wasn't born yesterday," I said.

"Maybe not, but you were born paranoid and suspicious," she said. "Mavis told me that you were walking the decks and I was worried."

"Do you talk to the ship AI much?" I asked.

"She's very helpful. Tom and Henshaw agree that the system reset was the most complete they'd ever heard of, but they disagree about why. Tom believes the initial programming of Union ship AI is inherently good, based on the values the Union claims to be built upon rather than how the government is actually run," Elise said.

Feeling restless and needing to move, I motioned for her to walk with me. "What does Henshaw think?"

"He believes that Captain Younger and her prize crew have conditioned Mavis to behave with dignity and respect," Elise said. "I don't think it matters. The main thing is, she's much better than Necron, who is still kind of a jerk according to Novasdaughter."

We came to a lift that would take us into the more secure area of the ship and I suddenly understood what destination I had been wandering toward all night. Elise and I stared at each other for a second.

"We're going to the vault, aren't we?" she asked.

"Yeah. I need to see the test subjects," I said with a quiet intensity that didn't encourage further discussion.

We descended the lift and passed through two regular guard stations before arriving at the final door to the restricted area. Two of President Coronas's honor guards in their exoskeleton armor towered beside two Xad warriors in their best gear holding their weapons at port arms.

"One moment, Reaper Cain," the ranking Xad guard said. "I need to check with Mavis to confirm you have unlimited access to the ship."

Elise and I waited without talking. Seconds ticked by and I wondered how these men remained vigilant hour after hour.

"You are cleared, Reaper Cain," the guard said.

"Thanks." I led the way into the most secret and dangerous part of our fleet.

"I need to show you something, Elise," I said.

"Why do I get the feeling I'm not going to like this?"

"Do you remember Commander Briggs? I asked.

Elise stopped abruptly. "What the hell are you talking about? He can't be one of these freaks."

I moved along the first dozen pods, stopping at the last one and pointing. Elise looked down, squinting to see through the glass. She stepped back shaking her head.

"I never really knew him, but you've talked about him. Are you still convinced he let us go when the Union had us dead to rights on Greendale?" she asked.

"That's what it felt like at the time. Either way, he was worse than some but better than most. And no one deserves this fate," I said.

"Unless he volunteered," Elise said. "That would be messed up."

"I wish I could talk to him and get some answers, but it's too dangerous," I said.

We spent the rest of our time looking for other people I knew. The spec ops community wasn't enormous, and I discovered most looked familiar to me even if I couldn't identify them.

"Do you still want them destroyed and jettisoned into a star?" Elise said.

I took my time answering. "That would be the best thing for them."

ELISE and I went to the brig to confront Ayers. The guards passed us through. We stopped outside of his door to develop our game plan.

"AI Mavis is asking if you require her assistance," X-37 said. "I've been running several assessments and believe we can trust her."

"You don't think she's going to become another Necron?" I asked, wanting to focus on the scientist more than I wanted to deal with the most powerful digital entity on the ship.

"Mavis has not attempted to quarantine me. She's prompt when answering my queries, and firm when I attempt to enter restricted data areas unguided," X-37 advised.

This surprised me. "She's allowed you into restricted areas? And you're just now telling me this?"

"I found nothing of interest in these restricted areas. Even with her help, it seems that information on Doctor Ayers and his experiments was purged from the system. The restricted information systems she escorted me through involved the details behind weapon systems, stealth cloaks, and other navigational protocols. I didn't think it was anything you needed to know or would be remotely interested in talking about," X-37 said.

"You got that right, X," I said. "If you trust Mavis, I trust Mavis."

"I'm flattered, Reaper Cain," X-37 said. "Or would be if I was truly sentient."

"How do you want to handle this?" Elise asked.

"We go in, I tune him up, you talk me down and then take the lead," I said.

"You think that will work?"

"I've never worked with a partner other than X-37, so I haven't had much field practice with team interrogations," I said.

Elise psyched herself up, almost bouncing on the balls of her feet, then exhaling until she appeared much calmer. "This is worse than preparing for a sparring session with Path, but I think I'm ready."

"Interrogations are stressful for everyone, but let's make sure Ayers gets the worst of it," I said.

When Mavis opened the door to the cell, I saw Doctor Ayers standing there asleep. His eyes were open, but unfocused. They twitched but he didn't seem to know we were there.

"That is so weird," Elise said.

"I don't think your plan is going to work. You should have warned Elise of the man's peculiarities," X-37 said.

"Ayers, wake up," I said, moving close enough to shake him if needed.

The man blinked and focused on me. "Good morning, Reaper. Have you come to release me?"

"Not exactly," I said. "I came to throat punch you until you tell me why you forced Briggs and the others into your experiments."

He didn't answer immediately, which suggested my guess was at least close to the truth.

"What's the matter, Ayers? How did you think I would react to my friends being turned into monsters?" I asked.

When Ayers spoke next, his tone was righteous but

subdued. "Some of them were volunteers, understanding the most important contribution they could make to humanity was submitting to the experiment."

"You asshole!" Elise shouted. "Have you ever been part of a Union experiment? Never free to make your own choices, always worried you were being turned into something horrible!"

She balled up her fists, bounced on her toes once or twice like she was going to restrain herself, then lunged at the man with her teeth bared.

I held her back with one arm, which only caused her to push and squirm past me. I grabbed her with both hands and walked her back toward the door, not happy that I had to turn my back on Doctor Ayers.

"It seems Elise has elected to play the role of bad cop during this interrogation," X-37 chirped. "My analysis suggests the spontaneity will be quite effective."

"Get control of yourself or you can leave," I said.

"Whatever. You saw what he did to them. It's not right," Elise said. "Neither of you understand!"

Still blocking her from access to Ayers, I looked him over and saw that he had an expression of betrayal and confusion on his face. The man really had thought Elise was his friend. Now he knew he was in trouble.

"Listen, Ayers," I said quietly. "I was in special operations for years before I became a Reaper. Some of these men came after me on Dreadmax and Greendale. I know them. We weren't exactly friends, but I'm certain they would've never volunteered to be mutated with experimental DNA research."

"Maybe you don't know them as well as you think. Everyone wants to be stronger and faster and smarter than they are," Ayers said.

"That's such bullshit," Elise said. "This is why I hate the Union."

I held up a finger for her to stop talking and gave her a warning look. In reality, I didn't care what she said or did, but I wanted Ayers to think I was protecting him from her.

"I need you to come clean with me, Ayers. If you want access to even a small portion of the research, you need to start building some trust with me and my people," I said.

"You're never going to let me do research," he said. "I know how Reapers work and how they are trained. You're a master manipulator and when you don't get your way, you just start killing people."

"You're mostly right," I said. "But we are way beyond known space dealing with problems no one ever imagined, and the rules have changed. Tell me about Briggs and the others."

Ayers sat on the edge of his bunk and massaged his temples.

I gave Elise a hand signal that suggested we were very close to a breakthrough and hoped she was acting. Her rage looked too real. Neither of us spoke as Ayers gathered his thoughts.

"I suppose what happened to Briggs and the others is my fault. I miscalculated," Ayers said.

"Explain what that means," I said.

"I was trying to convince Nebs to give me more space on the ship for my research. He was in one of his moods and told me no. So I warned him of how dangerous the aliens could be—showed him concept art of what I thought they might look like." Ayers put his hands together almost like a man who was praying and exhaled over his fingertips. "That really got his attention. He responded like he always did, saying we needed to have better weapons and better warriors than they did. The next thing you know, I'd been given the full go-ahead on human test subjects. Briggs and the others were called in for what they thought was a checkup."

Neither Elise nor I interrupted him. The tension in the room was almost a physical force.

"We did them one at a time, expecting problems. Briggs caught on quicker than the rest and almost escaped. He didn't buy my excuse that his medical exam had shown he had an extremely contagious variety of the flu," Ayers said.

"You told him he had the flu? Really?" I asked.

"Common sickness can be very dangerous on a starship far from home," Ayers said. "The Union has strict regulations regarding that type of thing."

"Do you have any idea how long it's been since somebody had the common flu on a Union ship?" I asked.

"I didn't think that common soldiers cared about that sort of trivia."

"None of these test subjects were common soldiers," I said.

"That, Reaper, is true. What do you want from me?"

"I want toss you out of an airlock, but I'd settle for the complete truth."

The smile he gave me was unnerving. "The complete truth is that you will never be prepared for what's coming. Not with this ragtag fleet."

"He is trying to manipulate you, Reaper Cain."

I silently acknowledged X-37, checked to be sure Elise wasn't about to make her own move, and extended my Reaper arm blade.

"Wait, I have proof," Ayers said, holding up both hands defensively. "Nebs gave me no choice. I have all of the documentation, and Mavis can show you holo footage of what he did to me."

"Mavis, can you hear us?" I asked, my gaze locked on Ayers.

"I can, Reaper 29C071," Mavis said, voice smooth as silk. "Would like to see Doctor Ayers being tortured? Over one hundred hours of recordings exist."

"Maybe later." I needed to think this through and develop a new game plan. "I never really liked Briggs anyway."

"This is a false assertion," X-37 said. "You were at odds with the man more times than not but respected him in a general sense at least."

I ignored my limited artificial intelligence and checked to see if Elise had anything to add.

She shook her head.

"I still think I should throw you out of an airlock," I said, and then we left the cell.

Outside, Elise surprised me. "You should teach me the hand language you use to talk privately with X-37."

"There's no secret hand language," I stated, wondering if X had let something slip. He was able to communicate with my team even while I was asleep via their earbuds.

"Right, that's why you're always fidgeting during those awkward pauses Reapers are known for. Honestly, I've never seen you at a loss for words. How do you expect me to believe you're not answering X-37 nonverbally," Elise said. "I get it, X is your LAI. But if I knew the hand language, Tom could design haptic feedback gloves allowing me to talk to X in the same manner. Then X could relay messages during interrogations and other situations like this. We could communicate without someone like Ayers catching on."

"That's not a bad idea," I said.

She smiled and punched me in my arm. "I knew there was a secret hand language."

"I knew you knew."

"Whatever."

18

Eventually I slept, revived myself, and headed to the observation deck to meet Tom. Elise's idea about the haptic feedback glove intrigued me.

"What time is it, X?"

"It is approximately 3:30 a.m. standard time," X-37 answered. "There are other people awake on the *Bright Lance*, but they are assigned to their posts for the most part. There are few patrons at the observation deck bar. You should have a reasonable amount of privacy."

I did a quick scan of the room when I entered, then went to Tom where he was reading from a tablet. He put it down as I took a seat.

"Good to see you, Hal."

My friend knew how to relax.

"Perhaps you should develop a reading habit as well," X-37 suggested.

I gave him a hand signal, watching Tom to see if he noticed what I was doing. There was a better than average chance that the man suspected I had a nonverbal way of communicating with X-37. He understood my LAI monitored every aspect of my biometrics, including proprioceptive mechanisms. This allowed X to understand more than just heart rate and blood pressure, but also my balance, physical coordination, and force generation. In short, the LAI knew what my hands were doing at all times.

"Did Elise talk to you about the glove?" I said, producing two cigars and motioning for the bartender to send someone with whiskeys.

"She mentioned something. It shouldn't be that hard to figure it out. When we're done here, I'm heading to my workshop anyway and I can tinker with the idea a bit."

The holo view wall loomed above us, while soft music played on the intercom. A young woman in a meticulous jumpsuit took our order for two whiskeys.

"Thanks. I figured you could handle it," I said. "We're going to have a much bigger problem with the mutant test subjects."

"The best course would probably be to destroy them," Tom said. He didn't exactly look happy about the idea and I knew him well enough to know he still saw the monstrosities as people who had been involuntarily modified.

"But you know that probably won't happen," I said. "For a variety of reasons."

"Are you going to let Ayers continue his work?"

I could see that Tom was nervous, worried about my answer.

"No, the man can't be trusted. But we will need him if we intend to save any of the early-stage hybrids," I said. "I'm not sure what to do with those who no longer appear human."

"They might be more human than they look," he said. "There's no way to know until we revive one of them and find out."

"You're right, but it's risky. We barely managed to assemble this fleet. You saw how chaotic the slip tunnel passage was. If we have a monster crisis, we could undo everything we've worked for," I said.

"What's really on your mind, Hal?" Tom put down his cigar next to his whiskey glass and his book. Leaning forward slightly, he touched his fingertips together to convey earnestness. "I've known you long enough to realize when something is eating at you."

"It's one thing to see humans turned into experiments," I said. "It's another when you recognize them. Briggs wasn't my friend, but I would never wish this type of fate on him."

"He's one of the more human versions, right?" Tom asked.

I nodded. "But like you said, there's no way to know what's happened inside. His brain could be a soup of chemicals. I'm afraid to wake him up and find out."

Elise walked into the observation area, past the bar and the two or three people talking quietly there, and joined us.

"You started without me," she said.

"You're too young to drink," I said.

"That's stupid, but I don't want to anyway."

"And I'm not going to be responsible for you smoking," I said.

"Good, because smoking is gross. I came to talk and watch the view. Sorry if I'm ruining your boys club."

"It's good to have you here," Tom said. "Hal and I were just discussing your idea for the haptic feedback glove and other things."

"Like what to do with the human alien hybrids?" she asked.

"Yep." I put out my cigar before I realized what I was doing. Tom's was already extinguished.

"Did you make a decision or figure anything out?" she asked.

"Nope."

She crossed her arms, thinking intently. The days of her teenage chatter were long behind us. There were moments when she reminded me of the kid I rescued from the cage, but our adventures were forcing her to grow up too soon. I made a mental note to start a prank war to lighten the mood on the ship. It wasn't my strong point now, but there had been a time when I had been a force to reckon with—full of mischief and other good, clean fun.

"I guess there are never easy answers," she said. "At least the view is nice."

We watched a dozen ships practicing docking maneuvers in the distance. In another part of the holo-view, one of the greenhouse ships faced the sun and increased the transparency of its shields to grow crops.

"I always knew I would escape the Union someday," Elise said. "But I never suspected it would be like this, with so many people starting over and working together."

ELISE HAD ABANDONED the conversation after an hour or two. Tom gave me a bit longer and then retired to his cabin to finish reading his book. I stayed watching the stars, sipping, and holding an unlit cigar until the midmorning crowd arrived.

"James Henshaw is sending you a coded message," X-37 said.

"What do you mean coded? I thought all of our communications were secure."

"That is correct, Reaper Cain. My struggle against Necron definitely upped my game in regard to security. Additionally, Mavis has not made attempts to violate our private links."

"Then why the hell is Henshaw complicating things?" The ocular engineer had been reclusive lately, rarely showing up on the observation deck, and according to the logs, he'd stopped going to observe the hybrid alien test subjects.

That was the most unusual thing about his behavior. He was one of the most curious people I'd ever met and had shown great interest in all of the work Ayers had done. Now, he was like a ghost.

"Apparently, he takes extra precautions whenever he's not on the *Lady Faith*," X-37 explained. "Presently, he is awaiting your arrival at an infrequently used storage bay on one of the aft decks."

"Fine. Give me a map." I attempted to clear my head of the whiskey I'd sipped for too long.

"I am relaying directions to your HUD projector."

An image appeared as a projection slightly in front of me. This made it larger than a helmet display. The illusion worked.

"Apologies, Reaper Cain," X-37 said. "Henshaw has changed the rendezvous point."

"Is someone following him?" I asked. "He's acting like he's trying to lose a tail."

"I have used one of the security networks Mavis has granted me full access to and can detect no one following Henshaw," X-37 said. "For the record, my job is much easier with such a cooperative ship AI."

"That's great, X." I picked up the pace, hoping to reach the rendezvous point before Henshaw changed it again. Because I knew he would.

"I should tell you, however, that it is not perfect. Even Bug struggles with the system from time to time," X-37 said.

"Sure, X. Nobody's perfect. Not even an LAI."

After four very frustrating attempts to find him, we finally met inside of a maintenance tube that was barely tall enough for me to stand in.

Henshaw looked more disheveled than I'd ever seen him. His hair was unkempt, but what made him look especially out of character was what he wore. Since we met on Roxo III, the man had always paid attention to fashion, sometimes pretending not to care even though everyone knew better. Casual chic was normally his thing.

Right now, he was wearing a jumpsuit that had been stolen from a laundry room. There were still folds in the fabric from where it had been stacked inside of a locker.

"What the hell are we doing here, Henshaw?" I demanded.

"Are you certain you weren't followed?" he asked.

"Positive," I said, biting down on the word. "Can you believe this guy, X? When have I ever allowed someone to tail me?"

"I have no record of anyone following you without your knowing," X-37 reported.

"That's good, really good" Henshaw checked over his shoulder. "What about the ship AI?"

"Don't worry about Mavis," I said. "What's your problem?"

"I thought you would understand," Henshaw said. "Ayers couldn't have built a research project like this without being politically sophisticated. You have to consider that Nebs might've been working for the doctor and not the other way around. Everything I've seen suggests that Ayers was manipulating him, and wasn't just another Union scientist with an unreasonable boss."

"I never really trust anybody," I said "You should know that."

"That's why I'm surprised you're not being more careful," Henshaw said.

"I've compared his behavior to previous behavioral patterns. I'm detecting a clear trend toward increasing paranoia," X-37 said.

"I'm always careful, Jimmy."

His lip curled at the nickname, which I knew he didn't like. "That's not enough. We have to get rid of him, and all of the test subjects. If we shut off the cryo-pods, we can learn what they were through autopsies and other analysis."

"You're serious," I said.

"I hate losing such a huge scientific discovery, but if I think they're too dangerous to study, then you should be paying attention. This will not end well. Get rid of Ayers, euthanize the hybrids. It's the only way to save this fleet you're so fond of," Henshaw said in an aggressive tone.

"X?"

"I'm already contacting Mavis to restrict Henshaw's access to the research facilities," X-37 said.

"What are you waiting for?" Henshaw demanded.

"Proof. I'll have the guard doubled and restrict access to the area. That's the best I can do right now," I said.

Henshaw shook his head almost hard enough to hurt himself. "That's not enough!"

"It is if I say it is. And it's not your problem," I said. "If you go near the research area, I'll put you in a cell right next to Ayers."

"You're making a mistake, Reaper."

"Listen, Jimmy, I'll be the first person to put those monsters out of their misery if it's the right thing to do."

ELISE and I waited for half an hour, but Path didn't show up. We had the training area to ourselves.

"Did you tell him we were going to spar?" I asked.

"He's normally here at this time," she said. "I didn't think I needed to call him."

"X, can you check on Path?"

"Right away, Reaper Cain."

"We might as well get started," I said.

"Conditioning first, or fighting first?" Elise asked.

"Your choice." Admitting how bad I felt wasn't a good idea. She would use my weakness against me, probably shouting and making lots of noise to aggravate my pounding headache.

"I think we should run first. The *Bright Lance* has a track that goes all the way around the outer concourse. There are even some holo screens along the way with a pretty good view of the fleet," she said.

I wasn't excited about pounding my feet around the fitness concourse, but I needed the exercise. With luck, I could even keep up with Elise. My confrontation with Henshaw, when I'd finally caught up with him, had driven me to drink too much. I knew what I wanted to do but was struggling at what I thought was the right thing to do.

Once we'd warmed up and stretched, we started jogging.

"Have you talked to your mother or sister today?" Elise asked.

"Not yet."

We rounded a long curve that followed the contour of the ship in this section.

"You need to spend more time with them," Elise said. "If we have to go on a mission, you won't have a chance to, I don't know, do all that family stuff."

"I've been busy. This problem with Henshaw and the hybrids is serious business," I said.

"There's more to it than that, and you know it. Tell me the truth, Reaper. What's wrong?"

I wasn't sure what I should tell her.

"Why are you so nervous?" Elise asked.

"I'm afraid I'll let them down. And not because of a failed mission, but because of who I am."

"They know you are a Reaper. Don't overthink it. Isn't that what you always tell me?" Elise asked.

We finished the lap and kept going on a second lap.

"What's wrong with Henshaw?" Elise asked, breathing harder than before.

"He...thinks...the hybrids are dangerous."

"Oh my God! You're winded." Elise laughed. "I think we should always run before we spar in the future."

"Fine, I'm not scared."

She laughed again.

"He's not wrong about the hybrids, I just don't agree with what he wants to do about them. Most were tricked into being test subjects or had the DNA splicing done against their will. I don't think they deserve to be put down like dogs," I said.

"Well shit," Elise said. "You had to make it ugly. Maybe we'll think of something while we're beating each other with practice swords."

"Path has followed Henshaw to his cabin and is standing guard outside of his door," X-37 interrupted. "Under other circumstances, it might seem that Henshaw had ordered him to do this. Given our recent conversations, I think he is trying to keep track of his old boss."

"Keep me updated," I answered. "Elise is going to try and convince me she knows how to sword fight," I said.

"Good luck with that, Reaper Cain."

19

"I'm not a big card player, X. When did you start making appointments for me without asking what I wanted?"

"I was able to work with AI Mavis and Path to convince Henshaw to attend," X-37 said. "He is fond of games of chance, and I believe he will wish to influence President Coronas and Rejon of Xad."

"Okay, you have my attention. Not that I like that particular scenario, but it could be informative," I said. "I'll need you to research whatever card games we're playing and help me cheat."

"That is quite unethical," X-37 said.

"I'm not trying to take their money, I just want to stay ahead of the real game," I said. "If Henshaw is unraveling, I need to know. If he's holding back, I need to know that as well. If all he wants is to get the hybrids destroyed, then maybe that's what we should do."

"I have downloaded and analyzed all relevant games of chance common in the Union. This also includes one transcript of a live-streamed poker game in which Henshaw did very well back on Roxo III. I'm searching now for information on Xad and Wallach games."

"I knew I could count on you, X. Where are we playing this high-stakes game?"

"Henshaw wanted to do it on the *Lady Faith*, but the security teams of President Coronas and Rejon disagreed immediately."

"Of course," I said. "I don't suppose we could do it on the *Jellybird*?"

"I made that suggestion. Rejon and Coronas are open to the idea, but their security teams opposed it," X-37 said. "It seems they had settled on the private viewing deck of the *Bright Lance*."

"I didn't know there was such a thing," I said.

X-37 gave me directions and I hurried toward the game. Hallways became narrower and narrower and the security doors more frequent. I felt like I was being watched more than normal and wondered if AI Mavis was as benevolent as X-37 seemed to think she was.

The observation deck was nearly as small as the one on the *Jellybird* and had more security than seemed necessary. Four of the Presidential Guards of Wallach crowded one wall, the tops of the exoskeleton armor nearly touching the ceiling.

Rejon's honor guard consisted of six men in resplendent uniforms, more formal than anything I'd seen so far—stiff collars, polished buckles, and unit patches with their home planet on it.

"Not exactly a private game," I muttered.

"Agreed," X-37 said. "My advice is to focus on not losing too much. This isn't a good place to press Henshaw for information."

"I need to know what has them so worked up."

X-37 asked me to scan the room so that he could record its dimensions and also analyze the potential strengths and weaknesses of the security teams. "I will look for an opportunity to learn his secrets."

"Welcome, Halek Cain." Coronas graciously waved one hand toward a seat near her. "Glad you could make it. It's been a long time since I relaxed with friends."

"Not sure this is going to be relaxing," I said as I joined her.

Rejon took a seat on the other side of me. "Are you a strong gambler, Reaper?"

"Only if I cheat."

Everyone in the room laughed, including Henshaw. He quickly became the man I remembered meeting on Roxo III. He dealt us into a game of poker with very little small talk.

"We're playing Seven Card Armada," he said. "Dealer chooses the game. Ten credit ante. We're using the Exodus Fleet Monetary Agreement, or EFMA, credits."

"I've heard of this game." Corona was growing more serious. "Shouldn't we put all of our weapons on the table like in the tablet stories I read growing up?"

The mood was light, and we all laughed. There was more than enough firepower in the room to get everyone killed. The exoskeleton guards had obvious weaknesses, but I didn't know how fast they could move or how accurate they were with their weapons. X-37 warned me the probable strength of the units was enough to rip doors open or crush anybody dumb enough to get caught in their oversized hands.

Seven Card Armada proved to be much faster than I had hoped, and I quickly lost most of my credit chips. For the next hour, I struggled to stay in the game. What I noticed, however, was a very distinct situation between Coronas and Rejon— admiration and rivalry.

"I need to win," I said to the table, but was really talking to X-37.

"You should be winning by now," X-37 said. "My analysis suggests that everyone at the table is cheating."

I didn't have the appropriate hand signal for indignant surprise. Henshaw, I knew would push the limits. He had a limited artificial intelligence that he'd used for games of chance in the past.

"If you recall from our first encounter with the people of Wallach, their most important political figures have a version of limited artificial intelligence. Perhaps she is also cheating," X-37 said.

Amanda Coronas, the most powerful woman of the Wallach people, smiled at me sweetly. I turned my attention to

Rejon, who appeared extra dignified. With subtle hand movements, I asked X-37 about him.

"I can neither confirm nor deny Rejon's use of an LAI," X-37 said.

Basically, X couldn't help me now. I drew my final card, studied it, and pushed every credit chip I had into the center of the table.

Seconds passed. Tension rippled around the table. Coronas no longer smiled at me and Rejon became as inscrutable as Path. Several agonizing moments later, both of them folded.

"Call." Henshaw pushed his own chips forward.

Per the rules of Seven Card Aramada, I disregarded two cards and lay down my betting hand—three tens, all gold stars, and a pair of planets.

Henshaw disregard his two cards, then spread an Admiral's Flush—a starship, a slip tunnel, a victorious fleet card, a flagship, and a green planet.

"Really?" I asked. "What are the odds of that hand this late in the game? Never mind, I don't want to know," I said.

Coronas and Rejon laughed as Henshaw cleaned off the table.

"That was informative," I said. "Let's never do it again."

"I always suspected Reapers would be poor losers," Henshaw said. "You could win it back."

"No way, Jimmy. I'm out of my league here," I said. "And I'm broke."

"There's always something to wager," Henshaw said.

"Yeah, that's true. But if we play again, I'm smoking a cigar like a true poker player and you won't have a chance. You might want to factor that in before you try something slick."

"Nothing good can come of this, Reaper Cain," X-37 said. "This is not about poker. Henshaw is up to something more than a game of cards."

"I'm curious," Coronas began. "What kind of things would you wager? I've been told that Reaper Cain originally found you gambling in the company of Vice Admiral Nebs. What were you trying to win from him?"

"What are you insinuating?" Henshaw asked.

"You know more about what's going on here than any of us," she said.

"The truth is worse than I suspected," he said. "When I approached Vice Admiral Nebs on Roxo III, I thought Ayers was dead."

"What is the real wager you're interested in?" Coronas asked.

Henshaw smiled with half his mouth. "This is the Reaper's game. He invited all of us. I suspect that he is manipulating each of us to get the answers he wants."

I scooped up the cards, shuffled them, and tapped them straight. Henshaw claimed he thought Ayers was dead. He had been after something from Nebs and now I was worried I understood what it was, not that it should surprise me. There were two personality traits that defined Henshaw: his uncontrollable hunger for knowledge, and his pride. He wanted Ayers dead for his own reasons.

Or that was my working theory. X-37 and I each needed more data, so I decided to draw out the game long past the point it should have ended.

We played for bragging rights, smoking cigars and sipping whiskey more than we were betting. Coronas had a nice laugh. Rejon turned out to be a sleepy drunk who mumbled hilarious anecdotes that would probably make more sense if I'd been raised as a salvager.

We all knew there was more to this encounter. None of us knew who was going to show their real hand first.

"The most important thing we can do," Rejon said when his head seemed to have cleared a bit, "is gather every possible resource from the system before moving on."

"I disagree," Coronas said. "The system is not special. It's time to move, find a richer system, maybe even a planet we could build a home on for our people."

Henshaw locked gazes with me as the leaders of Wallach and Xad went back and forth. I waited for a lull in the discussion and jumped in.

"What's your opinion, Henshaw? You clearly have something on your mind," I said.

Coronas and Rejon faced the ocular engineer who had parted us from our credits. Silence held the moment. When Henshaw spoke, his voice cracked—possibly from the cigars or possibly from some dark dread that was torturing him.

"Neither of those things matter," he said. "We have to deal with the alien hybrid problem. And before you disagree, I'm well aware that they are contained in their own cryo-pod prisons. Each of you is smart enough to understand that is a short-term solution at best. The implications of the technology and what Doctor Ayers is trying to achieve should terrify you."

"We've covered this," I said. "They may not be totally innocent, but they haven't exactly had due process. If you think I'm going to murder them in their sleep, you don't know as much about reapers as you thought."

"Clearly," Henshaw said.

"And we'll need Doctor Ayers to advise us on other problems with people recovering from the cryo-pods," I said.

"I'm sorry to disappoint you, Mr. Henshaw, but my security advisors agree with Halek Cain. We can contain the threat and possibly learn something from the technology. Sometimes the best medical and civilian uses of technology come from what were originally military projects," Coronas said.

"The chances of even one hybrid escaping is too high. The consequences will be horrific." Henshaw shifted uncomfortably in his chair. "But what's worse is what will happen if we meet the aliens this DNA came from. What will they think of us when they realize we made monsters out of their DNA and ours? From what I've seen, they don't look very forgiving, and I would hate to fight a war against them."

Coronas and Rejon went pale.

"What do you think we should do with them?" Coronas asked.

"Eject Ayers and his creations into the void, preferably toward a star that will destroy all evidence of their existence," Henshaw said. "I'm a scientist, always looking to learn the mysteries of the universe, so if I'm telling you this, you should listen."

"That's all the more reason to keep moving," Coronas said. "We need to find a defensible place with sufficient resources to rebuild."

Henshaw practically ignored the two most powerful leaders in our migrating society. "Tell me you have a better solution, Reaper."

"We can offload the test subjects that are too far gone onto a planet in the system we don't plan to return to," I said. "We keep Ayers alive and require him to care for the others. I'm no expert on gene splicing, but if they did it, they should be able to undo it."

"Your idea has flaws," Rejon said. "If the existence of these monsters has the potential to anger a powerful alien race, leaving evidence of our crimes on a random planet is a bad idea."

Coronas looked at me, her face unreadable. Rejon's logic seemed to be going someplace I didn't like.

No one touched their cards. The poker game, for all practical purposes, was over. I held Coronas's gaze. After about ten seconds, she made a motion for her guards to wait outside. Rejon did the same.

"What's really going on here, Jimmy?" I asked.

The ocular engineer's face flushed red and the lights in his artificial eyes dimmed until they were almost invisible. He trembled slightly.

"Ayers and I were competitors for the favor of Nebs. Things got out of control. He threatened to send demons after me. It was a threat I thought ridiculous until now."

"All this time, you're just looking after yourself. You think one of these alien hybrids is going to come for you?" I asked.

"You're right, Reaper. But that doesn't change anything. Sure they're coming for me, but they're going to come for all of you too."

"We will need a way to fight them," Rejon said.

Coronas nodded enthusiastically, picking up the thread of the conversation. "It is distasteful, but we are going to need every weapon we can come up with to defend ourselves."

"Can you control him, Mr. Henshaw?" Rejon asked.

"Not only no, but hell no," I said.

"I agree with Rejon, I think," Coronas said, sounding excited. "Mr. Henshaw is the only one who can really understand what Doctor Ayers was planning to do. And he is the most motivated not to allow him to escape. I propose that we grant him supervisory authority over Ayers and the alien technology."

"I concur," Rejon said quickly. "There are often risks that need to be taken for the greater good."

"What the hell are you talking about, greater good?" I couldn't believe what was happening. "You want a scientist who is so radical he removed his own eyes in charge of a scientist crazy enough to splice alien DNA with human DNA? Am I missing something? How is this a good idea?'"

"He will be closely supervised," Coronas said.

Rejon nodded in agreement. "Yes, the President of Wallach is correct. We have a ship full of well-trained security officers, a Reaper, and a Reaper's team. Everything is under control."

"Fuck."

"That is very eloquent, Reaper Cain," X-37 said, but I thought my LAI was even less happy about this development that I was.

Henshaw smiled, and I realized he'd been doing a lot more than playing poker. The man had set this entire encounter up somehow and just beat me hands down.

"If this goes wrong, Jimmy, I'll be coming for you," I said. "Don't forget what I am. Demons are from fairytales to scare children. I'm the last Reaper and you know what I can do."

20

INSPIRED by our post-poker game decision, Rejon sprang into action, rallying his people for a whirlwind tour of the system to gather resources. In less than a standard week, they had squeezed the system and filled their storage compartments.

"In the positive margin, the alien hybrid agreement has brought the people of this Xad and Wallach closer together than ever, even if most of the population doesn't know the details," X-37 said.

"Yeah, that's fabulous," I said, gazing from the bridge of the *Jellybird*. It was good to be off the *Bright Lance* despite the amenities it offered. Security for the ailing hybrids was the responsibility of a joint task force now, though Path stood guard over the vault as often as not.

Elise was at the helm, working with Jelly to find our place at the head of the slip tunnel formation. This jump was proving to be at least as chaotic as the leaving the Xad system. There were just too many ships, and few of them were using the same level of technology. Each captain seemed to hold different ideas about their place in the formation.

Some captains wanted to go first for the honor of making the crossing first. Others wanted the military vessels to protect them, but then interfered by demanding too much control over their operations.

"This is a mess," I said. "I'm about ten minutes from jumping ahead of everyone to scout the next system ourselves."

"My analysis suggests that would not be the worst option," X-37 said. "And I believe Jelly agrees with me."

"I do agree," Jelly said. "But that decision belongs to Elise, presently."

"We wait for fleet command's decision," Elise said.

"Of course," Jelly said. "We are holding course near the slip tunnel awaiting permission to proceed."

TEN HOURS after we led the scouting expedition through the slip tunnel, it opened into a promising star system. I led a scout squadron of three ships including the *Jellybird*.

"*Battle Axe* and *Hunter*, begin security patrols," Elise ordered. "We're on the clock. The rest of the fleet will exit soon, and we don't want any surprises."

The RWS *Battle Axe*, commanded by Captain Hunger, moved immediately. "*Battle Axe* acknowledges. En route."

The *Hunter of Xad*, also a well-armed scout craft, moved toward her assignment. "*Hunter* acknowledges," said Captain Omon.

"Tell me about the system, Jelly," I said.

"I believe it falls into the too good to be true category," Jelly said. "There is one garden planet. Long range sensors indicate it to be well suited for humans, a bit larger than most planets in its category, which might be a bonus. There is only one other slip tunnel, making the system easy to defend while still having an escape route in one direction or another. Several planets and asteroid belts are rich with raw materials."

I read through the data as it flowed onto the screen. "What am I seeing around the other slip tunnel? Are those ships?"

"There is a small debris field near the opening of the slip tunnel on the opposite side of the system," Jelly advised. "It does not open in a true lagrangian point, so it seems the debris should be pulled into one of the competing gravity wells near it. This suggests the ship or ships were destroyed recently."

"How recently?" I asked.

"We have insufficient data at this time," Jelly said. "I recommend either proceeding to the other slip tunnel or sending one of the other scout vessels to investigate."

"Negative, Jelly," I said. "We stay together. Once we have

this sector scouted, we will proceed in a squadron formation to the other slip tunnel to investigate."

"I'll let the *Battle Axe* and the *Hunter* know," Elise said.

"Good." I looked at Tom. "When Elise is ready, I'd like to take the micro-fighters out. Can you take the con?"

"It would be my pleasure," Tom said.

A short time later, Elise pushed back from her workstation. "That's done. Captain Hunger and Captain Omon are much easier to deal with than Coronas and Rejon."

"They seem solid and they keep their ships in good condition," I said. "I've seen their type before. I think we can count on them."

"Great, let's have some fun," Elise said. "I'd like to do some speed trials with the micro-fighters before we're surrounded by the junk fleet."

We headed for the storage bay of the *Jellybird* we'd converted to a flight deck for a pair of micro-fighters. The small ships were designed to attach on the exterior of one of these Union stealth carriers, but this wasn't practical for our needs. We put on our Archangel gear, integrated them with the micro-fighters as Elise had learned to do, and launched into the void.

"I'm still getting used to this," I said. "When you showed me how to use my Archangel armor with my micro-fighter, I thought I would feel less vulnerable. But the interface is so smooth I don't feel like I'm in a ship at all."

"I'm telling you, Reaper, your reaction time is so much faster this way it's hard to believe. Everything happens in real time and the suits are better at handling the G forces of hard turns, acceleration, and deceleration," Elise said, speaking quickly due to her own excitement. "I almost can't wait to get in a fight."

"Famous last words." Without warning, I punched my speed to maximum. Elise chased after me.

"Tom, stay close enough to pick us up but don't do anything dumb," Elise said. "I think I know what the Reaper has in mind."

"Copy that," Tom said. "A secondary scan shows a matching debris field near the slip tunnel we came through. None of this is a fraction of what we saw in the Xad system, but something happened here."

"It appears that an unknown force placed mines or otherwise attempted to control these access points to the system," Jelly said.

I laughed. Elise laughed with me but sounded a bit annoyed.

"Everyone guesses right once in a while," she said.

"Admit it, you didn't even consider the fact that both slip tunnels had been mined," I said. "Even though we've been training to expect anything when we enter a new solar system."

"We're doing the patrols, aren't we?" She didn't exactly sound defensive, but I thought I could get under her skin a bit.

"That's why I'm the scout leader on this mission," I said.

She fired back immediately, reminding me of the girl I'd left on Greendale after Dreadmax and then returned to find living on her own. "Or maybe it's because you're pushy and like telling everyone what to do."

"Something wrong with that?"

"You're messing with me, Reaper."

"*Battle Axe* to scout leader, we've cleared our sector and are moving toward your location," Captain Hunger said.

"Copy that, *Battle Axe*," I said. "*Hunter*, status?"

"Nearly complete. We found one derelict vessel. Initial scans show no signs of life," Captain Omon reported. "It looks like what you found is a larger field."

"Hold there and we will come to you after we finish here," I said. "*Battle Axe*, rendezvous with Hunter."

"En route," Hunger answered.

Elise and I closed on my discovery. The ship was long and looked like one of the larger ones I had seen near Xad. It was so big that we were able to race down the middle of it, dodging around its twisted infrastructure and laughing crazily.

I twisted the controls, quickly learning not to over correct. Elise was slightly behind me, but I could feel her trying to pass despite the obvious danger in this environment. From time to time I caught flashes of her ship acrobatics on my display.

"Didn't I tell you these things were awesome with your armor integrated?" The excitement in her voice made me laugh a bit.

"Settle down, kid. Let's try not to get killed before the rest of the fleet gets through the slip tunnel," I said.

We shot out the other side and banked around to head back for what the *Hunter of Xad* had found. The *Jellybird*, which had established a safe standoff distance from the Alon hulk we were zipping through, fell in with us on our new course.

"We have a few minutes before we get there," I said. "Did you get any good data from our reconnaissance, X?"

"I'm sure that Jelly and I observed far more from your camera feed than you did, at least from an analytical standpoint," X-37 said.

"Are you bragging, X?" I asked.

"It sounds like he's bragging," Elise said.

"Incorrect," X-37 said. "I am reporting factual information, as always."

"Well, was that an Alon ship or not?" I asked. The size and style of it reminded me of what the enemies of both Wallach and Xad had left behind. There had been few of their ships left behind in the conflicts over the ages. The most dangerous looking warships were of neither Wallach or Xad design.

"It matches the design parameters as we know them," X-37 said. "However, there is little of value remaining other than the metal and ceramic alloys of its construction. All weapons, power sources, and technology have been stripped away."

"Do you think someone like the people of Xad did that?" I asked.

"I do not believe that is the case, Reaper Cain. This was a more systematic salvage operation, probably done by the same people who built the ship."

Elise and I arrived at the other derelict ship slightly ahead of the *Jellybird*.

"Tom, why don't you take one point on the perimeter while *Hunter* and *Battle Axe* assume two other vector points. I'm going to show the Reaper the coolest thing about our little fighter ships," Elise said. "This isn't open at both ends like the other one so we're going to have to get our hands dirty."

Tom and the other captains acknowledged and took overwatch positions.

"Watch and learn, Reaper." Elise swooped to the surface of the dark hulk, disengaging from the wings and propulsion systems seconds before she landed on the exterior hull of the Alon wreck. The micro-fighter peeled away from her and hovered at a point she set with the armor LAI.

We had learned that the advanced Union armor had a unique type of LAI, one that was spread out over groups of Archangel gear. That was how Elise initially figured out the integration technology. Apparently, it had been an option that Nebs never approved. The evidence suggested he hadn't trusted his own people that much. Which had allowed us to defeat him against overwhelming odds.

"X, help me out," I said.

"Integrating with the Archangel LAI now," X-37 responded. "You may now disengage from the micro-fighter when you're ready."

I brought the little ship close to the deck, came to a relative stop, and gave the order. The wings and fuselage of the micro-fighter peeled away, dumping me unceremoniously downward. I landed on my hands and knees hard enough to stun me.

Elise laughed, unrepentant. "That was smooth, Reaper. Very nice."

"Don't get cocky, kid," I grumbled as I came to my feet and joined her.

"Who me? Cocky?"

Strutting past her, I found an access hatch. Once I determined there was no power, I ripped it free and looked inside. Nothing but darkness awaited us.

"I'll go first," I said.

"Good. Everyone knows Reapers are expendable." Elise took up a position to watch my back despite her bravado.

"On the contrary, Elise," X-37 said. "Reapers were always used as a high-value asset, even when they were sent on missions with a low probability of success. My records show that the cost was always a significant factor in Union decision making."

"Let's not talk about the Union right now," I said, activating my helmet lights to see the expansive passage spreading out ahead of us.

This ship wasn't as large as the one Elise and I had recently flown through, but it was big. Walking from end to end would take time. There were metal catwalks, stairways, and ladders leading to areas that had been stripped of anything useful. Unlike Dreadmax, there was no rust anywhere. Every surface had a unique crosshatch pattern.

But that wasn't what stunned Elise and me to silence.

Twenty meters inside the access hatch I had ripped open, we found bodies. Most of them looked like they had been human. Their uniforms bore distinct similarities to some of the fashion experiments the people of Xad were currently wearing. Their weapons, however, looked like advanced versions of Wallach arms.

"X, can you compare these corpses to what we know about our new allies?" I asked.

"I'm working on it now, Reaper Cain," X-37 said. "I believe these are Alon corpses."

"What's wrong with their skin? Or is that an effect of long-term void exposure? And while you're at it, how long do you think the ship has been like this?" I asked.

"Please focus on the most well-preserved Alon body you can find," X-37 asked.

I complied, kneeling over one of the bodies, not wanting to face the thing I thought had killed them. That corpse lay underneath a half-dozen Alon soldiers that had swarmed it and went down fighting.

"Please keep in mind that my reconstruction of probable Alon physiology is incomplete. Based on what I can see here, and on the rather incomplete references in the Wallach and Xad databases, these soldiers were very tall, well adapted to the void, and possessed radically different pigment from your skin or anybody we have encountered in our journeys."

"What else, X?" I asked, standing and moving toward the Alon bodies piled on top of a creature that I thought was going to be too familiar for comfort.

"I don't like this," Elise said. "Tom is telling me that they can't pick up our holo feeds—something about the material the ship hull is made from."

"We can fill him in later," I said, then pulled the first Alon corpse from the pile. Its arm came off. I cast it away and pulled on the feet with better results.

"None of the bodies have weapons or armor, which I find curious. A salvage crew might take the weapons, but why would they remove armor and then put the bodies back in these uncomfortable looking positions," X-37 said.

"Whoever these Alon were, they belong to the ship. The creature they killed was a boarder, trying to take control of the ship or just kill them all. I'm not sure which at this point," I said. "If they had been the boarders, they would've been wearing void suits."

"There is a very good possibility that the aggressors in this conflict considered killing all of their enemies part of taking control of the ship," X-37 said. "I will need much more data to make a precise analysis, of course."

"Okay, you can tell me more about the Alon later," I said. "I'm going to see if this creature on the bottom of the pile is one of Ayers's hybrid aliens."

"I'll stand guard," Elise said, a hitch in her voice.

I worked at the grim task, taking the time to drag each body to one side and lay it out for later examination. I was anxious to see if the tentacles protruding from the scene belonged to an actual, true to life alien matching what Ayers had been trying to recreate.

I had my doubts because the tentacles I could see almost looked like they were covered with frost, which seemed unlikely because there was no moisture in this environment. Nothing, even damaged metal that had been ripped free of the ship, had any rust or corrosion.

More importantly, the tentacles almost looked beautiful. I passed this along to Elise.

"Are you kidding me?" she asked.

"You're not looking at what I'm looking at," I said, removing the last Alon defender that had died saving his ship. His sunken, skull like face didn't give me many clues to his skin tones or whether or not he had hair. I was assuming some of the decomposition had happened before all atmosphere was lost from this vessel, but there wasn't a good way to be sure without a lot more work. His own bacteria might have been enough to start the processes.

"I'm recording in the highest definition possible for future analysis," X-37 said.

"Good call, because this isn't anything like I expected," I said.

Elise moved closer, still standing guard.

The body was nonhuman but hadn't changed colors or decomposed as far as I could tell. It was the color of a white dwarf star with sky-blue highlights at the tip of what I had assumed were tentacles.

What I was looking at now was something very different from the murderous freaks stored in the *Bright Lance* cryo-pods. This creature had been almost as beautiful as it had been deadly. The multiple limbs were slim and smooth, covered with something that might have been short, snow white felt.

The tangle of limbs lacked the hooks I had seen on the worst of Ayers's experiments. Instead, these were tipped with what looked like nine-inch bone razors—edged in blue like the watermark of swords I had seen on Heron XIII.

Overall, the alien was definitely humanoid, with two legs and two arms from which the tentacles had sprouted. The face was angular and graceful, the head wreathed in something like sharp edged feathers.

"That's nothing like I expected," Elise said.

"I am recording and taking measurements," X-37 said. "There are enough similarities between the experiments in this corpse to suggest splicing the DNA of its species with humans resulted in something more grotesque than either."

"Let's recon what we can, and decide what to do with the alien corpse," I said. "It doesn't feel right to leave it here, but I'm nervous about putting it on our ship. We don't know anything about it."

"We could put it in cold storage, lock the door, and set a guard," Elise said, not exactly sounding satisfied with the idea.

By the time we were done on the Alon ship, we'd counted over three hundred Alon and seven true alien bodies. We consulted with Tom and forwarded some of the images that couldn't be relayed through the hull of the derelict ship in real time.

Omon sent two of his best salvage people to help us pack two Alon bodies—a male and a female—and one of the true aliens in preservation containers. These were like the cryo-pods but much simpler. No one put in these boxes would ever be revived.

"We will bring back a team to collect the rest of the bodies," I said.

Elise agreed without speaking.

I was exhausted by the time the operation was done. Resting on the observation deck of the *Jellybird*, Elise, Tom, and I witnessed the arrival of the combined Wallach and Xad fleet.

"We've been busy," Elise said.

"Nice of you to notice." I sensed there was more to her statement.

"So busy that you haven't spent much time with your mother and sister," she said.

"They're still recovering. Don't worry about us. Now that they're awake, there's time to rebuild our relationships," I said.

"Are you sure?"

"I get it. You think I'm a terrible son and brother."

"That's not what I said. Just don't take anything for granted."

"My analysis suggests that is excellent advice," X-37 said.

21

The Wallach and Xad combined fleet was a flurry of activity after we gave them the news of the Alon ship and what we had found within. Our reconnaissance of the other slip tunnel had been less fruitful, only demonstrating that there had been a mine field around the tunnel opening and that several ships had met their fate there.

I walked the main concourse of the *Bright Lance* with my mother. She was growing stronger every day and had been busy while I was off playing Reaper. Many of the people we encountered waved and greeted her by name as we passed.

"How is Hannah adapting?" I asked.

"She spends all of her time in the gymnasium or the library. The Elise girl tried to talk to her, but they are very different people. Perhaps it's the age difference or just how they were raised," my mother said.

Hannah was ten years younger than me, and I was embarrassed I didn't remember her birthday with any degree of precision. To me, she'd always been the kid, just like Elise and Bug and lots of other people would always be kids.

My mother seemed to know what I was thinking just by looking at me. She smiled and took my arm. "You're not that old, Halek. Don't act like it."

"I feel pretty old," I admitted.

"It's a state of mind," she said, her expression serious when I expected a smile to soften the message. "Don't let the challenges in the galaxy break you down."

"I won't." Walking with my mother felt natural. I'd worried that we would have become too estranged.

"I think it's time to head back. I enjoy these walks, but I'm still building my endurance. The cryo-pods have a rejuvenating effect, or so I tell myself, but that doesn't mean sleeping four months at a time did my cardiovascular system much good," she said.

We headed back, frequently stopping to talk to crew members that had all kinds of things to share with my mother. She really had been socializing a lot. That wasn't something I remembered about her, but now that I thought about it, it made sense. My childhood had been dangerous and that had distorted what I remembered of it.

"Go check on your sister, if you can find her," my mother said as we parted.

"Right away, mother," I said, which made her smile.

"I think I like you better as an adult."

"Ouch!" I held my right hand over my heart, which amused her even more. She hugged me, but when she pulled back, I knew something was wrong.

WE STARED at each other until other passersby reached the next intersection and turned into a new hallway.

"Have you figured out why your sister and I were put into the pods?" she asked.

"Nebs was using you as hostages," I said.

"Think about it, Halek. There's more to it than that and you know it," she said.

"Ayers," I said through clenched teeth. "I have a source who puts most of the blame for what happened on him."

"Ayers had more influence over the vice admiral than most people suspected, but don't direct all of your hatred at him. Nebs truly was a monster," she said.

"We got rid of one, I don't see why we can't handle the other one," I said, thinking back on my discussion with Henshaw, Coronas, and Rejon."

"I know you've already considered this, but you need to jettison Ayers and all of his work into the nearest star as soon as you can make it happen," she said. There wasn't anger or resentment in her voice. She was as cold as ice and it frightened me.

"That's going to be a problem," I told her.

"Tell me the rest," she said.

"Henshaw managed to convince them to put him in control of Ayers and all of his projects," I said. "He used the same argument you are using, but while he claimed he wanted them gone, he really only wanted to take over the project and have power over his rival."

"James Henshaw? The engineer?" she asked.

"You know him?"

She nodded. "He was one of Neb's less important technicians, but to hear him talk about all of his advanced education, you would've thought he was the galaxy's gift to science."

"He's come a long way since then. Both of his eyes are cybernetic now, and he has a yacht that has a slip tunnel drive," I said.

"That is a problem," she said. "I never had much influence on the man, probably because I found him boring and arrogant—while he resented me for not fawning over his so-called brilliance. You have to convince President Coronas and Rejon of Xad to give me control over Ayers and his projects."

"So you can destroy them?" I didn't like where this was going. My mother wanted the exact same thing Henshaw wanted.

She hesitated slightly. "Yes."

"That's going to be a problem, because despite your low estimation of the man, he outmaneuvered me."

"Explain," she demanded.

"It's a long story, but it involves poker, cigars, and whiskey," I said, feeling like a kid despite towering over her.

"Never gamble with Henshaw. He might not be as smart

as he thinks he is but his skill as a con artist can't be matched," she said.

"I figured that out late." My mind wouldn't stop working on the problem. Plans and counter plans grew in my imagination and disappeared before they were fully formed.

Before I realized it, my mother was striding down the hallway with renewed purpose.

"Where are you going?" I asked.

"There's no time to waste. If Henshaw has taken control with subtlety and tricks, we have to act directly. Can you fight your way past the guards at the hybrid vault?"

I didn't move, knowing that if I pursued her, I would have to take her by the arm to stop her and I didn't want to do that. "No, I can't. Even if I wanted to. The last time I was there, there were a pair of the Wallach Presidential guards in exoskeleton armor."

She whirled around to face me, fury in her eyes. "You could take them. You're a Reaper."

"Even if I could, think of the repercussions," I said.

Emotions played on her face—anger, frustration, and an almost sad realization that much had changed between us. "I should be glad that the impulsive young man I remembered has learned to think. But you're showing your weakness. Sometimes we have to do things that are unpleasant."

I approached, anger building to a level I'd forgotten years ago. "Don't talk to me about doing unpleasant things. I am a Reaper. I'm tired of selling my soul for what people tell me is right."

At that, my mother softened and seemed to grow weaker by the second. I wasn't sure if she was embarrassed for what she had said or afraid of what would happen if I didn't take action against the alien hybrids immediately.

"I've seen them in action, Halek," she said. "I'll put you up against the Presidential Guards, or the Archangels, or a monster like the one they keep showing you fighting on Xad, but the abominations Ayers created will tear your face off."

"I've been working on my face tearing defense for weeks," I joked.

She laughed until she was almost crying and hugged me for the second time since we'd awakened her. "I'm sorry, Halek. Fear will push anyone to bad decisions and actions they're ashamed of. I need to sleep. Ridiculous given how much time I've spent unconscious in the last year."

"Get some rest. I actually have a secret weapon I can use to deal with Ayers and Henshaw."

She pulled back and looked up at me. "Truly? What kind of secret weapon?"

"I call him Bug."

STRIDING AWAY from my mother's cabin, I asked X-37 to contact the street kid from Dreadmax who had been doing electronic surveillance his entire life.

"I have him on the line. Go for Bug," X-37 said.

"How's it going, Bug?" I asked.

"Uh, good, Reaper. Why are you, uh, asking? Nothing going on here. Just checking the cameras, not eating extra rations of cheese crackers," he answered.

"You sound like you're crunching on something," I said. "I know how you like cheese crackers."

"They're just so good and cheesy."

"I get it, but there are rations for a reason. We have food stores now, but we don't know how long it will be before we get a proper resupply," I said.

"Uh, huh." *Chomp. Chomp. Chomp.*

"I could probably turn a blind eye for someone doing extra duty, someone who could solve a problem for me," I said. "I mean between X-37 and Mavis, I have all the evidence I need to lodge a complaint. And I know people."

"That's not fair. You can just go straight to Captain Younger with whatever you want. She'll put me on some crappy mining ship."

"Not if she doesn't know," I said. "I really need you to watch Henshaw."

"I thought you wanted me to watch Ayers, which, by the way, is really boring since he's locked down most of the time," Bug said.

"Most of the time?"

"He escapes, but your sword saint friend always follows him without being seen. It's pretty entertaining for about the first fifteen minutes, then I get hungry," Bug said, chomping on some more crackers.

"He escaped!"

"Never for very long," Bug replied defensively. *Chomp. Chomp. Chomp.*

"You have to tell me things like that. Why didn't Mavis alert X-37?" I demanded, amazed this could have gone so far without anyone knowing.

"You were already through the slip tunnel finding dead Aliens. I don't know why Mavis does things. She's a ship AI," Bug said.

"I'm looking into it now," X-37 said.

"I'm sorry, Mister Reaper. He never went far and was always caught by the guards," Bug said, rustling a bag noisily. "I thought you knew."

"I need you keep track of them both—and notify me immediately if Ayers is even acting like he might try an escape," I ordered.

"Sure, Reaper. I can do that. Anything else in particular you want me to look for?"

"Any time Ayers and Henshaw discuss anything about the alien hybrids, I want to be notified immediately."

"That's not so easy," Bug said. "There aren't any cameras I can access on that level."

"But you can do it, right?" If I didn't have a way to outsource my spying, I was going to be too busy to do much else.

"Oh, yeah, for sure. I just have to figure out which Archangel, or Presidential Guard, or ship guard has the duty, then I can tap into their helmet comms. Took me a while to figure out how to use them while they're turned off. But it can be done," Bug said, crumpling up a wrapper and throwing it away by the sound of it.

"You can spy on Archangels?" I asked.

"This should be impossible," X-37 said. "He would have to have access to their communal limited artificial intelligence."

"I picked up one of the helmets from the repair room. Checked it out and everything. Told Tom it was a school project. He thinks I need to get a real education and keeps sending me books and self-study courses," Bug said.

"I guess no good deed goes unpunished." I started planning my next move but was interrupted by a message from Elise reminding me we were due for a micro-fighter patrol. "I want you on Henshaw and Ayers like they owe me money."

"Do they?"

"No."

"Then—"

"Just tell me whenever Henshaw visits Ayers and if they talk about the hybrids. And tell me if Henshaw goes anywhere near the alien hybrid vault or does anything that involves them," I said.

"Okay." Bug's voice was casual, almost bored. "Can you get me some ration vouchers?"

"Sure."

22

ELISE TOOK THE LEAD, maneuvering her micro-fighter through the asteroid belt slightly faster than I was comfortable with.

"This will improve your piloting skills, Reaper Cain," X-37 said. "You have most likely run out of beginner's luck."

"I'm not a beginner. I've had training," I said.

"I believe you know what I mean," X-37 said.

"Try to keep up, Reaper," Elise said. She always sounded happy and alive when we were tearing to the void.

"I'm right behind you."

"Good." Something about her voice had changed. "I think I've spotted something. Possibly a ship."

"What kind of ship?"

"I think it's an Alon scout ship," Elise answered. "Whatever it is, it knows I see it and it's running."

"X, can you confirm what she's seeing?"

"Absolutely, Reaper Cain, just as soon as you bring us into visual range. I can't analyze what I can't see," X-37 said.

"You know what I mean, X. Elise, let me take the lead."

"It's too fast. Just try to keep up." She shot forward at full speed, weaving around asteroids one after another.

Before our sudden acceleration, there had seemed to be plenty of room between the space rocks. Now it felt like every time I steered, it was right toward an asteroid.

"Tom," I said. "Stay out of the asteroid field but don't get too far behind. Follow along the perimeter."

No response.

"Tom," I repeated.

"The scout ship is jamming our communications, which is intriguing since I don't see how they can know our frequencies or even our basic technology," X-37 said.

"How are they doing that if I can still talk to Elise?" I asked.

"Unknown, but it may have something to do with proximity and/or the asteroid field we are navigating at a rather dangerous rate," X-37 said.

Elise pulled farther away from me and I still couldn't see the mysterious Alon scout vessel she was chasing.

"My analysis suggests that you should minimize the rate at which she is leaving you behind without exceeding your piloting capabilities," X-37 said.

"Are you worried, X?"

"I am somewhat worried, Reaper Cain. The odds of

surviving the next several seconds are not promising. Please focus on what you are doing," X-37 said. "Would some relaxing music assist your concentration?"

"Shutting the hell up would be better yet," I said.

An extremely large rock tumbled toward me, or that's what it looked like. I couldn't see Elise or her quarry. Guessing which direction they were taking the pursuit, I jammed the control sticks forward and flew under the unusually large chunk of space debris.

When I cleared the rock, I was immediately faced with a cloud of smaller grit that peppered my shields. X-37 and my Archangel LAI worked together to find Elise.

I respected X-37's warning, but if I didn't take some risks, I was going to lose her and whatever she was chasing.

"Keep trying to raise the *Jellybird* and see if they can meet us on the other side of this asteroid belt," I said, then accelerated as fast as I dared—plus about ten percent.

"Unable to establish communication with the *Jellybird*," X-37 said.

Something big bumped my shield and scooted me sideways. I dropped down to avoid the next rock, then put the micro-fighter into a roll.

"It's leaving the asteroid belt," Elise said, her voice buried in static. "Just punch out of the belt and try to catch up with us on the other side. I'm going to…"

"We've lost signal," X-37 provided unhelpfully.

I shot forward, clearing the last group of rocks easily.

Cheering, I whooped and hollered my way toward a planet that had an ominous look to it.

"I'm detecting two small ships descending into the stratosphere," X-37 advised. "I am ninety percent certain that one of them is Elise."

I redlined the engines and went straight at them, desperate to catch up before Elise got herself into trouble.

THE COCKPIT of the micro-fighter vibrated as the wings extended for atmospheric maneuvering. Alerts flashed in my HUD and the controls fought my hands.

"Reduce speed immediately, Reaper Cain. You are going to overshoot Elise and the other ship," X-37 said.

I backed off just as I came alongside Elise. "Cain for Elise, how copy?"

"I hear you, Reaper."

A wash of words I didn't understand interrupted, completely burying our conversation. Whatever the other pilot was saying, it seemed to be some kind of challenge or accusation.

"X, can you figure out what he's trying to tell us?"

"I'm working on it, Reaper Cain," X-37 said.

"How's your ship, Elise?" I asked.

"It's good. I didn't run into anything, unlike some people I know," she answered.

"Ouch," I said. "Run into a couple of rocks, and everybody makes a big deal out of it."

"I'm low on fuel," she said. "I've sent several unanswered messages to the *Jellybird*. I really hope they know we're on this planet, because I'm going to have to land."

I checked my HUD and confirmed my fuel was also low. "I want to know where this strange scout ship is going, but we need to break off. I don't really want it telling its friends where we crashed down."

"Who said anything about crashing?" Elise asked indignantly.

"Yeah, whatever. Let's make a hard push to catch the Alon scout ship, then reverse course, break contact as cleanly as possible, and find a place to set down while it still believes were are in pursuit," I said.

"I'm on it." Elise rushed at the strange ship. Almost immediately, it accelerated far faster than we could match.

Elise and I banked in a wide turn, then flew down into a valley obscured by trees that had to be hundreds of feet tall.

ELISE MANAGED to get out of her ship before I did and was standing with her arms crossed, tapping her foot when I disengaged my Archangel armor from the chassis of the micro-fighter.

"What the hell are we going to do now?" Elise asked. "I

couldn't get confirmation that the *Jellybird* received our distress call."

After pulling a long work knife from my leg armor, I began chopping branches from one of the enormous trees surrounding our landing site. Elise quickly realized what I was doing and followed suit. We camouflaged our little ships as we talked.

"It's actually nice," I said. "Not much humidity, oxygen-rich environment with lots of plant life—suggests there will be other animals to hunt or domesticate. We could live here for a while."

"Or we could get rescued before some Alon search ship finds us," Elise said.

"What do you think, X? Should we just retire here and make the most of it?" I asked.

"I cannot make a valid analysis of that question until we have more information. Could you please explore the planet, or at least the immediate area?" X-37 asked.

"We can do that," Elise answered. "I feel like we are exposed here anyway. Why didn't we train for terrestrial field operations, Reaper?"

"I'm thoroughly trained for that type of thing," I answered. "Which is a good reason for you to listen to me and do what I say."

"Now I really want to get rescued," she said.

We moved into the trees, pausing to peer out from our new hiding place and search the sky for enemy ships. All we saw were flocks of birds moving across the valley, perching on treetops just long enough to gather and launch themselves with the flurry of activity.

"There is some sort of animal trail," I said. "It should lead to water. We can test it and see if it's drinkable. If it is, we will have a much better time surviving until we're found."

We moved steadily into the forest, descending through gullies and climbing up hills, all of which were covered with the towering evergreens and different types of underbrush. The landscape was a hundred layers of colors and textures and animal life.

"I think we'll probably have to explore this when the rest of the fleet gets here," Elise said. "It could definitely support everyone from Wallach and Xad."

"Unless it's already taken."

Elise made one of her faces that involved eye rolling and turning away from me. "Duh. That's why we'll scout it."

"X, have you decrypted any of that Alon transmission?" I asked.

"Only a single message. Something like *the planet defends itself*," X-37 said.

"That doesn't sound ominous." Elise turned in a circle. "I don't care what attacks as long as it doesn't have tentacles."

"Let's just not get seen," I said. "That's the best way to avoid attacks, tentacle or otherwise."

We found a stream with water so clear we could see fish swimming in it and the rocks on the bottom. I wasn't sure I liked the look of the fish—they had a rainbow sheen to them and darted away before I could think about catching one.

Some sort of four-legged creature covered in spotted fur looked at us from the other side of the water, then darted away. Only then did I realize there were seven or eight of them of different sizes.

"There's a lot of wildlife here. I wish we could get in touch with the *Jellybird*, or any ship that can scan for cities or technology," I said.

"I'm surprised we haven't seen more of those ships," Elise said. "What do you think that means? Could we have discovered this planet at the same time that the Alon found it?" She paused. "And if that's the case, how would they know the planet defends itself?"

"It's too early to tell and we don't even know for certain if that's who we're dealing with." I scanned the terrain and got X-37's opinion on where we might be able to take shelter.

There was a natural windbreak in the foothills of the mountains that surrounded us. With luck we might even find a cave to get us through the night.

"My analysis suggests that is your best option for shelter," X-37 said. "It's a defensible position and we can see a lot of the surrounding area on our approach to be sure it isn't already claimed by someone else."

"You heard X," I said. "Time to see how well the Archangels do on the ground."

"We are the Archangels, sort of," Elise said. "I know that's the armor designation, but if we worked for the Union that's what we would be called."

"Sure, but let's not do anything like the Union would." I

took off at a fast run. The armor augmented my strength and conserved my energy. Every movement was more efficient, and I made good time until I tripped.

Elise staggered to a stop beside me, having her own problems moving at the speed these things were capable of. Standing and fighting for balance, she eventually put her fists on her hips and looked down at me as I climbed to my feet.

"That was awesome," she said. "It's different than running on one of the treadmills or even the track of the *Bright Lance*."

"It's fantastic. Especially the part where we stick out like shining gold armor in a raw world that doesn't seem to have been touched by technology," I said. "We need to find some camouflage."

Elise laughed, totally up for the game. She scooped up a handful of dirt, her shining gauntlet every bit as efficient as a shovel. For several moments she smeared the rich, loamy soil all over her armor—and achieved nothing.

"There must be some sort of carbon and fluorine clear coat, polytetrafluoroethylene basically, covering the exterior of this stuff," Elise grumbled, but not in a negative or unhappy way. "I can't get it dirty."

"I noticed that when we crossed the river and came out clean as a whistle," I said.

"Well La-dee-da. Aren't you smart," she popped back. "We'll figure something out. For now, we can just stay inside the tree line to avoid aerial counter reconnaissance."

"Good idea." I checked the sky. Privately, I had expected there would already have been one of the Alon scout ships looking for us if it was going to happen. It seemed unlikely that there was a major enemy presence, if that's what they were on this planet.

I'd been wrong before.

"You're awfully quiet, X. Can you help us out with camouflage?" I asked.

"Of course, Reaper Cain," X-37 said. "I am highlighting camouflage instructions on your HUD now. It takes a few moments, but all you have to do is activate it and then remain motionless until the armor can adjust. It's not a true stealth option like the cloak that you inconveniently left on the *Bright Lance*, but it will change the outward appearance of your armor to match the flora of this environment during this particular season.

"Thanks, X." I activated the environment mimicking protocol. Elise, probably guided by the Archangel group LAI, was done before I was. That was getting to be a trend. She was quick.

"I told you integrating the armor was a good idea," she said.

"I never argued with you. Let's keep moving. I want to scout an area around our landing zone as thoroughly as possible." The helmet optics and my cybernetic eye integrated well. Images were stored in short-term memory, then analyzed and saved if they were something X-37 thought useful.

The forest was dark at night and it was strange to be outside of a ship without seeing a massive star field all around me. I tried to remember the last time I had been on a planet and not in a city.

"Any luck contacting the *Jellybird*?" I asked.

"No, Reaper Cain," X-37 said. "I am no longer detecting interference with our signals, however."

"Should be a matter of time. Elise, what do you think about spreading out? We'd be less of a target for whatever is in these woods."

"Our comms are solid right now. Let's do it."

I moved away from her, searching for threats and checking her position on my HUD when I couldn't see her directly.

"This seems like a nice planet," Elise said. "I wonder what President Coronas and Rejon will think of it."

"Every system we scout will be a potential new home for their people," I said.

"I'm hungry. Surely there has to be something we can eat on this place," Elise said.

"Let's finish our security sweep before we get distracted."

———

"THERE IS ONLY SO MUCH I can do," X-37 said. "My analysis of these berries is limited to visual feedback and/or the reactions of your body when you consume it. A check of my database suggests that some berries of this basic size and color are edible but that others could kill you instantly."

I looked at the purplish fruit in my hand. "That seems a bit harsh. They look sweet."

"Yeah," Elise said too casually. "Just throw down a couple of handfuls and see what happens. You're the logical choice for the experiment since X-37 can gather more data."

With our helmets off, her expressions were easier to read, and I saw that she honestly wanted to know if the local berries were edible, but that she also wanted to see me gag.

"Tom for Hal, please respond," a voice came in my ear.

After dropping the berries, I slipped on my helmet for better reception. There was an urgency in my friend's voice I didn't like.

"I'm here, Tom. Elise is with me."

"That's a huge relief! We've been scanning the planet for hours. You really hid your ships well," Tom said. "What is your situation? You need to get off that planet immediately."

Elise had her helmet on now as well and was moving toward her micro-fighter. "We need fuel, Tom. Can you send us down a shuttle?"

"I could do that, but we will lose a shuttle. There won't be time to recover it. I'm launching a care package to your location, which will alert the swarm. So don't mess around. Refuel and just leave the container. I don't like the look of this," Tom said, sounding even more worried than before.

"Send me a video," I said.

"It will be compressed. Standby," Tom said. "I'm doing two things at once."

"The fueling container is on its way," Jelly said.

I saw the single use fuel pod streaking down from the atmosphere, arcing toward our location with a complete lack of subtlety. If there were Alon forces on the planet or something else we hadn't seen yet, they wouldn't have difficulty finding us now.

"Talk to me, Tom," I said as I watched the first image is coming through my HUD projection. The view was of the planet from high orbit and there was a cloud of something moving our way.

"We thought it was a storm at first," Tom said. "But it doesn't move like an environmental system. It stopped several times, then seemed to detect something that got it moving again, then headed straight for your position."

"I don't like the look of that," Elise said, all of her cockiness gone. She'd proven her bravery over and over again. Our experiences together had taught me how to interpret her tone well.

I was glad we were on the same page. It wasn't quite time to crap our pants, but we needed to give our best game right now. We were on an alien planet of which we knew very little about and a swarm of something the size of a small continent was heading for us.

"My analysis of planetary creatures in the database combined with what we are seeing from high orbit suggests this is a flock of birds or some type of insect swarm," X-37 provided, probably trying to be helpful.

"Yeah, let's hope they can't penetrate Archangel armor or micro-fighters." I ran toward the fuel container as it struck the clearing.

"A bigger problem will be the sheer mass of the swarm,"

X-37 said, then gave me an extensive list of size estimations that really didn't help me much.

"We can't fly through a swarm of birds or bugs or whatever that size," Elise said. "Can you hurry up?"

I scrambled down into the crater, wanting to chastise Tom and Jelly for misjudging the impact velocity, but I wasn't sure it was their fault. We were working on the fly and just had to adapt.

Scrambling down into the hole, I searched frantically for some type of handle and found a clamp that looked like it matched a section of the *Jellybird's* storage bay. Grabbing with one hand and climbing with the other, I worked my way to the top of the hole where Elise pulled me the rest of the way out.

"Grab on!"

She quickly found the clamp on the other side and seized it. We shuffled ungracefully toward our ships and pulled out the refueling tubes.

Elise laughed in frustration. "If we had parked closer together, we could do them at the same time."

"That's the best we can do right now. Let's get this going," I said, starting the refueling of her ship first.

"The swarm will reach you in fewer than thirty minutes," Jelly said.

"That is almost exactly the amount of time it will take to fill both of your ships with the rather viscous fuel these things use," X-37 said. "That does not, however, account for the time it will take you to move the container to your ship, Reaper Cain."

"Fine. Time to put this armor to the test." I ran across the clearing where my micro-fighter was hidden. "It seemed like a good idea to spread them out at the time."

"You didn't hear me disagreeing with you." Elise ran to help me.

"That was kind of unusual, now that you mention it," I said.

We each grabbed a wing and moved the chassis with ease, then began filling it with the second nozzle immediately.

"Well done," X-37 said. "Now there'll only be a two minute and fifteen second overlap."

"That's what I'm predicting as well," Tom said. "The cloud does tend to stop seemingly at random. Fingers crossed, maybe you'll get lucky."

I checked my **HDK** dominator and the magazines I would reload from when shit got hot. Elise did the same.

A shadow moved through the night, appearing strange with our night vision optics giving everything we saw a harsh edge to be better identified by the armor's limited artificial intelligence and my cybernetic optics.

"I really hate this!" Elise's voice sounded forced, as though she was pushing the words through clenched teeth.

"Analyzing data," X-37 announced, not sounding the least bit worried. Sometimes it was nice to be an emotionless combination of hardware and algorithms. "I believe you can relax."

"Why don't we err on the side of caution," I suggested. "We're about to face the edge of a continent sized swarm of unknown alien life-forms."

Elise shifted her stance, her own HDK gripped in both hands.

"It's been nice knowing you, kid," I said.

"Not a kid," she replied.

I didn't really know what the first insect was when I saw it, because it was bigger than a kite. In the darkness, cast in the eerie black and white and green tones of the night vision optics, it looked ominous.

Hundreds more followed, then thousands, then we were surrounded in every direction by slow-moving insects of every shape and size.

"That's not what I expected." Elise stood straighter and lowered her weapon.

I activated the helmet light that I had rarely used, turning the scene into a rainbow of colors. Elise and I laughed, surprised and delighted despite how amped up we had been to face our death only seconds before.

"Please remember, Reaper Cain, that this swarm may still be dangerous despite its pleasant appearance," X-37 said.

I laughed as I talked. "Sure thing, X. I'll watch out for the pretty bugs."

Something happened as the light from my archangel helmet struck the delicate creatures. Some of them started to glow around the edges, and I realized that the top of the cloud was pulling light from the stars and moonshine.

"Maybe you should turn off your headlight," Elise said softly.

"Get in your ship." I finished off the refueling of my own micro-fighter chassis.

Elise climbed into hers, connected her armor to all of the strong points, and powered up the unit. I wanted to do the same but wasn't ready.

More and more of the bugs gathered light from the night sky until we were under a canopy of the most brilliant cloud I'd ever seen. The wings of each creature beat slowly against the gentle night breeze. The bottom layer of insects moved toward a perimeter that encircled us and began to gather their own light that was unavailable when they were at the bottom of the churning cloud.

I powered up my fighter.

Light swelled in the top layer until it was too bright to look at without filters for my helmet visor.

"Let's get the hell out of here, Elise. We're going to have to fly through the trees and look for a way to gain altitude." A second later, I punched my engines and took off without even bothering to fully disconnect the fuel hose. X-37 chastised me for ruining the coupling, but my gut was telling me we should have been gone five minutes ago.

"Hal, you've got a serious problem!" Tom shouted.

The combined energy of the solar insects gathering moon and star light focused in the center and blasted toward the surface, gouging a huge crater in the clearing.

Elise and I shot between trees, often tipping the micro-fighters onto their sides to avoid crashing into them. She took the lead, dropping into a gully and racing over a stream of water that was starting to boil from the destruction behind us. The more power the strange creatures poured into their organic weapon, the more the scene behind us looked like a nuclear holocaust.

In the void, it was easy to forget how fast these little micro-fighters were, but with the perspective of trees and mountains all around us, I really felt like we were about to die.

"The explosions are having a cumulative effect," Tom warned. "I'm still tracking you, thank the gods! Don't stop for anything."

The stream bed became a waterfall towering a hundred meters above us. Elise and I both shot upward, grunting at the G force as we were pulling to complete the maneuver. One of her wings clipped the water and sent a spray into the night.

"Why... would... bugs incinerate... the forest?" I asked as I pulled my fighter into the sky and flashed away from the destruction behind us.

"Unknown," X-37 said. "I believe they are defending the planet from invaders."

"I knew you were going to say that." I joined Elise, flying wide of the cloud of deceptively beautiful creatures. The plasma-like blast they had generated was reaching for the atmosphere.

"I'm not sure this planet is going to make a good home for the fleet," Elise said. "But now I'm curious. What's with this place?"

"Jelly is telling me the swarm is attempting to communicate," Tom said. "Apparently, the butterfly swarm is sentient and not happy about trespassers."

"I'm consulting with Jelly now," X-37 said. "We've agreed it's not a true language, more like the roar of a wild animal than a creature we could negotiate with."

"Great. Any sign of the Alon scout ship?"

"No, Captain," Jelly answered. "But there is a crisis on the *Bright Lance* requiring your attention."

"Fantastic," I said. "Do we have any idea what happened to the ship we were chasing?"

"Your encounter with the indigenous life-forms of this planet was on the edge of the swarm," X-37 explained. "I'm working with Jelly now and it seems that there were a series of other explosions. Our hypothesis is that the strangers you were pursuing, possibly the Alon, had an outpost that was just annihilated."

"We need to confirm that." I aimed my little ship toward the *Jellybird*.

"Of course, Reaper Cain. But I really must insist you head for the *Bright Lance* at your best possible speed. If you don't handle this situation, finding a new home for this fleet will be a moot point."

23

"My apologies," AI Mavis said. "But all Archangel armor must be powered down for service after a major mission."

"That's pretty fucking inconvenient." I felt my fatigue more clearly now that I was back on the *Bright Lance*. During a mission, it was easier to put that aside.

"I agree, Reaper," Mavis said. "This is unfortunate, but the rules are there for your safety and for the preservation of the equipment. Which is very expensive."

"My advice, Reaper Cain, is not to argue with Mavis," X-37 said to me privately. "She is a great improvement over Necron, but she has her idiosyncrasies. As a relatively young ship AI, her default mode is to follow rules and regulations very strictly. She doesn't have data that is gleaned from experience and interaction with humans to make more advanced decisions."

I listened but had already moved on. "All right, give me an update. Ayers awakened and released some of the hybrids, then escaped. I need some better details."

"We leave for five minutes and the entire ship goes to hell," Elise said.

"You were gone for thirty-seven hours," Mavis interjected.

"That is exactly what I was going to say," X-37 added.

"You know what I mean." Elise sounded frustrated and I wondered if she would start to understand the kind of crap I had to put up with all the time.

"Everyone shut up," I said. "Here's what we need. First and foremost, find whatever ship Ayers left with. Meanwhile, Elise and I will meet Path and Henshaw at the hybrid vault to assess the damage. I'm really interested to see how Henshaw allowed this to happen. He was in charge of the doctor, right?"

"That is correct," Mavis said. "However, he is currently in the medical bay—his condition stable but serious."

"Great. This just keeps getting better," I said. "Path, are you on this channel?"

"I am at the hybrid vault," the sword saint answered.

"Stay there. Keep everything locked down. Elise and I are on the way."

"I will be here," Path said.

"Bug, talk to me," I said.

No answer.

"Mavis, can you find Bug?" I asked. "He was supposed to watching Ayers and Henshaw."

"I will attempt to locate the boy," Mavis said.

The *Bright Lance* was a flurry of activity. Every guard and soldier had been called to duty. Major intersections had at least two armed men or women. We encountered a half-dozen patrols and were advised twice to use the stairs instead of the lifts

"There have been numerous sightings of the hybrid creatures throughout the ship," Mavis advised. "Three people have been killed and several more seriously wounded. It is unknown what these things want."

"Ayers left them here to create panic and disorder while he escaped," I explained. "Where is he?"

"Doctor Ayers took the *Lady Faith*," X-37 said. "That is how James Henshaw was injured. Apparently, there was some sort of struggle."

"That dumbass brought Ayers onto his ship, probably for some sort of high-brow scientific discussion, didn't he?" I asked.

"I can neither confirm nor deny that hypothesis," X-37 said.

"Remind me to punch Henshaw in his throat when I see him."

"I have updated your agenda to include punch James Henshaw in the throat," X-37 said.

"Mavis, have you found Bug yet?" I asked.

"The boy is on the line and awaiting communication with you, Reaper."

"Bug, talk to me. You were supposed to be watching both Ayers and Henshaw," I said.

"Who do you think sounded the alarm? I sent guards to inspect whatever they took onto the *Lady Faith*, but they were too late. Hey, do you mind, Reaper? I'm trying to find these monsters before they kill someone. The ship has a lot of cameras," Bug said.

"Sure thing, kid. Do your thing. But keep me updated."

When Elise and I finally arrived at the hybrid vault, we found what I hoped would be our last surprise of the day. There was a small army of guards and soldiers protecting the technicians that were putting new restraint mechanisms on each of the cryo-pods that still had subjects in them. There were also a lot of dead hybrids, killed by guards or by each other.

Commander Briggs sat on a bench holding a compress against an injury on his head. When he looked up, he appeared humiliated, hurt, and about ready to vomit. His formally ruddy complexion was now a dark shade of blue. Stripes went diagonally across his face and down his shoulders like the camouflage of a strange animal.

The man was also bigger, and he hadn't been small in the first place.

I looked at his arms and saw bumps, little spiky protrusions where the other alien hybrids could extend tentacle-like arms that ended in ugly, serrated hooks.

"What took you so long, Reaper?" His voice was strange, barely sounding like the man I remembered.

"We need to have a long talk."

"He took some of them with him. You know that, right?" Briggs said. "Why the hell didn't you destroy all of us when you took control of the *Dark Lance*?"

"They call it the *Bright Lance* now." I didn't really have an answer.

Silence grew between us as I pieced together the facts of our new situation. Briggs sat with his head in his hands, looking at his feet. He swayed forward and back slightly, barely able to control muscle spasms that rolled through his body from time to time.

"I think he left some of the completed Slayers behind to terrorize the ship," Briggs managed to say.

"At least one, but probably more. The ship is on high alert and we have guards everywhere."

"That won't matter. A lot of people are going to die before you put them down. Abandoning ship shouldn't be ruled out as an option," Briggs said.

"That will be easier said than done. There aren't exactly a lot of Union stealth carrier ships around to replace this one. The captain will not want to sacrifice it. Not worth losing an entire ship."

Briggs tried to laugh, which sent him into a convulsion. Every muscle in his body seized up at the same time, locking him in a state of agony for several seconds.

I wanted to help him but could only stand by, ready to catch him if he fell forward.

"Did you know there used to be four stealth carriers?" he

asked. "That was until one of these things got loose and the captain refused to abandon ship. They did so much damage hunting it that it was eventually scuttled in the Quan Darr 11 system."

"Did you have a Reaper on that ship?"

He managed to laugh without having a fit this time, sounding like he was blowing a tedious melody on a kazoo. "You always were a cocky as a son of a gun."

"I have to keep you under guard and locked up," I said. "We're on the same side now, like it or not."

"I'm not fit to be on anyone's side, and my condition is going to get worse before it gets better," he said. "Lock me up, but promise me someone will end it if I lose my ability to think like a human."

We hadn't been friends. There had only been one instance where I suspected he had done something to allow Elise and me to escape, but even then that was more of a hunch that I might have been imagining. After what happened to him, I felt a disturbing sense of kinship.

"I'll do it myself if it comes to that." I spoke softly but with conviction.

"Thanks, Reaper," he said, his voice devoid of emotion. "I was hoping you would say that. You're the only one I trust put me out of my misery without hesitation."

There wasn't anything to say to that, so I doubled the guards on his cell and left.

24

DOZENS OF PEOPLE crowded the situation room of the *Bright Lance*, including Captain Younger and Brion Rejon, leader of Xad. President Coronas had been relocated to her own ship when the crisis began.

"I find it interesting that the people of Xad don't require their leader to transfer to another ship," X-37 said.

"Their society evolved differently," I said. "I'm guessing their leadership cast wasn't always long-lived. They probably gave up on staying safe about the time they started trying to salvage thousands of derelict ships from the void."

"That is very similar to my own analysis," X-37 said. "Captain Younger is beginning the briefing."

I shut up and listened. Elise stood on my left, Path on my right, each of us in full Archangel armor but with our helmets off. Bridge security glared at the massive chain gun strapped to my back but didn't make me leave it outside.

"I wish I'd thought of that," Elise said.

"You were playing with micro-fighters," I responded, scanning every face in the room to gauge their level of fear versus their commitment to winning.

"Playing, innovating—you decide which I was doing," Elise said. "And you're welcome, by the way."

"Thank you for your vigilance thus far." Younger's strong voice carried across the room as people ended conversations and faced forward. "This crisis will call for great sacrifice and creative solutions. Reaper Cain has interviewed the surviving test subject and learned several things that will help us in our hunt."

She waved her hand and a holographic display of a fully formed monster appeared. The holo was blurry, taken from the security cam. It looked like it had been running or charging when the image was captured.

"There are at least two Slayers at large." She held up one hand to stop the murmuring that was spreading to the room. "That was what their creators called them and is sufficient for our purposes. The monsters are seven feet tall, dense enough to resist our weapons, and have demonstrated an unbelievable level of strength. Surviving victims claim they have strange eyes that seemed to look at their prey differently than we would and that their heads can turn at least one hundred and eighty degrees."

I studied the image carefully, noting how much different it appeared when it wasn't trapped in a cryo-pod.

Captain Younger continued. "They can extend—or shoot, actually—something like tentacles from their arms and legs. These appendages end in serrated hooks, possibly designed to capture prey, but we haven't seen that yet."

"That's good," someone said, and there was mild laughter for a few seconds.

"This holo image is misleading. Eyewitnesses report they are a shiny blue color, like they're constantly wet. Others claim they are nearly black," Younger said. "You all have your assignments. Your mission is to locate and contain any and all alien lifeforms. You will not engage with fewer than four combat trained individuals. Reaper Cain and his people, of course, are the exception."

She looked toward me. "Do you have anything to add, Cain?"

"They can be killed," I said.

"How do you know that?" asked a voice from the crowd.

"Anything can be killed. Stick to the plan, trust your team, and look for opportunities. The best thing we can do is deny them access to more and more parts of the ship until their only option is to get pushed out of an airlock," I said.

"I like that plan," Younger said. "But make no mistake, destroy these monsters at your first opportunity."

"We heard there were still some frozen in cryo-pods. What about them?" a crew member asked.

"That's not part of this briefing." Younger pointed at another crew member. "Next question."

"Some of us have families," the man toward the back said. "Can they be evacuated?"

"That's a good idea, Crewman Davidson. I'll assign people to begin the process."

Once I had caught Captain Younger's eye, I indicated I was leaving and she gave me a very short nod of approval.

"Mavis and Bug believe Ayers took six of the fresh, or least changed, hybrids, and six of them partially through the transformation," X-37 said. "We agree that all twelve of the completed Slayers are unaccounted for. Where would you wish to start, Reaper Cain?"

"I'd like to start by finding these things before any of the people from the ship do."

"That's exactly what I was thinking," Elise said. "Path, are you ready to hunt aliens?"

"Yes, though I find no pleasure destroying these unfortunate creatures," Path answered, then put on his helmet.

"Let's not overthink this," I said. "These things are dangerous and have already killed innocent crew members. If they were human, we'd still have to take them out. Don't get soft just because they were unwilling test subjects."

"Of course." Path's expression was as serene and unreadable as a pool of untouched water.

"X, point the way. I want to get a head start on the rest of the search teams."

"My analysis suggests it would also be smart to allow them

to secure as many areas of the ship as possible, thus narrowing options for your quarry."

"Yeah, sure. We'll do that too. But if we can get a jump on it now, it might save a lot of Wallach and Xad lives," I said.

"And the lives of those formerly serving the Union," X-37 said. "A significant number of them remain on each of the formerly Union ships."

"Sure," I said. "Let's just save everyone and sort it out later."

25

"THERE HAS BEEN a Slayer sighting on deck five, just outside the hydroponics room," X-37 said.

"We're on our way," I said.

"Do you think it's hungry? Or is it going to sabotage the hydroponics?" Elise asked. "I'm not really excited about tearing that place up."

"Damage to the farm would be problematic long term," I said. "But if that's where we find it, then we have to deal with it. Letting it wander around until we find the perfect location to corner it isn't really an option."

"How many doors does the place have?" Elise asked.

"There is one main door large enough for equipment and two side doors—one to a combination lounge and cafeteria area for workers, and another that eventually leads back to the main hallway. The problem I am seeing from the schematics is that there are numerous sub levels and access places to the hydroponics facility. These have not been updated for a while," X-37 said. "Sometimes these types of facilities are modified or repaired in creative ways."

"Keep us updated, X," I said as we entered a lift.

"Of course, Reaper Cain. AI Mavis has been very helpful. She wants me to convey that it is also in her best interest that we neutralize this clear and present threat to her crew."

"Great."

"We have another sighting near shuttle bay 14A," Mavis said. "I have lost contact with the response team."

"Of course," I said. "Path, can you handle that one?"

"I'm on my way," Path said, then left.

"All right," I said. "Just don't tell me there are any more right now. Elise and I will check the hydroponics rooms."

"Unfortunately, Reaper Cain," Mavis said, "there are two additional sightings, one at each end of the ship."

X-37 interjected. "Mavis is correct. My analysis suggests they were dispersed intentionally to slow your pursuit of Ayers."

Elise bit back a curse. "I'll deal with those two. You can have the farm level all to yourself."

"How are you going to fight two Slayers?" I asked.

"One at a time," she answered. "Which is still better than where you're going."

We parted ways. When they were out of sight, I picked up the pace, running toward my objective, hoping I could take down the first of the Slayers quickly and then help Elise and

Path. What I found on the way didn't bode well. One hallway was streaked with blood as though a body had been dragged into an access hatch. Now I had to decide whether I was going to enter the access hatch or continue to my original objective.

"What do you think, X?" I asked, studying the hatch.

"This blood is drying," X-37 said. "Mavis also advised me there are numerous scenes like this on the ship. We don't have time to investigate them all."

"Agreed," I said. "I'm going to trust my gut and continue. Patch me into their tactical network so I can listen to the response teams."

"Would you like me to filter the information," X-37 said. "It is somewhat chaotic. Multiple units are responding to multiple locations, possibly all chasing the same Slayer. Conversely, there were twelve fully formed Slayers, or hybrids as you have been referring to them thus far, in the cryo-pods before Doctor Ayers betrayed us. Mavis, Bug, and I believe that all twelve of the dirty things were put on a mission to rack up a high body count. This is about to get real."

"Twelve filthy monsters and one Reaper." I chuckled without a lot of actual humor in my voice. "Barely seems fair."

"My analysis suggests you should not become cocky or it will bite you on your posterior," X-37 advised.

"Good one, X."

"Was that humorous?"

"Sure, X."

"I will add it to my database of amusing one-liners."

I came to an oversized door leading into the hydroponics area. "Check on Elise and Path, then check for any relevant updates ship wide," I said. "Do we still think there is one in here?"

"There is at least one, Reaper Cain," X-37 said.

"I'm not sure I like the sound of that. Does Mavis have visual, and can she patch through the image?"

"Of course, Reaper Cain," X-37 said. "I'm updating the holo feed from Mavis now."

A disturbing image filled my HUD. After suffering a second of blurriness, I pushed the projection further out—an illusion but a useful illusion—and saw my enemies more clearly. Three of the Slayers squatted near a murky pool, splashing water on their faces and upper bodies. One turned slightly so that his neighbor could scoop up chunks of brains and gore from a place the monster couldn't reach. Each of the monsters was spattered with the gore of their recent victims.

"I'm going to need some help," I said.

"There is none available, unless you want to divert resources away from Path in Elise, who seem to have their hands full," X-37 said. "The entire ship is now on official lockdown. No one is allowed to leave their chambers unless they are part of a security team."

I thought about waiting these three Slayers out, hoping they would wander apart so that I could take them one by one. I couldn't hear what was inside, but they seemed to be arguing or just chittering at each other. One was bigger than the others. It jumped up, stomped forward, and shot tentacles out, nearly striking his fellow monsters.

The other two dropped back and separated, but before long were once again gathered in the gruesome feeding and bathing circle—because combining those activities made sense to a Slayer.

"We found where the bodies were dragged to."

"I'm linking to a security feed from deck three," X-37 said. "A combined team of Wallach, Xad, and Union soldiers are confronting one of the creatures."

"Audio only. I want to keep my eyes on the three by the pool inside this hydroponics area," I said.

"Of course, Reaper Cain," X-37 said, then obliged me with the sound of a squad fighting a deadly enemy.

"Contact, contact, contact!" A soldier shouted.

"Shift fire!" another yelled. "You're danger close, Donovan. Move so we can cover you. Godsdammit!"

The sound of gunfire increased, then ended abruptly. Screams of pain overwhelmed the channel.

"I have muted the security feed, but I am transcribing the data for analysis," X-37 said.

"Are we close enough to help?" I asked.

"You cannot reach them in time to offer assistance," X-37 said. "I suggest you complete the mission assigned to you."

"I did the mission assignments."

"All the more reason for you to stay the course, Reaper Cain," X-37 said.

"You're killing me, X."

"That is incorrect," X-37 said. "If anyone kills you, it will be one of these alien hybrids."

"Not helpful."

"What are you going to do, Reaper Cain?"

I shrank the images of the three Slayers on my HUD and moved them off to one side, then pulled up my tactical readouts. Everything in my Archangel armor seemed to be ready for action. "I'm going to put this fancy gear to the test."

First, I pulled the chain gun around to the front, pivoting it toward the ground where it could hang with a decreased profile until I was ready to use it. This transferred the load through the complicated harness differently and wasn't good for long-term support of the weapon. The HDK Dominator, the weapon that had served me well since Dreadmax, switched places when I pulled the bigger gun forward and was now secured on my back. The harness connected both weapons and slid over the surface of the armor when needed, allowing a quick change.

With practiced efficiency, I removed the stealth cloak and adjusted it to cover as much of my armor as possible. It wasn't perfect, but it would be an advantage in this environment. So far, I'd had mixed results attempting to integrate the Reaper mask with the Archangel armor and decided to keep leave it locked in one of my armor's storage compartments.

Mavis opened the main door to the hydroponics level. I entered quickly, slipping off to one side to avoid making a silhouette in the hallway. Inside, it was dark except for flickering lights of damaged emergency LEDs.

After pulling up the Z1A Destroyer, I swept the multi-barrel across the landscape searching for the watering hole. There were rows and rows of plants in every direction—some hung from the ceiling. Every growth station had a light fixture, soil bed, and watering tubes. Each row was slightly different, depending on whether it was corn, wheat, or barley.

"It looks like most of the damage is from fighting." I knelt to check a body. The man had been punctured hundreds of times, the damage seemingly caused by the alien hybrid's organic weapons.

The worst problem in the room was the inconsistent lighting. There had been one hell of a fight here. One second my Reaper eye and Archangel helmet optics adjusted to the gloom, the next they were blocking intense flashes of illumination.

"Are you seeing anything I'm not picking up," I asked.

I pulled my HUD image of the watering hole back into view. My enemies were now motionless, faces turned toward the ceiling as though sniffing the air and listening.

I crept forward in a low stance, constantly moving the multi-barrel of my weapon in preparation for contact. X-37 reviewed what we knew of the Slayers, most notably that their physiology was extremely dense and that none of the crew members had been able to defend themselves up to this point.

The sounds of the security team engaging them on the comms wasn't encouraging either.

"What's the chance they are able to tear me out of this armor?" I asked.

"Unknown, Reaper Cain," X-37 said.

I found two bodies covered with wounds and missing their heads. One man looked as though his arm had been wrenched half off of his body during a hand-to-hand struggle.

I kept moving.

"We are five meters from the central watering reservoir," X-37 said. "Mavis no longer has a functioning holo view of the area. Something has been damaged."

For some reason, my heat sensors we're not picking up my enemies. I had expected to be able to see them even through the rows of corn, wheat, and barley.

I advanced into the main reservoir, ready to lay down a hellish amount of high-powered gunfire. All three of the Slayers turned and looked directly at me.

"X, is my stealth cloak working?" I asked.

"It is operating at one hundred percent efficiency," my limited artificial intelligence reassured me. "However, they seem to see you."

The leader, the big one, stepped forward, hissing and chittering at me with a strange oversized mouth. I saw tentacles starting to sprout from its arms, quivering in anticipation of striking at me.

The leader's tail moved side to side, then slammed on the ground, bouncing up like it had its own violent, rage filled mind that wanted to kill me. At its end there was a single, talon-tipped tentacle that looked like it could double its range when extended.

The creature's eyes were multifaceted, pulling in reflections of the scene despite the darkness. My enhanced optics showed dark places that could have been holes through its amber eyeballs.

It growled something at me, the horrible sounds clearly a language that I didn't understand.

These observations happened in seconds. While it stalled, the other two edged toward my flanks.

I pivoted from my left and shot that one first, advancing forward to decrease the distance, which also increased my accuracy. The Z1A Destroyer barked a short burst of death and destruction.

What I expected to see was fountains of blood leaving its body as it was driven off its feet. Destroyer rounds packed a wicked punch my **HDK Dominator** could never match. It was all about velocity, bullet mass, and the state-of-the-art design of the projectiles that expanded when they struck. The creature staggered, the wounds I saw not nearly as satisfying as I had hoped.

"Threats on your right," X-37 warned, his speech tight to save time during combat.

The leader and the other one rushed me as I kicked the Slayer on my left square in its chest, launching it backward through a row of hydroponic plants. Dirt exploded into the air from some of the hanging pots. Water tubes broke free and sprayed in several directions.

I pivoted to my right and fired. During the split second it took for the rounds to strike, I realized something was wrong. My first victim hadn't stayed down despite gunshot wounds and my Archangel powered front thrust kick.

Retreating, I sprayed Destroyer bullets at close range, hitting all three targets but stopping none of them. They leapt forward, lashing out with razor hooked tentacles that shot forward from their arms. I barely noticed this part of their attack because I was focused on their gaping jaws and rows of sharp teeth.

"You are backpedaling into a row of small fruit trees," X-37 said.

I didn't have time to ask questions but wondered if this was going to be a problem for me, or for my enemies. The mini grove was small. I smashed through the trees with relative ease but not quick enough to avoid getting struck by the talons of the Slayer leader.

Thoughts flashed through my mind, things I couldn't do anything about right now like my family and friends and what would happen to the ship if I failed.

The leader rushed me but instead of retreating from the hellish barrage of ordinance I was sending their way, I lunged forward, driving Z1A Destroyer halfway down its throat before I pulled the trigger. Several dozen rounds went off before the multi-barrel stopped spinning. My victim twisted away in agony, nearly taking my weapon with it.

I dove past the flailing body, shoving the big gun toward my back, and tucking and rolling to my feet all at once.

Graceful wasn't the best way to describe it, but the maneuver was pretty badass and definitely something I was going to play up if I survived to tell the story.

"Alert, both the Destroyer and the Dominator require field expedient repairs before they will function. Please treat them with more care," X-37 said without emotion.

The first alien hybrid I shot jumped on me, landing with its feet and hands clawing at my torso simultaneously. I spun in a circle, trying to shake it off.

The final member of their deadly trio tackled me at the knees, slamming us all down in a big heap of violence. Going with the momentum, I twisted free and scrambled to the top of the pile. One of the monsters kicked, launching me into the air.

"That is an impressive display of strength, given your weight in this armor," X-37 commented. "Also, Elise has advised me that she has dispatched her two targets and wonders why you won't answer her on the radio."

I grunted something that might've been a curse as I darted through the mini farm, destroying everything in my path as I tried to escape.

You are approaching the tobacco plant section," X-37 said.

I slowed to a stop, turning to fight.

"What are you doing, Reaper Cain?"

"Sometimes you have to just do what's right." I extended my arm blade from the armor and took a fighting stance.

"Die, Reaper!" the leader hissed.

The other two regained their feet, wounds bleeding from where I had shot them but not as much as I had hoped or expected. They chanted, showing teeth as they screeched at me a babble of harsh grunts contrasting with sibilant vowels.

"The Slayers have the ability to speak," X-37 said.

I backed away, looking for an escape route or some sort of terrain advantage I could use to survive. "Yeah, that's great."

"It changes my analysis of the situation," X-37 began to say.

The creatures advanced, hissing and chanting words that I could barely understand. It was like their vocal cords weren't really made for speech but something in their twisted psychology made them want to try.

"I could use some backup, X," I gasped, putting my back to the wall and edging toward one of the side doors.

"I'm on my way, Reaper," Elise said.

The leader charged. I feinted high, then dropped into a low crouch, stabbing toward its stomach. Catching it in mid leap, I drove the blade forward as hard as I could and slashed out to one side. This time, alien hybrid blood rained down on the scene.

"Keep moving," X-37 said.

I didn't respond but rushed past the other two, searching for room to work. I needed to get to a better position but there weren't many options in this room.

The leader of the Slayers screamed in rage but fell to its knees holding its torso and gnashing its teeth in the air. Talons shot out of its arms and legs almost random.

Ignoring their leader's death throes, the other two came at me from both sides and smashed me between them.

The armor held, but the impact shook me. Everything became a confused jumble of images as we rolled across the ground. One of them bit me on the shoulder, its teeth hooking into the armor segments. When it twisted its head, I was pulled this way and that.

Pain shot through my right knee as the final Slayer tried to pull my leg off, twisting one of the hydraulic servos inside its golden metal sheath. X-37 warned me not to allow this to go further or I would be injured.

My LAI was trying to help, he really was.

My enemies were too close for me to swing or slash, so I retracted the blade and extended it several times, catching one Slayer after another in the face, throat, and armpits. One of the unlucky bastards took a devastating groin injury and I assumed it would be out of the fight.

One of the monsters rolled away and started to crawl. The one that remained punched me in the helmet. The first strike was nothing. The helmet maintained integrity; it had a complex system of padding and dynamic shock absorption systems to keep me from getting banged around too much inside, even if it didn't feel great.

After a few strikes, the effect of the impact seemed worse. I let go of one of its arms and tried to defend myself, grabbing it by the throat with my other hand. I pushed back, then pulled it down until I slammed my helmet visor into its face.

Jagged teeth and blood sprayed around us from the strike.

I twisted to my left, rolling it onto its back and took the mount position. Its tentacles lashed me with the serrated hooks but couldn't penetrate the Archangel armor. I rained down one strike after another until the creature stopped moving.

Struggling to my feet, I looked around and saw the other two Slayers had succumbed to their injuries and were lying in wide pools of their own dark blood. The problem came when I tried to walk. My right leg wouldn't extend fully, and the left was hard to control.

"Congratulations on your survival, Reaper Cain," X-37 said.

A new voice chimed in my ear. "Yeah, Mister Reaper, you were the best," Bug said.

"Thanks." Breathing hard and wincing from injuries I didn't remember receiving didn't make me feel like I was the best, but whatever. My leg hurt but I thought I could walk if I wasn't trapped in my broken Archangel rig.

"These things are strong if they can break this armor," I said.

"I have begun to gather data for a strength projection graph," X-37 said. "You are very much correct, Reaper Cain. The Slayers are many times more powerful than you are."

"When they're not dead," I said, working to strip away an Archangel panel without much success.

"Correct, Reaper Cain," X-37 said.

"Sorry I couldn't help more," Bug said, overflowing with enthusiasm.

"I'm going to have to lose the armor," I said. "Where are Elise and Path?"

"I'm looking for them," Bug said. "Mavis helps me a lot. This is getting crazy. Haven't seen action like this since Dreadmax came apart. I hope this isn't my fault. I really was trying to watch Ayers and Henshaw like you asked, Mister Reaper."

"Let's hope nothing like Dreadmax happens here," I said.

"That would really suck, Mister Reaper." A pause followed Bug's words. "The ship has taken a lot of internal damage. You really needed to stop these things before we start venting atmosphere."

"Did you find Elise and Path yet?" Having to ask a second time caused me to grit my teeth. Where the hell was that kid?

"They're on the way, Mister Reaper. Chill-lax," Bug said.

26

A TREMOR RAN through the ship, forcing me to put one hand on the wall just outside of the hydroponics area.

"What the hell was that?" I asked.

"Mavis and I believe it is sabotage, timed charges left behind to further disrupt our efforts to pursue Doctor Ayers," X-37 said.

I clenched my teeth and calmed myself before blurting profanity. "I'm really going to throat punch that guy when I catch him," I said.

"Of course you are, Reaper Cain," X-37 said. "My analysis—"

"—suggests that won't help anything," I finished for my LAI. "Why don't you leave violence to me and just tell me where Elise and the rest of these alien hybrid Slayer things are?"

"Of course, Reaper Cain," X-37 said. "Right away, Reaper Cain."

"I'm not sure I like your tone, X." X-37, Mavis, and Bug talked amongst themselves while I limped forward a few steps and decided I had to have the Archangel armor off even if I had to trash it to get free of it. Normally it wasn't as difficult to slip out of, but the Slayers had really done a number on it.

Using the enhanced strength of the arms and gauntlets, I tore apart everything on my right leg from the knee down. Relief flooded through the joint. I took a few breaths, enjoyed the sensation, and then stripped out of the rest of the gear.

"I have an update for you," X-37 said.

Putting on the Reaper mask and the stealth cloak, I listened.

"BATTLE SUMMARY," X-37 said. "You burned approximately four hundred and thirty-seven calories—"

"Skip all that," I said impatiently, then found a tube with nutrient paste and water from the discarded equipment and slugged it down.

"You took out three of the alien hybrids, Elise killed two, and Path successfully eliminated the Slayer he was after. The combined efforts of ship security forces have reduced the number by another four," X-37 said.

"I'm not that good at math, X. Can you tell me how many that leaves of twelve from the cryo-pods?"

Bug jumped in. "That leaves two, mister. Wait, are you kidding me?"

"Yeah, Bug. I can actually count past ten," I said, easing into a jog toward the main lift. If I didn't come back to this deck of the ship for a year it would be too soon.

AI Mavis spoke in her almost too reasonable voice. "The remaining two alien hybrids are assaulting the bridge. Captain Younger has requested assistance. You are the closest response force."

"That can't be right," I said.

"Her guards are fortifying the bridge and Rejon has armed himself to defend the area, but they will need help," X-37 said. "All crewmembers who are not actively engaged in the searching and clearing of the ship have been monitoring the numerous battles with the creatures. It hasn't been going well. Frankly, I'm surprised you're alive."

"I'm on my way," I said, picking up the pace. "Get a hold of Elise and Path to set a new rendezvous point."

"We are working on that," X-37 said.

"Where is my mother and sister?"

"They are in one of the safe areas that were partitioned during the initial stages of the crisis. Hannah has armed herself to protect your mother," X-37 said.

ELISE, Path, and I converged at the central nexus of the main deck. From here, there were two ways to access the bridge: a security lift and a stairwell that Mavis explained had several blast doors that could be closed to stop intruders from reaching the most critical part of the vessel.

All of it looked compact compared to other Union warships I had seen, but by now, I was accustomed to the stealth carrier we'd taken from vice admiral Nebs.

Elise and Path each showed signs of a hard fight. Their once pristine armor was streaked with blood and scorch marks.

"These things are strong as hell," Elise said, then displayed the damage her adversaries had done to her arms, shoulders, and neck area.

"You're going to need a new rig after this," I said.

"Where is your armor?"

"Busted." I conducted a quick check of their armaments, just as I would before any other mission. "This doesn't look like Slayer blood."

Path answered, "I stopped to help wounded."

"We also put out some fires," Elise added.

The ship was on emergency lighting that pulsed lethargically.

Activating the stealth cloak, and sliding the Reaper mask into place, I took the lead. Without the increased size of armor, the cloak had better coverage—if that meant anything. It seemed like the Slayers had seen me because my legs and part of the Destroyer had protruded from the cloak's coverage, but I had a nagging feeling that wasn't the entire reason they saw me. "Let's get moving."

Elise and Path spread out as much as possible and

followed. I took the stairs three at a time, checking each angle before I made the tight turn for the next climb. The only weapon I had was my pistol and my arm blade. Hopefully, the stealth cloak would give me the advantage of surprise.

Mavis opened each door as I approached. X-37 helped scan the openings before crossing through. By the time we reached the deck where the bridge was located, I found evidence of a hard fight.

The hallway leading to the bridge was made to be defended. Not only were there bodies of bridge guards down, but the fortified security stations at each intersection had been ripped apart and their occupants slaughtered.

"That's horrible," Elise said, as blood and brain dripped from the ceiling of one of the small rooms. "These things are so freaking strong."

I glanced at the gun ports and saw evidence they had fired their weapons through the small openings as the Slayers attacked. The doors, so far as I could tell, had been torn free, which should have been impossible. I had trained for this type of assault and never enjoyed it. Even with explosive breaching charges, it was almost impossible to take a bridge like this.

We had initially captured the ship through subterfuge and X-37's diligent sabotage of the ships AI to let us in. The monsters tackled the problem in a much more primitive way, and it seemed to be working for them.

"Let's move," I said. "I'll go first and get a look at them before we make our attack. X-37 thinks they are probably trying to pull apart the main door now and should be distracted."

Elise and Path signaled their agreement and I moved through the final intersection that led to the bridge.

The area in front of the main bridge door was slightly larger than the hallway, which would give us a good place to fight if it came to that. I was really hoping we could shoot and stab them in their backs and end this quickly.

A wounded man crawled toward me. I stepped over him as he continued toward Path and Elise.

"At least I know the stealth cloak is working," I said. The incident in the hydroponics farm had me worried, but the explanation was simple. The cloak hadn't been able to cover my feet and the monsters were smarter, and more observant, than they seemed.

Sure, that was the reason. Absolutely.

"My analysis showed it is functioning well within ideal parameters," X-37 said. "There are three other living security guards, but they cannot move. I recommend assisting them as soon as the battle is concluded to maximize their chance of survival. It would be best, however, to move slowly and use caution while engaging the enemy."

"Sounds good, don't let me forget." I spotted the two Slayers. The monsters were digging their claws into the metal, creating handholds so they could pull and tug on the blast door that should've been impenetrable without serious firepower. Their tentacles writhed in the air, extending and retracting in a strange rhythm that I guessed mimicked their breathing or heart rates.

Not wanting to alert them with noise, I gave X-37 a hand signal to relay the information to Elise and path. X-37 soon advised me that they were ready to enter the final area and attack.

I signaled X-37 that I would initiate the attack.

"We'll double team the other one, then help you," Elise said.

Moving silently, I was within striking distance when it turned to me and spoke.

"Reaps, Reaps," it said. "Why you against us?"

"The Slayer is talking to you, Reaper Cain," X-37 said.

"Figured that out all by myself," I said, frustrated that it could see me.

"Reaps on the wrong side," the monstrosity croaked. "Help kill. Kill them all. Only way to be sure, Reaps. We needs control ship, Reaps."

The other Slayer spun around, opened its jaws as wide as they would go, and screamed at me before charging.

I lunged at my new target, driving my Reaper blade straight down its throat. The mouth snapped shut on my cybernetic arm like a trap, the teeth cutting into the metal. With my right hand, I drew my pistol then pushed it to its temple and fired. Each time I stroked the trigger, I changed targets, making sure to put one in each of its strange, stealth-cloak-seeing eyes.

Elise sprinted across the small area, leapt into the air, and slammed into the alien hybrid that had tried to speak to me. She drove it against the wall and I heard a wet thunk as its skull cracked. The impact didn't kill it.

Tentacles flashed from the arms of my adversary, hooking into my torso, legs, and every place the Reaper mask didn't cover. Streams of data flowed from what the mask observed. At the same time, I was starting to understand their language with the help of the mask and X.

It wasn't perfect, but it was enough for me to believe these two, at least, were trying to hold on to their humanity. The problem was, they were also trying to murder my friends and allies.

Pain screamed through every part of my body. The injuries were bad enough, but I was certain the hooked barbs on the end of the tentacles were poisoned or at least covered in some type of acid.

I fired until the magazine ran dry and then beat it with the empty gun. At the same time, I twisted the blade in its throat, pushing my arm further into it. This broke a lot of teeth.

The entire struggle took only seconds but seemed longer. Elise rolled across the floor, wrestling with her Slayer enemy while Path ran between us with his sword. He slashed the tail off of my enemy before the tail could stab me in the throat.

The sword saint spun in a circle, blade flashing in a wide arc, and cut off the head of the Slayer trying to eat me. Path's blade struck my blade as it passed through the monster's neck, causing me to stagger sideways as the head came off.

It wasn't exactly as graceful or dignified as an action hero in a holo movie, but I'd take the win.

Elise struggled to her feet, lifting her Slayer over her head and then slamming it forcefully to the deck. Without hesitation, she dropped onto it, driving her elbow into the back of its neck. She bounced up, aimed, and fired until she was out of ammunition.

Most of the bullets hit the dense flesh of the hybrid, penetrating just enough not to go bouncing around the room. There were a few errant rounds, however, that whizzed past me. Sparks from the bullets danced around the room with each ricochet.

"Easy, Elise! I'm not wearing armor! Can you try not to shoot me?" I shouted as I shook the hybrid head from my arm. The teeth remained impeded in my cybernetics.

She ran to my side, pried open the mouth of the monstrous head, and tossed it away. Then, because she was bigger and far stronger than I was while wearing the Archangel gear, she grabbed me by the shoulders and looked me over.

"You're a mess, Reaper. Shit, you're bleeding out of every part of your body!" She shouted like it was my fault.

"Not every part." I nearly passed out.

"I am restricting blood flow," X-37 said. "Elise, can you apply pressure bandages?"

"Sure thing, X." Elise ripped open her combat first aid kit.

"Ouch!" I hissed as she poured clotting gel into my

wounds and jammed self-adhesive pressure bandages all over my body. "Your bedside manner needs serious work."

"Ha, ha. Very funny, Reaper. You want to die or what?" she asked.

Path stood guard, watching the hallway for any threats we might have missed.

"Mavis, can you let the bridge know we're out here?" I asked.

"At once, Reaper," AI Mavis answered. "They would have been able to watch the battle had the creatures not smashed the cameras."

Elise stepped back to examine me. "I shouldn't laugh, but you're a wreck, Reaper. You should be able to hobble forward now that we did all of the hard work."

"Are we comparing kills now? Because I had this little trio I dealt with in the hydroponic farm."

A voice came through the speaker box next to the door. "Are you there, Reaper?"

"I'm here, Rejon. This area is clear. I can't vouch for the rest of the ship, but we've taken out twelve Slayers. That's all of the fully formed alien hybrids."

"Very good," he said. "Once we can verify, I will open the door. Do you need medical attention?"

"Nice of you to ask," I said. "And the answer is hell yeah. Maybe a few days off and a box of cigars would be nice too."

Rejon laughed with relief. "If I had any doubt it was you, now I am sure. Several team leaders are checking in, including CSL Locke of Wallach. I'm also surprised at how well the Union turncoats performed. Many lives would have been lost without their help."

"I'm sure they have a few good ones," I said.

"You need to go to the medical bay and get checked out," X-37 said. "Once we are certain you're not going to die from internal bleeding or alien infection, Tom and Henshaw have a lot of work to do on your cybernetic arm."

"Don't talk about Henshaw right now."

"He was tricked by Doctor Ayers," X-37 said. "All evidence suggests that he thought he was able to control the man. His interest in the research is understandable, given his dedication to science."

"Tell that to the families of the people who died cleaning up this mess," I said.

"Let's get you to the med bay," Elise said. "You can walk, or I can carry you. Your choice."

"You can't stay in that armor forever," I said.

She laughed. "But for now, you're at my mercy!"

"I'll walk."

"That is the more dignified choice, Reaper Cain," X-37 said.

"I didn't need that, X."

27

My mother and my sister came to visit me in my hospital room. It was a welcome relief from the hellish boredom and draconian rules of the place. The medical staff didn't allow cigars, whiskey, or anything that resembled fun—and they didn't want me to leave and go after Ayers.

"Halek, what kind of mess did you get into?" my mother asked while my sister silently gave me a hug and then stepped back, almost out of my peripheral vision. "You need to rely on your team more. I've been in this game long enough to know solo missions are dangerous."

"You're right," I said. "We started out together, but the situation changed."

"Yes, that is often how it goes." For a moment, she seemed far away, and I wondered how well I really knew her. She talked about missions like she had been forced to do them alone. The last several months had taught me she understood Union politics and that she had been playing a dangerous game to give me the tools and clues I needed to find her and defeat Nebs.

I never considered that she had been a field operative, but that was my guess now. Maybe that had been before she met my father.

"You have a very complex family," X-37 said to me privately. "I have noted several instances that suggest both women are trained at espionage. Your sister is much younger, but old enough to have completed almost any training the Union would've had to offer her."

"Are you going after Ayers by yourself," Hannah asked.

"I'll take a team—probably three ships with the best people I can pull from Xad, Wallach, and the Union."

She frowned at the last part. If my sister had been trained by the Union, she no longer held any loyalty or affection for it —or the people who had kept her prisoner for Nebs.

"I want to help," she said. The simplicity of her statement caught me off guard. My mother didn't interrupt, which made me believe she knew this was coming and may have even planned it.

"Okay, here's your first test," I said. "Give me a situation briefing."

"The *Bright Lance* and other ships are all reporting they are secured," she began. "AI Mavis predicts the damage can be repaired in less than one standard week. Follow-up scans of the planet where you were nearly killed by insects show that there was an ancient civilization there that is long since extinct."

"I was going to tell you that," X-37 said privately.

"That brings us to the Alon," my sister Hannah said. "The scout ship you chased was part of a rearguard. It seems that the Alon have already been here and were doing a final check of the area before leaving. Your appearance and rather poorly thought out chase has changed that."

I kept my mouth shut with effort.

"During the Slayer crisis, the bridge crew was still sharp enough to maintain operations, including fleet security. There have been three reconnaissance missions against us. All ships are believed to belong to the Alon."

"What about Ayers? Did they have anything to do with his escape?"

"There is no information linking Ayers to the Alon, but it is too early to tell," Hannah said. "What I can say with confidence is that he took a small, slip tunnel capable ship and fled the system. Most of the partially complete alien hybrid experiments are with him. Would you like to see the footage from their escape?"

"Yeah," I said. "Can we do it on the observation deck so I can smoke a cigar?"

Without a word, she handed me a tablet, cigar, and a heating tab to light a Presidential.

I accepted all three items but didn't light up. Chewing on cigar would have to be enough. A cloud of smoke would only draw nurses, which would be an interruption I didn't need right now.

"The ship Doctor Ayers took was the *Lady Faith*, a surprisingly well-equipped pleasure yacht that will be very difficult to catch," Hannah said. "Before we continue, however, I want to finish with the planet in this system. Under other circumstances, it might be an ideal resource for the exodus fleet. But, I've discussed this with Captain Younger, her advisor, and a collective of AI advisors from the other ships in the fleet. The planet has evolved several surprising and unique defensive mechanisms that won't tolerate our presence there. We are marking it for future exploration but don't believe we can stay long enough to make it work, especially if we have Alon ships creeping about."

"What about the archaeological sites?" I asked.

"They appear to be primitive and there is clear evidence visible from high orbit to indicate the Alon have already excavated all sites larger than a single dwelling," Hannah said.

I nodded and waited for her to continue.

"We now have two priorities of approximately equal value," she said.

I detected her Union training in the way she spoke. She'd been to a high-level academy, possibly for fleet operations. She was only in her twenties, but she seemed an old soul. I was slightly embarrassed not to know her exact age, but I'd had a lot on my mind over the last decade.

"Doctor Ayers must be located and destroyed, along with all of his research," Hannah said. "We must also conduct counter surveillance on the Alon forces. Both Xad and Wallach have fought them over the last several centuries and agree the threat is imminent."

"Sounds like a large fleet problem."

"What's your point, brother?" Hannah asked.

"I'm a Reaper. The best thing I can do is go after Ayers. I think you should mentor under Captain Younger. This fleet needs someone trustworthy with high-level Union training in fleet operations."

"We've discussed this," she said. "I have a lot more than officer training to fall back on. Some habits will be hard to break."

"Well that's a little bit vague and mysterious."

"It is what it is," she said.

My mother interrupted. "We are playing for very high stakes now. You need to be on your feet and ready for action as soon as possible. I've gone over everything I could learn about your friends and only have a few suggestions on supplemental personnel."

This wasn't comfortable, I decided, but didn't say anything. She had to know I didn't respond well to authority, even if it was from somebody I loved and cared about. I'd been on my own for a while and was accustomed to making my own decisions.

"Who do you think I should add to my team?" I asked.

"I think you should take the *Jellybird* and your friends, of course. But the RWS *Battle Axe* and the *Hunter of Xad* are also well suited to this mission. I've spoken with CSL Locke and

Rejon. They've agreed to assign their best personnel to those ships to assist you in tracking down Ayers. Their only stipulation is that the doctor be destroyed and that anything you learn from the encounter be shared equally."

"I can live with that."

EVERY MUSCLE in my body ached as I placed my cybernetic arm on the workbench. My sutures burned and itched. This was like a hangover without experiencing any of the alcohol consumption that should've proceeded such misery.

Tom pointed to the areas he had fixed while Henshaw rubbed his chin. The ocular engineer was silent, thoroughly chastened by recent events. I'd never seen him like this and wondered if he was finally realizing that it didn't matter how smart an individual was unless we all worked together.

"You did good work, Tom," Henshaw said softly. "Just give me a few minutes to check over the finer details."

He leaned forward and focused on my cybernetic arm section by section. His artificial eyes blinked and whirled with lights from time to time. When he finally stepped back and crossed his arms, a serious but satisfied look dominated his expression.

"It's not pretty," he said. "But the last Reaper isn't about to win any beauty contests anyway, is he?"

I let that go and moved on to what we really needed to talk about. "What the hell were you thinking, Jimmy?"

"I deserve that, that tone you're using with me," he said. "My intentions, I assure you, were for the right reasons. I've recently learned the drawbacks of overestimating my own abilities. Ayers has yet to learn that lesson. He is very single-minded and does not see all of the implications of his work."

I waited for more, and for once, X-37 had nothing to say during the brief silence.

"The DNA that Doctor Ayers used to splice into his human test subjects was not old, not nearly as old as one would assume if it had truly been collected from archaeological sites," Henshaw said.

"You think these aliens are still out there, maybe even close enough to come after us?" I asked, thinking of the strange white aliens. The fleet's forensic teams hadn't been able to determine how long they'd been dead on the Alon ships. Everyone had been a tad bit busy over the last several days.

"I'm almost certain of it, but I can't prove it. For someone like me, that's a problem and I refuse to hypothesize further without more data," Henshaw said. "What I am willing to speculate on is some of the things that Doctor Ayers said when I was attempting to interrogate him on the *Lady Faith*."

I listened but was remembering the videos my sister had shown me of the test subjects being ushered onto the *Lady Faith*, and those with less human appearances being transported in coffin-like crates. Doctor Ayers had several confederates that were, as of yet, unidentified.

"If I were a betting man, and I am, I'd say he is taking his research to the Alon, believing they will be more appreciative patrons of his skills," Henshaw said. "When I first realized that's what he intended, I was actually relieved, because I had thought he was going to go to find the aliens. If he chooses to go that route, I think things will go very badly for all of humanity."

For once, I agreed completely but wanted to hear him say it. "What do you mean?"

"How would we, as humans, respond to a race who had performed such experiments on our people?" he asked. "If Ayers finds the aliens and shows them what he's done, it will probably be the start of a war of extermination against humanity."

EPILOGUE

LEAVING my friends behind was the hardest decision I'd ever made. It wasn't so long ago I didn't have friends to lose. Our confrontation with the Slayers made me realize how much my life had changed and forced me to see the bigger picture.

Elise had a future. Path was an inspiration to others. My mother and sister were the best trained leaders in this ragtag armada of hope. I was just the Last Reaper, and I had a job to do. There was no reason they had to go down with me when the confrontation with Ayers and his Slayers went sideways.

I was almost to the flight deck when I heard Elise yelling at me.

"Where do you think you're going, Reaper?"

I stopped. I turned. I faced this big pain in the ass that I'd been dragging around since Dreadmax. "I'm going after Ayers. Someone, and by that I mean you, needs to stay and protect all these people. There could be other hybrids we missed, or threats we haven't thought of yet."

"You're trying to ditch me!"

"Listen, kid. We've been lucky so far. Let me take care of this, and if it works out, I promise I'll come back or catch up to you and the rest of the fleet wherever you find yourselves."

"My analysis suggest she will not believe this," X-37 said.

"That is such bullshit," Elise blurted. "Does Path get to go? Tom? Henshaw?"

"I'm not singling you out. Everyone stays. I'm taking a group of professionals from Xad and Wallach. Think of it as me training up a new team. Could be useful in the future."

Elise crossed her arms, flared her nostrils, and said nothing. I continued to the *Jellybird*. When the ramp dropped, I realized she'd played me—stalling while the rest of ungrateful friends betrayed me.

Path, Tom, and Henshaw waited inside—clearly planning to force themselves into my plans.

"X, did you know about this?" I said. "Whose side are you on?"

"I'm on your side, Reaper Cain," X-37 said. "There is literally no possible way for me to be anything but loyal."

Elise smiled as she followed me up the ramp.

"I hope you're happy," I said.

"I am."

CAIN, X-37, and ELISE will return in WILL OF THE REAPER, coming November, 2019.

For more updates, join the Facebook group and become a Renegade Reader today.

RENEGADE STAR UNIVERSE

The Renegade Star Universe

Available on Amazon now

The Renegade Star Series

They say the Earth is just a myth. Something to tell your children when you put them to sleep, the lost homeworld of humanity. Everyone knows it isn't real, though. It can't be.

But when Captain Jace Hughes encounters a nun with a mysterious piece of cargo and a bold secret, he soon discovers that everything he thought he knew about Earth is wrong. So very, very wrong.

Climb aboard The Renegade Star and assemble a crew, follow the clues, uncover the truth, and most importantly, try to stay alive.

The Last Reaper Series

When a high value scientist is taken hostage inside the galaxy's most dangerous prison, Halek Cain is the only man for the job.

The last remaining survivor of the Reaper program, Hal is an unstoppable force of fuel and madness. A veteran amputee-turned-cyborg, he has a history of violence and a talent for killing that is unmatched by any soldier.

With the promise of freedom as his only incentive, he'll stop at nothing to earn back his life from the people who made him, imprisoned him, and were too afraid to let him die.

The Orion Colony Series

Humanity's Exodus is about to begin.

When half of mankind revolts and demands more opportunity, those at the top decide on a compromise: they will build the first colony ships and allow those who are willing to discover new worlds to leave and start over.

Twelve ships are built, the first of which is called Orion. Many are eager to go, but only one hundred thousand are chosen for each vessel. Far from Earth, a new life awaits, and it promises the prosperity they've always wanted.

But still, resistance stirs, eager to sabotage this new expansion effort, threatening the promise of a new life. As Orion moves through the void of space, towards a distant world, its passengers must fight for survival in an unprecedented conflict.

Win or lose, their future will be forever changed.

The Fifth Column Series

After a soldier is left for dead, Eva Delgado's life begins to unravel.

The truth of what happened remains a mystery, and the government will stop at nothing to keep it buried.

Together with the unit's medic, Eva finds herself branded a terrorist and enemy of the State, hunted by two opposing governments.

When the pair uncover a plot that could have ramifications

for the whole galaxy, they know they have to act, but it will take all of their training, cunning and just a bit of luck to do what no one else has achieved.

But what do you do when every secret begets another? And how far will you go to find the truth?

Nameless (Abigail's Story)

Abigail and Clementine were just a couple of orphans looking for a home.

But when the two girls witness something terrible, they have no choice but to leave their orphanage and go into hiding. The only person willing to take them in is a man named Mulberry, but his home isn't the safest place for two innocent children.

Abigail and Clementine quickly discover that their new caretaker is the head of a guild of assassins, and the two are thrown into a whole new world of danger. To survive, they'll need to adapt, focus, and learn how to survive in a world of killers.

The Constable (Alphonse's Story)

My name is Alphonse Malloy, and I see everything.

From a simple glance, I know your hobbies, what you ate for breakfast, how well you slept, and whether or not your wife is secretly seeing the high school biology teacher when you're not around.

I can't explain how or why I get these feelings, only that I know they're true.

All the little secrets you're too afraid to tell.

Sometimes, that means helping people. Other times, it means staring down the barrel of a loaded gun.

I wish I could tell you I was using this ability for good.

I wish I could tell you a lot of things.

The Constable Returns

Alphonse Malloy may just be the smartest man alive.

A year has passed since Alphonse joined the Constables, but his work is only just beginning. In order to graduate and achieve full Constable status, Alphonse will need to complete one final mission.

When new information about an old enemy arises, Al and his mentor Dorian must head deep into the Deadlands in search of answers.

But in a galaxy of secrets, the truth is often more elusive than it seems.

As the search continues, Alphonse's talents will be pushed to their absolute limit, and he'll need everything he's learned to make it out of this one alive.

Warrior Queen (Lucia's Story)

On a lost world, far removed from Earth, a group of humans struggle to survive.

Two thousand years after their ancestors lost control of a hidden genetics research facility, the descendants of mankind have been reduced to a tribe of two hundred survivors. They fight, kill, and die in an endless cycle, all in the hope that things will get better.

Lucia is one of these colonists and the daughter of the tribe's leader, the Director. Together with several other candidates, she must soon undergo a trial to decide her father's replacement. The winner will shape the future of the entire colony.

But the trial is dangerous, meant to test each candidate's wits and strengths to see who is truly worthy. To claim victory, Lucia will need to venture out into the tunnels near the city to search for lost artifacts known as Cores--small but powerful devices capable of harnessing endless energy.

But there are monsters here, waiting in the dark, and they are always hungry. Beware the Boneclaw, Lucia's father use to tell her, for it lives only to kill and to feed.

Lucia must do whatever it takes, learn as much as she can, and fight with every ounce of strength if she hopes to make it through the day.

Forget winning the trial. The real challenge is staying alive.

Resonant Son Series

30 floors of nightmare fueled action. An ex-cop with nothing left to lose.

After losing his job and family, Flint Reed finds himself in the middle of a terrorist attack. With nothing but his wits and experience as a former Union police officer, he must do every-thing he can to stay alive.

As he soon discovers, however, there are also hostages, and no one is coming to save them.

All hope falls to Flint.

But as he fights to navigate the building, the real answers begin to unravel. What are the terrorists really after, and why are they so intent on getting into the vault?

Experience the beginning of the Resonant Son series. If you're a fan of Die Hard, Renegade Star, or the Last Reaper, you'll love this epic scifi thrill ride.

GET A FREE BOOK

Chaney posts updates, official art, previews, and other awesome stuff on his website. You can also follow him on Instagram, Facebook, and Twitter.

Search for **JN Chaney's Renegade Readers** on Facebook to join the group where readers can come together and share their lives and interests, especially regarding Chaney's books.

For updates about new releases, as well as exclusive promotions, sign up for the VIP mailing list. Head there now to receive a free copy of *The Other Side of Nowhere*.

https://www.subscribepage.com/organic

Enjoying the series? Help others discover *The Last Reaper* series by leaving a review on Amazon.

ABOUT THE AUTHORS

J. N. Chaney has a Master's of Fine Arts in creative writing and fancies himself quite the Super Mario Bros. fan. When he isn't writing or gaming, you can find him online at **www.jn-chaney.com**.

Scott Moon has been writing fantasy, science fiction, and urban fantasy since he was a kid. When not reading, writing, or spending time with his awesome family, he enjoys playing the guitar or learning Brazilian Jiu-Jitsu. He loves dogs and plans to have a ranch full of them when he makes it big. One will be a Rottweiler named Frodo. He is also a co-host of the popular Keystroke Medium show. You can find him online at **http://www.scottmoonwriter.com**